THE DIXIE APOCALYPSE

THE DIXIE APOCALYPSE

RICHARD FOSSEY

BROWN BOOKS
PUBLISHING GROUP

The Dixie Apocalypse

Brown Books Publishing Group
Dallas, TX / New York, NY
www.BrownBooks.com
(972) 381-0009

A New Era in Publishing®

Publisher's Cataloging-in-Publication Data

Names: Fossey, Richard, author.
Title: The Dixie apocalypse / Richard Fossey.
Description: Dallas, TX ; New York, NY : Brown Books Publishing Group, [2022]
Identifiers: ISBN: 978-1-61254-574-5 (paperback) | LCCN: 2022938136
Subjects: LCSH: College teachers--Louisiana--Fiction. | Generals--United States--
    Fiction. | Martial law--United States--Fiction. | Farms--Louisiana--Fiction.|
    Hunger--Louisiana--Fiction. | Survival--Louisiana--Fiction. | LCGFT:
    Apocalyptic fiction. | Action and adventure fiction. | BISAC: FICTION /
    Dystopian. | FICTION / Action & Adventure. | FICTION / Southern.
Classification: LCC: PS3606.O74947 D59 2022 | DDC: 813/.6--dc23

ISBN 978-1-61254-574-5
LCCN 2022938136

Printed in the United States
10 9 8 7 6 5 4 3 2 1

For more information or to contact the author, please go to
www.RichardFossey.com.

To Kim

It's true, I suffer a great deal, but do I suffer well?
—St. Therese of Lisieux

PROLOGUE

How many years has it been since I received a Social Security check? How long has my city been under martial law? When did my neighbors start carrying handguns? When was the last time I saw a policeman, drove a car, or drank a cup of coffee?

PLAYING WITH GUNS

I left the farm compound before dawn and headed up River Road for the farmers market in Baton Rouge.

I departed early because I had farm produce to sell, and I wanted to get to the market in time to grab a good space. I was riding my old e-bike, a cargo-bike model, sturdy enough to haul my freight: four bushels of sweet potatoes.

It was a cold, autumn morning, and a chilling breeze swept over me from off the Mississippi. I was wearing my sturdy Carhartt canvas coat with the hood pulled up.

I was peddling along just before daylight, and I felt vaguely uneasy. The road was deserted, and had a menacing quality in the pre-dawn darkness. Fog from the river drifted over me; I could see nothing clearly. A clump of weeds looked like a mugger crouching on the roadside. Trees and fence posts appeared as plunderers carrying weapons.

I was armed, of course. Almost every adult carried a gun in those days . . . and quite a few teenagers. Most went open carry, displaying their handguns on their belts or in shoulder holsters.

But I had a different philosophy. I didn't want people to know I carried a pistol. Since the new times began, I had seen several petty squabbles end in bloodshed because someone pulled a gun. Most times, it seemed to me, those incidents would have ended peacefully had the angry parties not brandished their firearms.

I always kept my gun concealed, but it would have been foolish not to have some kind of protection in this lawless time when many people were hungry and the strong preyed on the weak. My Glock 19 Compact was stowed in my backpack along with my lunch and a spare fifteen-round magazine.

I sang to myself just to make a little noise—some old gospel song from my childhood. I had given up on the religion of my youth when I converted to Catholicism, my wife's religion. But gospel tunes still rattled around in my head—optimistic songs I had learned in Sunday School, songs that assured me I was going to heaven.

The river levee was on my left, blocking my view of the Mississippi River. Louisiana State University's Veterinary School building was on my right. It was abandoned many years ago. Once air-conditioning stopped, that building, like all the other buildings on the LSU campus, became uninhabitable.

Ahead, the Interstate-10 bridge spanned over the river. In the old times, this bridge had been jammed day and night with cars and commercial trucks—trucks hauling stuff made in China for Americans who didn't make anything anymore. It was always cheap stuff, stuff we often didn't need in the first place.

But those days were over anyway. Today, it was virtually a foot-bridge—no vehicles at all. Up ahead, River Road was blocked. An enormous RV—one of the old gas-guzzling behemoths—stretched halfway across the crumbling asphalt. Someone had torched it years ago during one of the riots. It had burned down to the bare metal, and all the tires had melted in the fire.

In the old times, such a scene would have been shocking. If a wrecked or burned vehicle blocked a public street, the police would quickly dispatch a tow truck and have it hauled away. But now the people of Baton Rouge lived in the "new normal," and those who survived in this harsh new time were accustomed to seeing thousands of burned wrecks strewn all over Baton Rouge—mostly cars, but also buses, trucks, and RVs.

I had peddled past this particular wreck many times, but always in daylight. Today, in the shadowy light of the early morning, the blackened carcass looked sinister. And there was something new: a downed pecan tree lay across the road. Together, the RV and the tree completely blocked my way.

Suddenly, I was frightened. This was a perfect place for an ambush, especially at this hour.

Feeling foolish and scared at the same time, I stopped singing, and I slowly coasted up to the obstruction to see if I could get my bike through. I felt my heart racing and my stomach clenching. My senses told me something malevolent was waiting for me.

Just as I rolled to a halt, a woman stepped out from behind the RV and pointed a revolver at me—one of those models made to look like an Old West six-shooter.

"I'm taking that bike, motherfucker," she said. She was blonde, in her early thirties, and wearing an LSU hooded sweatshirt.

I was scared, but I told myself to stay calm. I guessed the woman was one of the hundreds of ex-LSU students who lived in Tiger Land, an enormous slum of rundown apartment complexes that were built near LSU for college students. When the university shut down and the federal student-loan program collapsed, many of these students were left stranded in Baton Rouge. Some of them became pilferers and shoplifters, but most were not dangerous. I didn't think this woman would shoot me, so I pretended she wasn't pointing a gun at me.

"I'm headed for the farmers market," I said. "Are you hungry? I've got some sweet potatoes you can have. In fact, you can have my lunch."

"Get off the fucking bike, asshole, or I swear to god I'll blow your head off!"

Sometimes I think fast in a crisis, and sometimes I don't. Today, I took a couple of seconds to figure out how I might make it out of this situation alive: My robber was carrying a revolver, not an autoloader. What caliber? Ammo for some handguns had been hard to find for years; millions of them had become no more than paperweights. Maybe her gun wasn't loaded, or maybe she had a few bullets, but not many.

3

If she were alone, which she appeared to be, she would need the gun to protect herself. Maybe she wouldn't waste a bullet to get my bike. Maybe she wasn't a murderer.

I weighed one more factor: my backpack had Kevlar plates sewn into the lining, and could be converted into a bulletproof vest in a few seconds. I had bought it years ago during my prepper phase. Bulletproof backpacks had been popular with the rich people who bought them for their kids back in the days when mass school shootings were common.

I always wore this pack when I traveled alone. I had no idea whether it would stop a bullet. Even though it came with a money-back guarantee, that was no good to me at all unless the woman shot me in the back and the bullet made it through.

Regardless of the risk, I couldn't give up my bike without a fight. I had bought that e-bike years ago for $1,500. Now it was probably worth twenty thousand paper dollars, or maybe two ounces of gold. I couldn't walk back to my people and tell them that I had meekly turned it over to a robber.

I edged my bike around while I talked, and set the peddle assist at the highest level. The woman kept calling me a motherfucker and telling me she was going to kill me.

A sudden instinct told me to bolt. I hit the throttle on my cargo bike and headed back down River Road. I was too close to the woman, and I knew it. If she chose to shoot me, she wouldn't even have to aim.

And she did shoot me. She shot me in the back, and the wallop was terrific, like I was hit by a hammer. But the Kevlar plates in my backpack stopped the bullet. I lost my balance and lurched forward, rolling off my bike. Sweet potatoes went everywhere.

I struggled out of my backpack and fumbled through it to find my Glock. I realized then that I had never learned to shoot the damn thing. Bullets were too expensive for target practice, and I had only shot it a couple of times.

The Glock had no manual safety, and I knew a bullet was in the chamber. I found the gun and pulled it out of my backpack. I pointed it directly at the woman and pulled the trigger. I pulled it twice.

Both bullets hit my robber in the chest—one hit right on the U of her LSU hoodie, and the other struck the L. She fell backward on the pavement. Blood seeped through her sweatshirt and trickled from her mouth and nose. She gasped and gurgled for a bit, but I knew I'd killed her.

The gunfire made my ears ring, and my ribs ached like they were broken. And then, before I could collect myself, a man came running from behind the RV. He was a big man, about the same age as the woman, and he headed right toward me. I braced myself for a collision.

But the guy wasn't running at me—he was going for his companion's revolver. When he got to her body, he knelt, picked up the gun, aimed it at me, and tried to pull the trigger. It was a single-action gun, which required him to cock back the hammer before firing. I guess the guy didn't know that.

He fumbled with the gun, groping for the safety lever with his fingers. I shot him once in the head from two feet away. His head exploded, and I was instantly splattered with his blood and brain matter.

I suppose I went into shock. For a few seconds, I viewed the carnage as a detached observer—as if I were watching an action movie. Numbly, I noticed that the man's hair was tied up in a man bun and that the woman I shot was wearing open-toed sandals. I felt my heart pounding and wondered if I was going into cardiac arrest.

Now what?

In a few minutes, the shock wore off, and I went into full panic mode. I had lived through the new times for years without hurting anyone. Now, in the space of about ninety seconds, I'd killed two people.

I considered dragging their bodies over the levee and dumping them in the Mississippi. Would the current sweep them downriver, or would they remain motionless in the backwater along the shore, bobbing like corks at the end of a fishing line? I thought about burying them under the levee, but I didn't have a shovel.

Did anyone witness the shootings? I wondered. I hadn't seen anyone, but there might have been some homeless wanderer sheltering in the veterinary school building. From one of the upper floors, a person could easily have seen what went down.

Should I report the shootings?

I couldn't dial 911 on my cell phone because I didn't have a cell phone. Those magic gadgets had disappeared years ago. In any event, there was no more 911; Baton Rouge didn't have a police force anymore.

Just as well. If this had happened during the old times, a SWAT team would have shown up in an armored vehicle. I probably would have been arrested and charged with murder. Maybe the police would believe I had shot in self-defense, or maybe they wouldn't. I might have gotten labeled as just another grey-haired old guy who had gone postal because he'd lost his retirement savings in the stock market crash.

On the other hand, the absence of a police force was not necessarily good for me. Local vigilantes occasionally took the law into their own hands, particularly when someone was accused of rape or murder.

Armed mobs had hanged a few people off the I-10 bridge. A couple of times, when they didn't have a rope handy, they just pushed their victim off the span into the Mississippi.

Most of these vigilantes were elderly people—the ones who had watched too much *Gunsmoke* when they were kids. The old folks got surly when the government stopped sending out Social Security checks. If the geezers found out I had shot a couple of people, they might track me down and kill me.

And then there was the army, which was in charge of security in Baton Rouge now.

Should I report the River Road incident to the military?

We were all under martial law in the new times, and the army occasionally held drumhead court-martials to deal with looters, arsonists, and murderers. Since the army had no prison facilities, the sentence was often death by firing squad.

Which do I prefer, I asked myself: *hanging, drowning, or a firing squad?* I decided I would rather be court-martialed and shot by the army. At least I could expect some rough form of due process and an accurate firing squad.

In the end, I decided not to tell anyone what I had done. I gathered up my sweet potatoes and went on to the farmers market like it was an ordinary day.

I left the bodies sprawled in the road. I also left the woman's pistol, which was still clenched in the dead man's hand. After all, I didn't need another revolver. My family had a five-gallon bucket full of revolvers back at the farm compound, which we kept in our armory on the off chance we might find ammo for one of them.

Before leaving the scene, I crossed over the levee and washed the blood and brains off my canvas coat in the brown water of the Mississippi River. I knew that cold water could dissolve a bloodstain in fabric, and I was grateful that the river was frigid.

As I stood on the levee bank, I saw a great blue heron standing in a shallow backwater a little upstream from me. I didn't startle it, and it didn't move. I think it figured I was harmless.

As I walked back over the levee, a line from *Gone with the Wind* came into my mind: "I can shoot straight," I said to myself, "as long as I don't have to shoot too far."

COLONEL MERSKI ABSOLVES
ME OF MY SINS

I walked my bike around the wrecked RV and peddled on up the road to the farmers market. I passed by several abandoned warehouses where cotton bales were once stored.

I rolled by the old Water Campus building that was cantilevered over the river. The Water Campus—where brilliant environmental engineers, hydrologists, and marine biologists once worked to control the Mississippi River and save the Louisiana coastline . . . which was disappearing at the rate of one football field every hour.

All those experts were gone now, and the lower Mississippi River did what it damned well pleased. Hurricane Maxine destroyed the river levees around New Orleans, allowing the river to spread out like a giant glass of spilled chocolate milk into the Gulf of Mexico. The Army Corps of Engineers had controlled the flow of the Big Muddy for more than a century with a series of dikes and spillways, but in the end the river broke free.

Peddling at a sedate pace, I glided under the I-10 bridge and through the ruins of downtown Baton Rouge. A sprawling camp of homeless people sheltered itself under the giant river bridge, but I saw no one among the tents and cardboard shacks. The homeless people were still sleeping.

Soon, I arrived at the Red Stick farmers market, which was one of the few institutions to survive the burning of Baton Rouge. All through the riots and urban violence, people still grew food crops and sold them at the farmers market. It was October now, and local truck farmers were selling autumn crops: sweet potatoes, pumpkins, mustard greens, and such.

The farmers market was located where it had always been—on Fourth Street across from St. Joseph's Cathedral. The Cathedral had also survived the riots, some would say miraculously. As buildings all around St. Joseph's were being looted and burned, the Knights of Columbus showed up with their deer rifles and 12-gauge shotguns and defended the cathedral.

I was told the knights built a wall around the cathedral by turning abandoned cars and trucks on their sides. They held out more than a week until the Eighty-Second Airborne arrived, surviving on jambalaya and gumbo that they cooked over propane burners.

Some of the rioters tried to persuade the army to arrest the knights for murder because they had killed a few people who tried to get over their barricade. Most of the casualties had died from gunshot wounds; the knights had fried a turkey before one of the assaults, and they poured boiling peanut oil on one rioter.

But the army wasn't interested in arresting the knights, who had quickly endeared themselves to the soldiers by holding a big fish fry and handing out Bud Lights that they had managed to keep refrigerated using their hurricane generators.

All that happened years ago. Today was a fine autumn morning at the farmers market, and I found willing buyers for my sweet potatoes. I sold some for silver and traded some for a crescent wrench and a can of WD-40.

Around midmorning, a Cajun guy wearing camouflage from head to foot walked up to my booth carrying a case of muscadine wine.

"Whoa there, buddy," I said jokingly, poking fun at his camouflage ensemble. "You scared me sneaking up on me that way. I thought you were a bush! Is it deer-hunting season already?"

"*Cher*, it's always huntin' season these days," he replied. "If I see a deer, I'm gonna shoot it, an' I ain't waiting on no big buck. I'm a meat hunter now, and there ain't no game rangers around to stop me."

He introduced himself as T-Boy Bienvenue and offered to swap four bottles of his wine for a bushel of my sweet potatoes. Knowing how Louisiana wine usually tastes, I turned him down. But Bienvenue was persistent. "You will love dis wine," he assured me. "It pairs well wid blacken' redfish an' asparagus."

"But I don't have any redfish or asparagus," I countered.

"Then it makes a nice dessert wine. Just pour it over bread pudding. I put plenty of cane sugar in it to make it semi-sweet."

I was still dubious, and when Bienvenue upped his bid to eight bottles of wine, he overplayed his hand. "Look," I said, "my family doesn't drink wine. We're all beer drinkers. Why don't you try unloading your wine at one of the parish churches? I'll bet your semi-sweet muscadine would make great communion wine."

"You think my wine is good enough to be the blood of Christ?" he asked incredulously.

"I don't know why not. I'm sure you've sipped some bad-tasting communion wine over the years. I know I have. I'll bet your muscadine wine is better than most."

As Bienvenue considered my suggestion, I noticed Father Kerry walking by. He wore a long, close-fitting, black cassock and a three-peaked biretta—the garb of a conservative Catholic priest.

I pointed Father Kerry out to Bienvenue. "Here's Father Kerry," I said, "the pastor at St. Joan of Arc. Why don't you see if Father Kerry will buy your wine?"

Taking my advice, Bienvenue picked up his case of wine and caught up with Father Kerry. He must have gotten a cold reception because he returned a few minutes later, and he still had all his inventory.

"Father Kerry turned me down," he reported, "and he was kinda rude about it."

"I'm sorry, T-Boy. I should have warned you about Father Kerry."

"He's kind of a *couyon*," I added, using the Cajun word for a foolish or crazy person. "I think I might have given you a bad suggestion."

"No, *bon ami*. I know Father Kerry," Bienvenue replied darkly. "He's not a couyon. He's the *Rougarou*."

Bienvenue's remark shocked me. The Rougarou is a mythical creature of Cajun folklore, a kind of werewolf with the body of a human and the head of a wolf. He is said to stalk the cane fields and swamps of South Louisiana at night and suck the blood from humans he catches unawares in the darkness. As I understood the legend, the Rougarou preys only on Catholics. Louisiana Protestants had no fear of the Rougarou, and didn't believe he really existed.

I scanned Bienvenue's somber face. He was not joking.

"The Rougarou? What do you mean by that, T-boy?"

Bienvenue reflected for a few seconds before answering. "Let's just say that if Father Kerry gets into heaven, then you and me, we definitely gettin' in."

"Here," he added and handed me a bottle. "Take dis. It's *lagniappe*."

"*Merci*," I replied, which exhausted my Cajun French vocabulary. "Why don't you take a dozen sweet potatoes. Pick out some big ones. Also *lagniappe*."

And so we made a trade after all, and T-Boy and I parted on good terms.

A little later, I looked up to see Colonel Francis X. Merski, the commandant of Fort Sharpton. He was dressed—as usual—in combat fatigues and wore a sidearm, and he was accompanied by two armed soldiers also dressed for battle. The soldiers carried assault rifles at the ready, and their vests were stuffed with magazines for their rifles. Both wore wrap-around sunglasses, which the Baton Rouge soldiers seemed to favor.

"How's it going, Willoughby?" Colonel Merski greeted me cheerfully. "You're peddling potatoes today, I see."

We shook hands. I remembered to grip his hand as hard as I knew he was going to grip mine. Merski had grown up in Chicago in a Polish-American family, and he still spoke with a slight Chicago accent. He was a stocky guy with a buzz haircut and a ready sense of humor, but everyone knew he could be dangerous if you messed with him. It was well known in Baton Rouge that Merski had given his troops a standing order to shoot anyone who challenged the army's authority.

"I'm down here looking for a birthday present for my niece," Merski said, as if he had to explain himself. "Are any of those hippie artists around here today selling jewelry? I don't want to give her a pumpkin. That's what I gave her last year."

I liked the colonel, and we had become good friends in spite of the fact that we were two completely different kinds of men. Merski had spent his entire adult life in the army. He'd served a couple of tours in Afghanistan during that decades-long conflict—a "cluster fuck," as Merski described it. He had fought insurgents in California, and was among the troops that came to Israel's relief just before the global economy went south.

I, on the other hand, had never served in the military. I had been a lawyer in the old times, and then a college professor. When the petroleum economy began winding down, nobody needed lawyers, and they needed college professors even less. People who had carpentry skills became a lot more valuable than people who just talked. Unfortunately, I had no skills other than writing and arguing, and I couldn't feed myself that way.

But I discovered I had a talent for gardening and animal husbandry, and I cultivated those new skills. Otherwise, I would have starved.

"I see your cargo bike is still running," Merski said. "I wish I could get a few of those for the garrison. I wouldn't have to feed so many goddamned horses."

I had made up my mind to keep mum about the people I shot on River Road, but I trusted Merski. On a sudden impulse, I told him what had happened.

"As a matter of fact," I said, attempting to conceal my anxiety, "a couple of bandits tried to steal my bike on River Road this morning."

Merski immediately switched from his jovial demeanor to his military mode. "Tell me what happened," he said. An order, not a suggestion.

I briefly told him how things went down and that I had shot two people dead. It was a big deal for me, of course. I had never shot anyone before.

It was not such a big deal for Merski. I'm sure he shot a lot of people over his thirty years in the military, including a few in Baton Rouge. Although the rioting had come to an end, the city was still under martial law. Merski ordered summary executions for anyone who committed a serious crime, and sometimes he performed those executions himself.

"Were they comancheros, do you think? Or pickers?" Merski asked. Comanchero was the name people applied to gangs of rapists, armed robbers, and murderers that skulked around outside the city. They were vicious killers who sometimes tied up their victims in the swamps and left them for alligator bait. It was rumored that some of the comancheros were cannibals.

Pickers, on the other hand, were generally harmless souls who scavenged through old buildings and panhandled on the streets. But the pickers could be dangerous, too, especially if you encountered a hungry one with a gun on some lonely road.

"I think they were pickers," I replied. "They didn't seem very proficient with firearms."

Merski laughed. "I'm sure you're right," he chuckled. "If they had been comancheros, they would have shot your happy ass, cut your legs off, and eaten them for lunch."

I gave him a weak smile, but I knew he was right. I had survived the morning because I had been waylaid by amateurs. Had they been comancheros, they would have killed me.

"Keep this to yourself," Merski told me after he had heard me out. "Don't even tell your family about this. Remember: confession may be good for the soul, but it can be mighty hard on the neck."

He turned to one of his bodyguards and issued a terse order. "Sergeant Rutledge," he said, "Mr. Burns just told me that he saw a couple of bodies on River Road near the old veterinary school. Take a squad down there and dispose of the corpses in the usual manner. If you find a gun, throw that in the river too. I want you to write up your report as a murder-suicide. God knows that's common enough these days."

And that was that. My anxiety lifted immediately. At that particular moment, I didn't care that I had killed two people. I was just relieved to know I had gotten away with it.

Colonel Merski abruptly changed the subject. "Will," he said, "you've been serving as my civilian commissary officer for some time now. I've got a new requisition order I'd like you to fill. You'll need to go to Houston to get what I need."

I had indeed become Merski's unofficial commissary officer, rounding up supplies and materials for his garrison. Merski commanded an infantry battalion of about six hundred soldiers, both men and women. Many of his troopers had families—spouses, children, and assorted relatives—bringing the total military community in Baton Rouge to well over a thousand people. It was Merski's job to keep everyone fed and clothed, and to find the equipment his garrison needed.

Merski found it more efficient to employ me as a civilian to buy or barter with various vendors than have the army do it. "You look harmless," he had observed when we first met, "and you're a good bullshitter. I think people with things to sell would rather deal with you than a soldier carrying an assault rifle."

I liked working with Merski. He appreciated what I was doing for Fort Sharpton, and he paid me a small stipend in silver—not the nearly worthless paper money that was still circulating.

"I want you to take the Red Ball Express to Houston tomorrow," he said. "I'll have my requisition order ready for you and a list of what we need. Be at the Fort Sharpton gate at 0500 hours. I'll send a couple of soldiers to accompany you.

"Don't bring your Glock," he added. "You've shot enough people this week."

LOOKING BACK ON THE APOCALYPSE: THE FOUNDING OF LÂCHE PAS

After selling all my sweet potatoes, I climbed on my e-bike and headed back to Lâche Pas, which was the name my family gave to the 160 acres we farmed south of Baton Rouge.

Lâche Pas is a shortened form of a Cajun expression, "Lâche pas la patate," which translates to "Don't let go of the potato," or more loosely, "Don't give up."

I passed by the burned RV where I had been ambushed early in the morning. Merski's soldiers had disposed of the bodies and the revolver. They'd even mopped up the blood on the asphalt and cleared the downed pecan tree from the road. For a moment, I allowed myself to believe that the morning's trauma was nothing more than a half-remembered nightmare.

Peddling along, I thought back on all that had happened to me and my family in the new times as we responded to the stock market crash, the plagues, the hyperinflation, the riots, and the terrorist attacks.

In happier days, I had lived with my wife and children on LSU Avenue, just a couple of blocks from the LSU campus. I had recently retired, and I spent my time puttering in my vegetable garden and writing scholarly articles that hardly anybody read. My wife and I made plans to travel; Ireland, Greece, and Nova Scotia were on our bucket list.

Then Hurricane Maxine slammed into New Orleans one August day, and my wife and children were swept off the Bonnet Carre Causeway and drowned.

And so I was alone as the world began slipping into chaos. In the years that followed Hurricane Maxine, a series of calamities rocked the American economy, each one pushing society closer and closer toward collapse.

First, worldwide reserves of petroleum dwindled, causing energy prices to skyrocket. Gasoline became so expensive that people couldn't commute to work from the suburbs, and suburban homes became almost worthless.

Food prices shot up, and food shortages became common. For the first time since the Depression of the 1930s, many Americans went hungry, and the federal government began giving away basic commodities like flour, cooking oil, rice, and beans.

Unfortunately, a lot of Americans didn't know how to cook. They had gotten used to going out for dinner, ordering takeout, or heating up prepackaged meals. I remember standing in line to get my monthly allotment of commodities and saw the guy in front of me shaking his head when he received ten pounds of flour and five pounds of cornmeal.

"What am I supposed to do with this shit?" he asked. "I ain't no Betty Crocker."

Then the plagues came. Scientists had developed a vaccine for the coronavirus that appeared in 2020, but new virus strains emerged that were resistant to the vaccines. Death rates rose for each new variant. Millions of people died each year, just as medieval Europeans died of the Black Plague.

Hunger, disease, and despair fueled urban violence. Rioting, looting, and arson destroyed large swaths of American cities, making them unlivable. Municipal services broke down, electricity became unreliable, and garbage pickup ceased. The police stopped showing up at crime scenes; instead, they hunkered down in their precinct buildings behind bulletproof windows and fortified doors.

Besides all this, climate change made the natural environment less predictable and less benign: hurricanes became more frequent and more destructive, rising ocean levels threatened coastal cities, and prolonged droughts endangered the nation's food supplies.

America's enemies saw all this turmoil and exploited it. Terrorists slipped across the nation's southern border with explosives and weapons of biological warfare. Then when American society was already under tremendous stress, foreign saboteurs set off small dirty bombs on the East Coast, causing millions of people to die from radiation poisoning. New York and the mid-Atlantic states became virtually uninhabitable.

In the aftermath of this calamity, American society imploded. The courts ceased to function, state legislatures stopped meeting, and Congress disappeared. Urban violence became so intense that federal troops were called in to restore order in dozens of American cities and impose martial law.

Millions of Americans gave in to despair in the new times. Suicide rates went up just as they did in Germany in 1945 when the Russians invaded. Life lost its purpose for many people, and they ceased to believe that things would ever get better.

Killing oneself was not difficult in those days; there were plenty of guns around. Ammunition was expensive, but all a person needed to commit suicide was a large-caliber pistol and a single bullet. A depressed individual who didn't possess a handgun could always borrow one for a few minutes from a sympathetic gun owner—a crude form of assisted suicide.

Ingesting drugs was another popular way to die because no one could say for sure whether a person committed suicide or accidentally overdosed. Opioids were cheap and readily available.

For years, I had lived in a state of deep depression after I lost my wife and children to Hurricane Maxine. Life lost all meaning to me. I lived one empty day after another as a burned-out professor.

Over time, however, my depression waned, and I adapted to the slow-moving catastrophe of America's meltdown as best I could. My monthly pension checks stopped coming, and then the government stopped sending me my monthly Social Security check. I began drawing down my savings just to buy groceries. But I did not despair.

Instead, I rose to the challenge of finding food and the things I needed to stay alive. I had always been a gardener, but then I began gardening in earnest. I plowed up my lawn to raise vegetables just as the Russians did during the Nazi siege of Leningrad.

Several elderly people lived in my neighborhood, and some of them begged me to plant vegetables in their yards and give them a share of the harvest. I couldn't say no.

Gradually, I became a sunrise-to-sunset gardener. Planting, watering, weeding, and harvesting took up almost all my waking hours as I went from one garden plot to another. I bought a rototiller for an exorbitant price, which I used to prepare the ground for planting.

I also owned a cargo-model e-bike sturdy enough to haul my produce to the farmers market to sell or barter. I could travel forty miles on it between charges, which allowed me to pedal around Baton Rouge to get the supplies I needed to keep my truck-farming operation going.

For a couple of years, I managed to feed myself and a few of my neighbors. I learned to preserve the food I grew—a skill my great-grandparents had mastered, but my generation had never acquired. I made tomato sauce from fresh tomatoes and cucumbers into pickles. I planted cabbages in my autumn garden and began making sauerkraut.

I started raising chickens. Several of my neighbors helped me fence off a vacant lot to accommodate free-ranging poultry, and I gathered the manure for fertilizer.

In spite of these efforts, I realized I could not survive over the long term by gardening and raising chickens, nor could anyone else living in Baton Rouge. City people simply could not grow enough food to get us all through the winter months.

As food became more and more scarce, people in Baton Rouge became desperate—particularly young people. Food riots broke out from time to time at the depleted grocery stores, and bands of looters ranged through affluent neighborhoods looking for food or valuables that could be traded for food.

In the winter months, many townspeople would eat anything. Ducks and geese disappeared from the LSU lakes and went into cooking pots. The squirrels that once gamboled through the live oaks in my neighborhood also went missing as my neighbors and I learned to cook squirrel meat and gravy.

During these years, Baton Rouge still provided municipal water service. People could drink the water from their kitchen taps, they could flush their toilets, and I could irrigate my garden plots. The town still had electricity, but it became quite expensive and less reliable. My home was fitted for natural gas, so I could cook my food even when the electric service was down.

I was part of an extended family of people who lived all over South Louisiana, and I tried to keep in touch with my relatives. Gordon McIlhenny, my brother-in-law, lived near New Orleans with his wife Laura, and we talked by phone every few days.

Gordon was a construction contractor. He owned just about every carpentry tool imaginable. He and Laura lived on a two-acre tract north of Lake Pontchartrain, and he mowed his lawn weekly with a small tractor.

Like many homes on the Gulf Coast, Gordon and Laura's home was elevated twelve feet above ground level as a protection against storm surges. Thus, their house survived Hurricane Maxine, which had destroyed New Orleans, but urban violence drove most of their neighbors out of their homes, and looters and vandals set fire to empty houses.

For a while, Gordon and Laura refused to be driven out, knowing their home would be destroyed by arsonists if they abandoned it. Gordon posted a sign in his front yard warning that the premises were protected by Smith & Wesson—the handgun manufacturer—and he wasn't joking. He packed a .357 revolver whenever he left his house, and criminals knew Gordon would defend his property.

But one day, Gordon called me to say that an armed gang of hoodlums had attacked his home. They didn't have the nerve to break down his front door; they didn't want to run the risk that Gordon would be waiting for them with a loaded shotgun. So instead, they slipped under his elevated house and fired bullets up through the floor. They also tried to set his house on fire.

"Laura and I are getting out," Gordon told me. "We've got to find a safer place to live even if we lose our home."

I urged them to come to Baton Rouge. "There are lots of empty houses in my neighborhood," I said. "The owners either died or disappeared . . . Why don't you and Laura move into one of those?" I suggested. "You can help me with the gardening."

Gordon agreed, and soon Gordon, Laura, and I expanded our garden plots and were selling vegetables. Gordon brought all his carpentry tools and his tractor.

Within a few months, other relatives had joined us in Baton Rouge, and we all managed to keep busy. My niece Allison and her husband Jerry had been restaurant workers in New Orleans before Hurricane Maxine, and they both knew a lot about preparing and preserving food. Sam Avery, one of Gordon's nephews and an ex-marine, became our family's armorer—keeping our weapons clean and in good order, and our ammunition secure.

We acquired a hog and fed it garden scraps. When it had grown to be around three hundred pounds, we butchered it under Jerry's supervision. We processed every part of that hog, including its feet, its ears, and its intestines, which we cleaned and made into sausage casings. As Jerry put it, we preserved every bit of that hog except its squeal.

By this time, Baton Rouge was under permanent martial law. The army established a fort around the state capitol building and named it Fort Sharpton. The soldiers moved their families and dependents into the Spanish Town Historic District, which adjoined the state capitol grounds, and they enclosed the neighborhood within the fort's perimeter with a chain-link fence topped by razor wire.

Years ago, I had read Alexander Solzhenitsyn's book *One Day in the Life of Ivan Denisovich*. I was impressed by the book's protagonist who survived Stalin's concentration camps by being resourceful. Denisovich learned a new trade—bricklaying. He earned a few cents repairing clothing and running errands for other prisoners. Most importantly, Denisovich cultivated a number of reciprocal relationships by being trustworthy and useful.

I decided to adapt Denisovich's survival skills to the new times. I established relationships with the few remaining merchants in Baton Rouge, and I won a reputation for being an honest trader.

In particular, I cultivated a relationship with Colonel Merski, Fort Sharpton's commander. Our family sold food to the garrison, and I occasionally sent the colonel a small gift: a basket of ripe tomatoes, a few jars of blueberry jelly, or some home-brewed beer.

Merski took an interest in our family's garden operation, and he occasionally dropped by to watch us at our work. One day, he made me a proposition.

"Will, your family has made a success out of the truck-farming business. You're raising enough food to sell, and you've won the respect of your neighbors. But wouldn't your farm operation be more efficient if you cultivated one large tract?"

"Yes," I agreed, "but no one in my family owns a farm."

"Well, I've been thinking about this, and I've decided to introduce a homestead program in East Baton Rouge Parish. There are thousands of acres of good farmland along the banks of the Mississippi, and no one is using it."

I told Merski I would love to farm the land south of the LSU campus—land that had once been cultivated by LSU's agricultural college—but LSU still owned that land, and there was no one around with whom I could negotiate a farm lease.

"You forget, Will, that Baton Rouge is under martial law. I get to make the rules now, and I'm going to deed you and your brother-in-law eighty acres apiece on the condition that your family farms the land and sells part of your harvest to the army at a fair price.

"This is an experiment," he added. "If you and Gordon can make it, I'm going to deed more farmland to other families. I estimate at least half of our population has to start farming in order to feed everybody, so we need a lot more farmers."

Gordon and I accepted Merski's offer, and we selected a plot of land near Louisiana State University, which closed shortly after the federal student-loan program collapsed. Our homestead was located not far from the weed-infested LSU golf course. Real estate developers had constructed subdivisions around it during the old times, but this plot remained undeveloped. It was fertile Mississippi River bottomland, perfect for growing crops.

The old Louisiana School for the Deaf, abandoned years ago, bordered this farmland on the south. We fenced in some of the deaf school buildings and topped the fencing with barbed wire. Under Gordon's supervision, we converted the structures into residences for our family members, and we built barns to shelter our animals and store our crops.

Gradually, Lâche Pas became a productive farm. We harvested garden vegetables, planted fruit trees and a blueberry plot, grew sugar cane and sweet potatoes, raised hogs, and brewed beer. In a few years, our family was largely self-sufficient, and we sold or bartered our farm products to obtain things we couldn't grow or make ourselves.

Colonel Merski was so pleased by Lâche Pas's success that he deeded land to other families who promised to develop productive farms. The army confiscated farm machinery that had been abandoned all over South Louisiana—tractors, planting machinery, and plows. He gave this equipment to the farmers, and he sold them some of the army's gasoline—just enough for us to run our tractors and other farm machinery.

In a few years, more than fifty farms were thriving on the east side of the Mississippi River. Before long, the farmers began raising enough food to feed their families and the military garrison. They even produced a surplus and sold food to people in the area.

Gordon and I owned Lâche Pas by virtue of the fact that Colonel Merski had deeded it to us and our family members worked it together. Over time, Gordon became the head of our family clan, with the power to accept new members to our community and to evict members who were quarrelsome or lazy. "This is not a summer-of-love commune," he said repeatedly. "Everybody must work."

Eventually, each family member found a niche. Allison specialized in growing fruit and making jams and jellies. Her husband Jerry supervised our livestock.

I took charge of the truck-farming operation and sold our excess produce. I also helped homeschool the children of Lâche Pas. And from time to time, Colonel Merski hired me to obtain things Fort Sharpton needed.

Within a few years, our community grew to twenty-two people: six married couples, seven children, and three single people. We considered ourselves very fortunate. We grew enough food so that we never went hungry, and we were gradually beginning to prosper.

In spite of the army's presence, Lâche Pas and the other farms remained vulnerable to criminal activity. First, there were the pickers—homeless beggars who occasionally committed acts of petty theft and burglary. Most of the pickers were harmless, but they sometimes robbed people at gunpoint or mugged them on the roads.

Second, armed bands of marauders roamed over the countryside. French-speaking people in South Louisiana called these bandits *routiers*, the name the French gave the mercenary soldiers who terrorized France during the Hundred Years War. Most people called them comancheros.

Besides these threats, we all knew that organized armies were fighting a vicious race war in the southern states to the east. White racists had organized the New Redneck Army, and African Americans had formed an army as well—the Army of the Nubian Nation.

Lâche Pas was safer than the farmsteads that were established downriver because it was located near Fort Sharpton. But even still, all the adults carried sidearms. We also had a collection of hunting rifles and shotguns.

Fortunately, Gordon and I had started hoarding ammunition back in the old times when ammunition could be bought online. Years before American society collapsed, we both had a vague foreboding that the apocalypse was coming. Gordon purchased guns and ammo in a variety of calibers, figuring ammunition for some calibers would become scarcer than others.

Based on advice from friends, who believed 9 mm ammunition would always be popular, I purchased one handgun—a 9 mm Glock, and I bought three thousand rounds of 9 mm ammunition. I also bought a twelve-gauge shotgun and a couple of hundred rounds of buckshot for it.

Gordon and I didn't believe we would ever need to shoot all that ammunition, but we knew it was becoming increasingly scarce and valuable in the new times. We figured we could sell ammo if we needed hard currency or use it for bartering.

I didn't tell anyone outside my family that I was buying bullets because I didn't want to embarrass myself in front of my friends. I didn't want people thinking I was some wacky-prepper or gun nut. But by the time our family established Lâche Pas, I was grateful to have a stock of ammunition for our guns.

Colonel Merski realized the farmers were vulnerable, and he encouraged us to form a militia, which we did. Gordon became the militia commander, and Merski's soldiers trained the farmers in basic infantry tactics.

As I peddled into Lâche Pas at the end of a stressful day, I looked over our family's fields and gardens. Our winter crops were thriving. Rows of mustard greens, collard greens, and turnips reminded me that my family would have green stuff in our diet this winter. We had also planted broccoli, cabbages, and brussels sprouts—crops not yet ready for harvesting.

Near the compound's security fence, I saw leaf lettuce growing. It was ready to pick, and we could eat fresh salads in the late fall. Inside the compound, our herb garden was flourishing, and Allison—who cooked most of our family dinners—could pick basil, oregano, parsley, thyme, and mint any time she needed spice for her cooking.

I walked my e-bike into the Lâche Pas compound, closed the gate behind me, and stowed my bike in the tractor shed. I smelled onions being sauteed and wondered what I would eat for dinner. Then I walked to our farm's armory—a small, windowless building with concrete walls and a steel door. Once inside, I retrieved my Glock from my backpack, removed the ammunition magazine, and replaced the three bullets I had fired. Then I cleaned the barrel with gun solvent and locked the weapon in the gun safe for the night.

Sam, our family's armorer, insisted that all our guns be cleaned on the same day we fired them and that their magazines be checked to make sure they were operable and fully loaded. Normally, I would ask Sam to perform these chores.

Today I did these tasks myself because I didn't want anyone asking questions about why I had fired three bullets from my Glock. Colonel Merski had given me good advice when he told me not to tell my family that I had shot two people on River Road that morning.

I was filled with gratitude that my family had adapted to the new times and that we had enough to eat, but the day's encounter with the bandits on River Road made me apprehensive about the future. Would we survive if the comancheros attacked us? Could we defend our farm if the Nubians or the Rednecks tried to conquer the Mississippi valley?

But I pushed these thoughts to the back of my mind as I walked over to our community pantry, found a mug, and poured myself a draft of cool apple cider. To the west, I watched the sun go down behind the Mississippi River levee. I sipped my cider and allowed my thoughts to turn toward Texas.

AMBUSHED ON THE
ATCHAFALAYA CAUSEWAY

The morning after the River Road shootout, I showed up at Fort Sharpton's front gate a little before dawn. A Red Ball Express truck was idling in the parking lot, having arrived that morning after an all-night run from Mobile.

My heart clinched in my chest at the sight of the bedraggled passengers who staggered off the truck. They had ridden all night huddled in the back of a flatbed trailer. They were dirty, poorly dressed, and weary, but they seemed grateful to find themselves safe in Baton Rouge without getting ambushed on the road.

A half dozen Fort Sharpton soldiers were processing the passengers in the parking lot. A couple of enlisted personnel were checking identification documents, and others were searching baggage for contraband. A medical officer conducted a brief health exam for all the new arrivals to identify anyone who was ill from COVID-37, the latest variant of the coronavirus.

I caught sight of Lieutenant Wilhelmina Barkley, who was standing apart from the hustle and bustle of disembarking Red Ball passengers. I headed over to her. "Hi, Mr. Burns," she said. "Sergeant Guadalupe Gomez and I will be your military escort on your trip to Houston."

Lieutenant Barkley was a middle-aged woman, probably in her late forties, with streaks of gray in her hair. She was a bit overweight, and her combat fatigues fit snugly. I knew her only slightly as a widow who was said to be a crack shot with a rifle.

I had not met Sergeant Gomez before. She was a trim woman with coal-black hair tucked in a bun under her military helmet. She and the Lieutenant were both armed with standard assault rifles and Beretta 9 mm pistols. Their camouflage vests were stuffed with extra ammunition magazines, and they both wore bullet-proof Kevlar vests.

The lieutenant handed me a fistful of army paperwork: requisition orders, travel vouchers, and a list of things that Colonel Merski wanted me to procure in Houston. The big-ticket items were cavalry gear: saddles (preferably western), bridles, saddle blankets, hoof picks, curry combs, and veterinary supplies. He also wanted me to buy large quantities of mosquito repellent, axes, hand saws, and two-man crosscut saws.

To my surprise, Colonel Merski also put disposable diapers on his procurement list. "Diapers!" I exclaimed in surprise. "How many diapers does he want and what sizes?"

"The colonel wants you to buy as many diapers as you can lay your hands on, in all sizes," Lieutenant Barkley answered. "He said it's a morale issue."

As we talked, I looked up to see Sergeant Gomez climbing onto a steel platform that had been welded to the back of the truck cab. The platform was fitted with a waist-high guardrail that made it look like the crow's nest on a nineteenth-century sailing ship. Two enlisted men handed her a M-240 machine gun, which she clamped to some fittings that had been bolted to the roof of the cab.

The Red Ball Express was a private trucking company subsidized by the military. Its official name, given to it by the army, was Civilian Auxiliary Transport System (CATS), but most people called it the Red Ball Express after the famous army truck convey system that operated in Europe during World War II. The original Red Ball Express ran truckloads of food, fuel, and ammunition from Atlantic seaports to frontline troops in France and Germany.

The present-day Red Ball operated dozens of trucks along Interstate 10 and a few other Interstate highways, hauling freight on flatbed trailers for the military and civilian merchants. In addition, if a particular truck had unused space, the truck line sold passenger tickets to civilians for a modest price.

Riding the Red Ball was a miserable way to travel because the passengers were required to ride in the back of the trucks' open-air trailers, protected only by a light railing. To make matters worse, the trucks did not stop for meals or restroom breaks. Blue portable toilets were usually placed on the very back of the flatbed trailers, which passengers would use in lieu of proper restrooms.

I noticed that Ernie Esperanza was our civilian truck driver for the run to Houston. I knew Ernie casually as an usher at St. Joan of Arc Catholic Church and a Fourth Degree Knight of Columbus. I didn't go to mass much anymore, but I had seen him a few times at Catholic functions all decked out in his fourth-degree regalia: admiral's hat with a feather plume, red cape, white sash, and dress sword.

Ernie wasn't wearing his plumed hat today. Instead, he showed up in a shapeless, green fishing shirt and frayed blue jeans. He had a holstered 9 mm pistol strapped to his waist.

"Hi, Mr. Burns," he called out cheerfully, and then immediately hit me up to buy a raffle ticket.

"Say, Mr. Burns, have you bought your raffle tickets yet for the church bazaar? We're giving away a barbeque pit—almost brand new."

"What's it going to cost me?" I asked.

"One silver dime or forty paper bucks. And your ticket gets you into the fish fry."

"That's a good deal," I said. "I think I've got a couple of dimes. I'll buy two."

Ernie finished our transaction and then climbed into the truck cab. "Saddle up!" he shouted. "We're burning daylight."

As a government contractor, I was privileged to ride in the cab with Esperanza. I squeezed in between Ernie and Lieutenant Barkley, who sat by the passenger door with her rifle barrel sticking out the window.

"Mr. Burns," Esperanza said, "this is your lucky day. This beat-up truck still has its windshield. It's cracked, I admit, but it'll keep the bugs out of your teeth.

"And that's not all," he added proudly. "The CD player still works." He handed me a vinyl carrying case stuffed with CDs.

"You got any Hank Williams?" I asked.

"You bet your cheating heart I do."

"How about Merle Haggard?"

"Oh, yeah. I've got some Merle CDs. And I got Tammy, Dolly, Lefty, and Willie. You are in for a treat."

I thumbed through Ernie's CD collection to see what other treasures it might contain. "Hey," I exclaimed in surprise, "you've even got a Wanda Jackson CD. She's the Queen of Rockabilly."

"Don't I know it," Ernie replied. "That Wanda CD is my most valuable possession." He slipped the disk into the Peterbilt's CD player, and soon we were listening to Wanda Jackson belting out "Riot in Cell Block #9," my favorite rockabilly song.

And so we were off. I heard Ernie muttering to himself as we pulled onto the I-10 bridge. "Our Lady of the Highway, pray for us." He made the sign of the cross.

I had long ago ceased being a devout Catholic, but I still went to mass occasionally. When I saw Ernie crossing himself, I instinctively did the same. Apparently, Lieutenant Barkley was also a Catholic because she too crossed herself without embarrassment.

"Oh ho!" Ernie exclaimed at these unexpected signs of devotion. "Three Catholics in a Peterbilt! What could go wrong?"

I was excited, I admit, to be on the road. I hadn't been in a motorized vehicle for more than a year. The Red Ball trucks only traveled at about twenty-five miles per hour, due to the miserable condition of the highway. It would take us eleven hours for us to reach Houston—only a four-hour drive during the old times.

Still, it was exhilarating to be headed west to Texas, where I had lived long ago in another time. I found myself wondering whether *Mi Raza Su Raza*, my favorite Mexican seafood restaurant, was still open on Houston's Richmond Street, and I thought about the remote possibility of getting a cup of real coffee.

"Lieutenant," I said, "I appreciate having you and Sergeant Gomez for protection. Maybe someday we can travel safely down the interstate highways without a military escort."

Lieutenant Barkley shook her head at my naivety. "Mr. Burns," she replied, "there will never be a day when you won't be running a risk if you're on the interstate. Conditions on the roads are getting worse, not better. Just last week, a Red Ball truck was hijacked west of Jacksonville. The driver and all the passengers were killed, and comancheros made off with the truck. Another truck was attacked outside Biloxi a few days ago. They didn't get the truck, but they wounded the driver and some of the passengers."

I had not known that the interstate highways were so dangerous. I listened intently to Lieutenant Barkley's words.

"Fact of the matter," she continued," the army won't be able to keep the roads open much longer. We don't have the diesel, and we don't have the personnel to ensure people's safety. Fort Sharpton is responsible for guarding the last operating oil refineries in Louisiana. We're also in charge of keeping the bridges open and patrolling the Mississippi River levees, but we don't have near enough people to handle all these jobs."

"But the road to Houston is safe, isn't it?"

"Probably. As far as I know, we've never had a hijacking on that section of I-10. But you never know. The causeway over the Atchafalaya Swamp is the most dangerous stretch of road— a seventeen-mile-long bridge with no roadside cover and no exits. If we get stopped up there, we'll be sitting ducks."

I realized then that I was distracting Lieutenant from her guard duties, and that she was becoming slightly perturbed. "I can't talk to you anymore," she said abruptly. "I have to keep my eyes on the road."

I've always been an optimist, so Lieutenant Barkley's dour assessment didn't bother me in the least. I was on the move on a pleasant autumn day, and I enjoyed being surrounded by forests and swamps as we motored along at a steady pace. Most of the trees were bare, and leaves were scattered on the roadside; but the palmettos and the wild magnolia trees were still green, and the leaves on the swamp maple trees had turned scarlet, adding a little color to the grey woodlands.

Like Lieutenant Barkley, Ernie was looking for signs of trouble on the road ahead. After a few minutes, he turned off the CD player, and we traveled down the interstate in silence.

Soon, I fell asleep, lulled by the rocking motion of the truck and the reassuring purr of the Peterbilt's diesel engine.

About an hour later, I awoke to find Lieutenant Barkley shaking me by the arm. "Wake up, Mr. Burns. We've got trouble."

We were on the Atchafalaya Causeway. Peering ahead, I saw a barricade stretched across the road, made up of all kinds of debris—tree trunks, wrecked cars, and oil drums. Behind the barrier were six or seven people, both men and women, and they were all carrying guns. *Comancheros!*

Esperanza stopped the truck a hundred yards from the roadblock and let the engine idle. He pulled his pistol from its holster, checked to make sure it was loaded, and laid the gun on the dashboard.

For about ten minutes, nothing happened. I think the comancheros were surprised to see Sergeant Gomez's machine gun perched on top of the truck cab and were debating whether to take us on.

I found myself wishing I had disregarded Colonel Merski's order not to take my Glock to Texas. *How comforting it would be to be holding a pistol.*

Then a couple of shots rang out from the barricade. A bullet slammed through the windshield and hit Esperanza in the face. He slumped over the steering wheel; blood spewed all over the cab.

Barkley was standing behind the open passenger door when the shooting started. "Rules of engagement!" she shouted.

"Copy that!" Gomez replied, and began firing the machine gun at the hijackers, shooting in short bursts.

Meanwhile, Lieutenant Barkley loaded the grenade launcher under the barrel of her rifle, and lobbed smoke grenades into the barricade. She was remarkably accurate. In just a few seconds, the barricade became almost completely obscured by smoke.

"Okay, Mr. Burns," Lieutenant Barkley said to me, "let's roll. We've got to get over that barrier and clear out the bandits, or we're going to die. Follow me and stay close."

Wait a minute, I thought to myself. *Isn't she supposed to be protecting me? I didn't sign on to fight robbers.*

"But Lieutenant," I protested, "I'm not weapons qualified." I think I was parroting a line from an old movie I had seen years ago: *13 Hours.*

Barkley must have seen the same movie, because she handed me her sidearm and said, "Now you're weapons qualified. Just point and shoot and keep shooting until you hit somebody. And don't shoot me." And then she sprinted down the causeway.

She was surprisingly swift for a middle-aged woman. I was a good twenty years older than she was, and I had trouble keeping up with her. But I did my best. I desperately yearned to keep Lieutenant Barkley's Kevlar vest between me and the flying bullets.

Sergeant Gomez continued firing the machine gun, which made a merry staccato sound—like popcorn popping on the kitchen stove when I was a kid.

When we got to the barrier, the Lieutenant plunged into the smoke. Guns went off and I heard men and women cursing and shouting in defiance.

Very timidly, I edged into the murk and watched the Lieutenant shoot our attackers almost methodically. She gave no one a chance to surrender, even though a couple of people dropped their weapons and shouted, "I give up!"

"Mr. Burns," she ordered. "Some guy is getting away. Shoot him."

I saw then that the comancheros had given themselves an escape route by hanging a rope ladder off the concrete guardrail. Their plan must have been to scramble down that ladder if their ambush went awry, and escape through the swamp. I spotted one bandit disappear down it into the murky terrain below.

I didn't want to stick my head over the guardrail and make myself a target for anyone standing below the causeway—a good way to get my head blown off, I figured. So I extended my arm over the railing and shot blindly in the general direction of the ladder. I wasn't even trying to aim the weapon.

"Burns," Lieutenant Barkley shouted over the thundering noise, "you can't kill someone you can't see. Get eyes on that bastard and shoot him."

I did as she ordered and peered down into the swamp. Some poor soul was clinging to the ladder about ten feet above the ground. He gave me a frightened, pleading look. "Don't shoot," he said. "I surrender."

I ignored his plea and began shooting. I fired several times without hitting him, even though he was only six or seven feet away.

I kept pulling the trigger just as Barkley instructed, and I finally shot the guy in the neck. He fell into the swamp face down in the water.

Suddenly, all was quiet. Lieutenant Barkley searched through the debris checking bodies, making sure no one was alive. A couple of comancheros were still breathing; she shot them both in the head.

"Okay, Mr. Burns, we're done here. Let's get back to the truck."

I gave her back her pistol. "I'm sorry, Lieutenant," I said. "I wasted a lot of your bullets. I'm a terrible shot."

"That's okay, Mr. Burns. Fort Sharpton has plenty of ammunition. We could shoot people every day 'til Jesus comes, and we wouldn't run out. It's food and gasoline—that's what we're short of."

WE ROLL INTO TEXAS

When we got back to the truck, Lieutenant Barkley climbed on the running board and checked Ernie Esperanza's vital signs. He was dead.

We found Sergeant Gomez in the back of the truck, administering first aid to two wounded passengers. Two other passengers were dead.

"Some bandits attacked us from behind," Gomez explained. "The poor passengers were sitting ducks. Nothing to hide behind except the porta-potty."

"How'd you hold them off?" Barkley asked.

"Well, the machine gun was clamped down, facing forward, so it was useless to me. So I fired at them with my service rifle. They bolted away right when I started shooting. A couple of them were trying to drag a chain across the road to block our escape, but they gave up on that idea once my bullets went whizzing around them."

"What a mess," Barkley said. "Gomez, be very careful, but go down to where you saw the shooters and make sure they're all gone. Take out anyone you find alive and dump all the bodies over the causeway. Bring back any weapons or ammo that you find.

"And if it's safe," she continued, rather cautiously for someone so sure of herself in a combat situation, "get one of the passengers to bring that chain back here. The army can always use a good chain."

Barkley and I walked back to the barricade. One passenger volunteered to help us clear the junk off the road. Five dead bandits lay sprawled on the pavement. Barkley ordered us to gather up all their weapons and search the bodies for ammunition before we dumped them in the swamp.

Our volunteer was a grey-headed man with braided, greasy hair. He was wearing a ragged New Orleans Saints sweatshirt and polyester pants. He might have been elderly, but it was impossible to guess how old he was. People aged quickly in the new times unless they ate regularly and had a safe place to sleep.

The guy picked up a pink .380 next to one of the female bandits, and slipped it into his dirty trousers. He then went through the dead woman's clothing and her child-size pink backpack—a Disney pack with an image of Snow White on the back. I saw him gather up a fistful of bullets for the .380; he only turned some of them over to Barkley.

I should report him to Barkley, I told myself. But I didn't. I couldn't. That raggedy old man would need a gun wherever he was going, and that small-caliber pink pistol would be useful to him. I figured he might sleep better at night if he had a loaded gun in his pocket.

It was now midmorning, and we were still ten hours from Houston. I pulled Esperanza's body out of the truck cab and put it on the flatbed trailer. I covered his body and the bodies of the two dead passengers with a tarp I found in the truck cab.

Lieutenant Barkley then addressed all the survivors. "Okay, here's what we're going to do: I'll man the machine gun in the crow's nest, and Sergeant Gomez will ride in the trailer with the passengers. She'll respond if we get attacked again from the rear.

"We'll put the two wounded passengers in the truck cab. Mr. Burns, you'll drive the truck. I'm not going to ask you if you've ever driven an 18-wheeler before because I don't think you have. And frankly, it doesn't matter."

I wiped away Esperanza's blood the best I could and crawled up into the driver's seat. No use telling Barkley that I wasn't competent to drive a commercial truck. She had put me in charge of getting us all to Houston, and I'd just have to figure it out. The old Peterbilt had eighteen gears. I finally found a gear that seemed appropriate for driving at twenty-five miles an hour, and soon we were slowly motoring down the interstate.

After we got rolling, we had no more mishaps. We made one stop at the army roadblock on the Sabine River. An army medic checked on the two wounded passengers, and told us to keep moving. A young, enlisted man with a West Texas accent tossed a case of bottled water into the back of the truck. "Y'all stay hydrated," he told the passengers. "And remember, all y'all are in shock."

Then we crossed the state border, and drove past the old welcome center where in the old times people stopped to go to the bathroom and get a Texas roadmap. The flagpole was still standing and flew an enormous Texas flag over a smaller American flag flying upside down.

I knew that flying a flag upside down was considered disrespectful and should only be flown that way as a signal of severe distress. *What does the army mean by flying the American flag that way?*

I drove on to Houston in absolute silence. Both wounded passengers stared vacantly at the passing landscape. I was curious to know more about them. *Where were they going,* I wondered, *and what are their long-term plans for survival?* I didn't try to talk with them, however, because I knew they were in shock. Instead, I concentrated on the road ahead. Debris often littered the highway—some too small to notice until too late. I didn't want to puncture a truck tire, which would leave our little group stranded on this dangerous highway.

I knew that Colonel Merski had given his troops a standing order to take no prisoners when dealing with the comancheros; after the ambush on the Atchafalaya Causeway, Merski's policy made sense to me. Lieutenant Barkley and Sergeant Gomez were outnumbered and fighting off an attack from two sides. They could not possibly take prisoners while fighting a life-or-death battle with a superior force of terrorists.

Still, I was shocked to see Lieutenant Barkley execute comancheros who were begging for mercy. I was also shocked at myself—how easy it had been for me to shoot a helpless man who was trying to surrender. Lieutenant Barkley ordered me to shoot the guy, and I shot him without a qualm.

After passing through the Sabine River checkpoint, I continued driving west on I-10 through the ruins of Beaumont and crossed the Trinity River and San Jacinto Bayou. About forty miles east of Houston, I began driving through vast suburban housing tracts. Almost every house was empty. When America was a nation of 330 million people, it needed those houses; now, with maybe only thirty million people, there were way too many dwellings.

I drove into the city's center during what once would have been rush hour, but I saw no vehicles on the road other than an occasional army truck. I drove by abandoned apartment complexes, condominiums, taquerias, Asian restaurants, and auto repair shops. I didn't see any open shops or stores—no one walking on the streets.

Houston, people once said, was a metropolis made possible by air conditioning. But when the power grid went down, the air conditioning went down with it. Now all these homes and businesses were uninhabitable.

The glorious Houston skyline looked like a monster cemetery, with each empty skyscraper now a glass-and-steel tombstone. No one took the elevator to the fortieth floor anymore. The elevators were no longer operational, the air conditioning had shut down, and the windows were designed not to open. They only served as reminders of the life that once lived below them.

In any event, there was no work for anyone to do in Houston's many office towers. No one needed corporate lawyers because there were no corporations and no law. No one needed financial services because the dollar was worthless. No one needed insurance because nothing of value remained to be insured. What people needed now were food and shelter, and food and shelter were not to be found in the sky towers of Houston.

Over a period of fifty years, Texans paved more than a thousand square miles of the South Texas coastal plains. Those plains once soaked up rainwater; now, a combination of rising sea levels and that fast-paced suburban development had turned parts of the city of Houston into nothing but a swamp in the new times.

Once the coastal plain was covered with concrete, there was no place for the water to go; every heavy rain became a flood event. Even before the economy imploded, old Houston neighborhoods that had never flooded became swamps after every heavy rainfall. Houses being rebuilt in those neighborhoods were erected on stilts—if they were erected at all—while some parts of Houston began taking on the appearance of Venice.

Then there were the riots, the arson, the looting, and the random murders. The recurring plagues, which always seemed to manage to stay a few months ahead of the newest vaccine, wiped out a good chunk of the population from the formerly fourth most populous city in the US. Houston became a big, dead city—home to nothing.

At last, I drove our truckload of misery into the city's core and rolled to a stop at the front gate of Fort Joplin.

LOOKING FOR SADDLES AND DIAPERS

I drove through Fort Joplin's front gate a little after sunset. It was a moonless night, but the sky was aglow with millions of stars—stars that Houstonians had not seen back when electric lighting had obscured the nighttime heavens.

We were now inside Houston's I-610 inner loop on the grounds of the University of St. Thomas, which closed long ago. The army had taken over the university grounds and parts of Montrose Avenue, including the old Chinese Consulate. A chain-link fence topped with barbed wire surrounded the fort's perimeter, and soldiers guarded the main gate, standing behind a wall of sandbags and manning a .50 caliber machine gun.

The army established Fort Joplin during the early years of the new times in an effort to guard the Houston oil refineries and quell the urban warfare that broke out after the dollar collapsed. The city of Houston was under martial law, but the army's authority only extended to the outer fringes of the Houston metropolitan area. Chaos continued to reign in large parts of Texas.

As our truck rolled to a halt, we must have looked like a scene from an old western movie—the stagecoach pulling into Lordsburg, arrows piercing its side, with Lieutenant Barkley playing the role of a weary John Wayne cradling his Winchester. The truck's windshield was pierced with bullet holes, as was the porta-potty. Mr. Esperanza's dried blood stained the driver-side door.

A trim captain stepped up and scanned our truck and its passengers with a flashlight. "Ah, jeez," he said. "I can see you ran into some trouble." Lieutenant Barkley said nothing until she had finished helping Sergeant Gomez unclamp the machine gun from the roof of the truck cab.

"We were ambushed in Louisiana," she explained, "somewhere around milepost 122. We lost our driver and two passengers, and we've got two wounded civilians inside the cab."

Medics moved in to put the wounded on stretchers and carry them to the base's infirmary. Soldiers began processing the other passengers and unloading military cargo from the flatbed trailer.

"How many attackers?" the captain asked.

"I'd say about a dozen. They barricaded the causeway to stop us, and then they attacked from both the front and the back of the truck. We killed six of them. The others escaped through the swamp. We think we wounded one or two who got carried off by their comrades."

"These people look hungry," the captain said as he surveyed the scruffy passengers who seemed to be in a zombie-like trance. "We've got nothing to eat at this hour except MREs, but I'll make sure everyone gets a box.

"I've got you and Sergeant Gomez booked into the Bachelor Officer Quarters, and we also have a room for your civilian contract officer—it's Mr. Burns, right?"

I nodded as the captain surveyed my bloody, dirty appearance. "MREs?" I asked

"Meals ready to eat. Pray you don't have to eat them for too long.

"We don't have hot showers right now," the captain said, "but you can take a warm shower tomorrow morning beginning at 0500. But don't linger in the shower," he added—looking directly at me, "or there won't be enough hot water for everybody else. Breakfast is served in the mess hall at 0600.

"Our commissary officer will meet you at the mess hall at 0800 to help you get the supplies you're looking for. But before you leave the base, you'll need to talk with General Mier, the post commander. He'll want a debrief from the three of you about the ambush."

I checked in to the BOQ, which had once been a college dormitory. I washed Esperanza's blood off my arms and hands, and picked through my MRE. I decided to skip the entre—vegetarian Mexican pasta—and nibbled a bit on an army chocolate bar.

My mind told me not to think about the day's events until I would be back home at Lâche Pas. Nevertheless, I reflected on everything that had happened to me since I left Baton Rouge early in the morning.

I have never considered myself physically courageous. I hadn't gone out for football back in my high school years in West Texas, in spite of the fact that boys who didn't play football were virtual nonentities. I had been frail in my youth, and I was afraid of getting hurt.

Yet Lieutenant Barkley had given me her Beretta, confident—apparently—that I could be useful in a gunfight. And I, unthinkingly, joined her charge on the comancheros' barricade.

It's true I shrunk back from exposing myself to a bullet when she ordered me to shoot one of our attackers who was trying to escape. But I eventually followed Barkley's orders and shot the guy. On the whole, I thought I had acquitted myself fairly well.

Then Lieutenant Barkley directed me to drive the Peterbilt into Houston, and I got the job done. I admit that my performance had been far from professional—I never got the truck out of one of its lower gears. God help me if I had been required to put the truck in reverse. But we had gotten safely into Houston, and I had parked the big rig without running into Fort Joplin's front gate.

I had killed a young man—a helpless young man. *Had that been the right thing to do?* After all, he'd looked harmless enough hanging from that rope ladder like a monkey.

Nevertheless, I concluded, I had done the right thing when I followed Lieutenant Barkley's order. That man chose to attack a truckload of innocent people, and he probably would've helped his comrades kill us all if the ambush had been successful.

I fell asleep wondering if the army would serve me a cup of coffee in the morning—that delightful elixir I had taken for granted in the old times. It was in very short supply in Louisiana, so some people had resorted to making ersatz coffee from roasted barley, chicory roots, or even ground acorns. But in my mind, the foundation of civilized life was a cup of strong, hot coffee in the morning; I dearly missed it.

I awoke early the next day and walked to the communal shower room. I steeled myself for a tepid sprinkle, but to my surprise, I was sprayed with steaming, hot water just like in the old times. Hot water—another foundation of civilized life.

The captain had warned me not to linger in the shower, so I quickly washed my hair and scrubbed the dirt, grime, and blood off my body. I was tempted to loiter under the shower stream and luxuriate in a sense of wholesome warmth and cleanliness, but I forced myself to turn off the spigot after five or six minutes.

Then I got dressed in my civilian-contractor outfit: a frayed, white Joseph E. Banks dress shirt and a pair of much-worn khakis that I bought at the Gap back in the days when America had clothing stores. I tried to remember the last time I had walked into a clothing store to buy something to wear. Was it ten years ago? Fifteen years ago? I couldn't remember.

I walked over to the mess hall for breakfast. The army did not serve me any coffee, but I did get a cup of black tea—steaming hot and caffeinated, not quite as good as coffee—and three pancakes.

The breakfast menu told me the army was on short rations. I took a single syrup packet from a metal bowl next to a sign that said: "Take one only. Personnel taking two syrup packets will be shot. Personnel taking three packets will be shot twice."

Lieutenant Barkley and Sergeant Gomez were midway through their breakfast when I sat down at their table. "Hello, soldier boy," Barkley greeted me cheerfully. "Did you sleep okay?"

"Yeah, I did, Lieutenant, but I think I've got some sleepless nights ahead of me. It's going to take me a while to process everything that happened yesterday."

42

"You two were magnificent," I added. "We'd have all been killed if you hadn't been with us."

"You did your part," Barkley responded. "I'm sorry I got you involved in the fighting, but we had to clear that barricade, and I didn't think I could do it by myself."

"I'm glad we made it out alive. It means a lot to me that you called on me to help out."

Fort Joplin's commissary officer showed up at that moment. I looked up to see an energetic-looking, young officer clutching a clipboard. He wore a starched khaki uniform, his shoes were shined, and his face was unlined with worry. He looked like had stepped out of the old times. *Does this guy iron his own uniforms?*

"Good morning, everyone. I'm Major Quezada. I went over Fort Sharpton's requisition list that Lieutenant Barkley shared with me this morning, and I think I can help you find what you need.

"I can see you're looking for equine supplies—saddles, bridles, and whatnot. The best place to go is Telephone Road. There are a couple of saddleries over there. Check out Zapata's saddlery and the Ortiz shop first. Both are run by Mexicans—real craftsmen, both of them."

Quezada nodded my way as he continued. "I've got a bike for you, Mr. Burns, and a bike for Lieutenant Barkley. We're sending along an MP to be your guide.

"Here he is, Corporal James Bonham," Quezada said as he turned toward a skinny young soldier wearing a camo-patterned uniform and a helmet liner bearing the stenciled letters MP. "You all are free to leave right after you meet with General Mier."

Corporal Bonham escorted us into General Manuel Mier's office, which was the former provost's suite at the University of St. Thomas. The room still contained the accouterments of academia: framed diplomas hanging askew on one wall, and a crimson-colored academic cap and gown hanging on a coat rack.

Standing in the provost's suite, I recalled a time when I was a young college professor who aspired to become a university provost. I had a strong legal background, good writing skills, and a knack for settling disputes and solving problems. I had handled a multitude of human resources issues when I had been a practicing attorney and possessed the guts to fire incompetent or lazy employees. Surely academia could use a guy like me.

But I eventually realized I was not cut out to be a university administrator. Universities never fired a tenured professor unless he committed rape or murder or said something politically incorrect. I knew faculty members who didn't even show up for work regularly or grade their students' papers. I knew a few who seduced their graduate students year after year, and several who suffered from serious mental illness. I even remember a couple of professors who were engaged in outright fraud.

The department chairs, the deans, the provosts, and the bureaucrats in the human resources bunker didn't want to do anything about dysfunctional faculty members. They just wanted a quiet life and a nice pension. They certainly didn't want to appoint a person like me who was willing to shake things up.

These thoughts depressed me for a moment; and I wondered, not for the first time, whether I had wasted a good part of my life pursuing an academic career. Academic life is supposed to be intellectually stimulating, but my life had become a lot more zestful and fulfilling in the new times. Growing food and working for Colonel Merski was considerably more satisfying than being a professor, and I was grateful that these troubled times had given me a new lease on life.

I shook off these thoughts as Lieutenant Barkley, Sergeant Gomez, and I filed into Mier's office. The general offered us a cup of hot tea, and then listened intently while Lieutenant Barkley briefed him on our skirmish on I-10. She praised Sergeant Gomez while minimizing her own role, and she even put in a good word for me.

Somehow Lieutenant Barkley's humility didn't surprise me. After all, a woman who is willing to charge a barricade while people were shooting at her is not a person who would brag about her courage. I was deeply touched by her generosity in giving me some credit for the causeway battle. I knew then that the Lieutenant was someone I could count on, and I was grateful that Colonel Merski had chosen her to protect me on my journey to Houston.

"We've got Mr. Esperanza's body in a walk-in cooler," General Mier informed us. "Army practice is to cremate the remains in situations like this. Do you happen to know if he was married?"

I was startled to realize that I had completely forgotten about Ernie Esperanza, whose blood I had washed off my arms only a few hours before.

I spoke up. "Yes, General, Ernie was married, and he had two children."

"I'll send Colonel Merski a message this morning by the Red Ball, briefing him on your fracas and listing your casualties. I assume the colonel will inform Mr. Esperanza's widow."

"Wait a minute," I burst out without thinking. "I don't think Ernie's widow would want him to be cremated. Ernie was a devout Catholic at his parish church back in Baton Rouge, and an actively participating Fourth Degree Knight of Columbus. I'm sure he would want a funeral mass and a knight escort to the cemetery."

I had clearly irritated General Mier. "Mr. Burns, what in the hell are you talking about? The army has no means for getting Mr. Esperanza's remains back to Baton Rouge. As you well know, that's at least a twelve-hour journey. How would you preserve the corpse? Not to mention there's not a single coffin in all of Houston. We've been burying the dead in mass graves or burning them in great pyres for several years. I see no reason for treating your truck driver any differently."

"But he's a Fourth Degree Knight, sir," I protested lamely, sounding, I feared, like a small child who had been denied a cookie. I felt my face turn red, embarrassed that one simple outburst made me look like a whiny old man who was living in the past, not the guy who had shot a comanchero the day before.

Yet I could not allow Ernie Esperanza's death to be dismissed so easily. I saw his face in my mind and remembered the pleasure he had taken in sharing his country music CDs with me in the Peterbilt.

I recalled Ernie's simple, almost childlike Catholic faith that was always evident during the mass when he would humbly grasp the host—the Body of Christ— and place it on his tongue. In my mind, he was a better Catholic than Father Kerry, our parish priest. Ernie accepted the mystical doctrines of the Church without question, and he strove to follow his Christian vocation, which, he would tell you, was to be a good husband and father.

I knew, too, that the bullet that killed Ernie could easily have killed me instead. I was sitting right beside him in the truck cab when the shooting started. It could have been me that was slated for a mass cremation this morning and not Ernie.

My mind flashed back to the sight of Ernie's bloody corpse slumped in the cab of the Red Ball truck. Who would tell his wife that her husband was dead? I remembered seeing Ernie's family kneeling every Sunday at the communion rail at St. Joan of Arc church, and I wondered how his wife would bear her spouse's death and how his children would survive without their father.

Then Sergeant Gomez jumped in. "Respectfully, sir, I can build a simple coffin for Mr. Esperanza. I just need some wood, a saw, and a few carpentry tools."

"So, Sergeant Gomez, in addition to being a machine gunner, you're a coffin maker?" General Mier replied skeptically, a touch of sarcasm in his voice.

"I was a frame carpenter, sir, in another life."

"We're in the new times now, Sergeant," General Mier responded. "There are too many dead to be dealt with in the old way. You know that, don't you?"

"I know, sir. But we still have to treat the dead with respect. Ernie Esperanza died doing a dangerous job—trying to get cargo and passengers to Houston. We can't just throw his body in a pile for burning."

General Mier let out a great sigh of exasperation. "So Sergeant Gomez can build a coffin. But you still have to preserve the body until you get back to Fort Sharpton."

Sergeant Gomez didn't have a solution for that problem, and I didn't either. But the sergeant's unexpected interjection had prompted General Mier to have a change of heart.

"Okay, team, this is what we are going to do: I'll send Sergeant Gomez to the motor pool. There are a couple of grunts there who are pretty crafty, and they've got carpentry tools. Houston has plenty of used lumber for a coffin."

He turned to Gomez. "Sergeant, can you build a coffin in one day?"

"Yes, sir," Sergeant Gomez replied crisply. "All I need is lumber and some tools, and maybe one skilled person to help me."

"Then we'll keep Mr. Esperanza's remains in the cooler," General Mier concluded. "I'll order someone to reinstall the icemaker so you can pack the body in ice on the trip to Louisiana."

"You've got ice?" I said in surprise. "Fort Joplin must have plenty of electricity."

"Yes, Mr. Burns, we've got electricity. You've heard of the Texas grid, of course. Parts of Texas are still getting electricity from that grid—mostly wind and solar-generated. The grid only provides about 10 percent of what we would need if we went back to the old way of living. But with strict rationing, we get enough juice for essential services. And I'm declaring ice for Mr. Esperanza to be an essential service—which means no warm showers tomorrow morning."

"Thanks, General," I said gratefully, my voice cracking just a little. "This will mean a lot to Ernie's widow and to his children.

"Burying the dead is one of the seven corporal works of mercy," I added gratuitously. "I learned that from Ernie."

"I understand that, Mr. Burns," General Mier replied in an even voice. "But it's gotten kind of hard to practice some of those works of mercy in the new times."

A few minutes later, Corporal Bonham returned, and soon we were peddling down Alabama Street on three olive drab Schwinn bikes. Lieutenant Barkley slung her rifle over her bike's handlebar, and Corporal Bonham carried a sidearm.

"My god," Lieutenant Barkley exclaimed a few minutes later as we came upon a cluster of bleak grey edifices. "What an ugly bunch of buildings! Is that a prison?"

"No," Corporal Bonham replied. "That's the University of Houston, or as Houstonians used to call it, Cougar High School. It closed a long time ago."

"That's probably a good thing," Barkley responded. "I would think it would be pretty depressing to be a student there. Doesn't look like anybody looted it, though. That's odd."

"Think about it, Lieutenant," Bonham replied. "There's nothing worth stealing at a college except the T-shirts in the bookstore. What would looters find if they broke into a professor's office? A dirty coffee cup, maybe? Some ungraded student papers?"

We turned left to pass under I-H 45 and on to Telephone Road. I had lived in Houston many years ago, and I was familiar with Telephone Road as it was in the old times. I couldn't help but reminisce a bit.

"The old Telephone Road was a magical place back in the petroleum era," I explained to Corporal Bonham and Lieutenant Barkley. "This is where the Texaco workers went to blow their paychecks. Lots of used car lots, dance halls, and bars. Lots of hamburger joints and cheap Tex-Mex restaurants."

Looking down the street, I could see Telephone Road had changed. Most of the businesses were closed, and some were burned out. The restaurants and beer joints were gone. But we found Zapata's saddlery with no trouble.

Plutarco Zapata greeted us from the back of his store, an elderly man with an air of dignity that some people acquire as a recompense for growing old. He did not seem surprised to see me and two armed soldiers walk into his shop.

"I'm a civilian contractor for the army," I told him. "We need western saddles—at least forty. We also need bridles, saddle blankets, and all sorts of farrier tools: curry combs, hoof picks, hoof nippers, and farrier's rasps."

Senor Zapata swept his hands around the shop. "We have what you see," he said, as if people came into his store every day offering to buy out his inventory. "We have six new saddles that we made here—expensive, but of good quality. We have ten used saddles that we've repaired and restored, so not as expensive. And we have four very cheap English saddles. We've got bridles, saddle blankets, and various farrier supplies, but we don't have veterinary medicine. You may be able to get those things at Senor Ortiz's shop down the street."

I spent the next half hour examining the saddles and bridles. Corporal Bonham did so as well. And while we scrutinized Zapata's goods, I discovered he was an Oklahoma boy who had grown up on a ranch in the western part of the state. He helped me look things over and made some suggestions.

"What do you think about those English saddles, Corporal?" I asked. "Do you think the Army could use those back in Louisiana?"

Bonham replied with surprising vehemence. "Absolutely not, Mr. Burns. Look at 'em. No pommels, no saddle trees, and no skirts. And hell, they're not even leather. These saddles wouldn't last a week in the Texas brush country or your Louisiana swamps. Besides, if you rode around here with a synthetic English saddle, people would laugh at you and your horse would die of shame. Hell, I'd rather be court-martialed and shot than put an English saddle on a horse."

"Okay, Corporal," I replied. "You convinced me. No English saddles."

In the end, I bought almost everything in Mr. Zapata's store with the exception of the English saddles, which Senor Zapata gave me at no charge.

"What would my customers say," he asked, "if they came into my store and saw nothing but English saddles not even made of leather? I would be humiliated.

"You can throw them in Buffalo Bayou if you like," he continued, "but I will only sell you the western saddles if you take the English saddles too. I curse the day I put those saddles in my shop."

"Okay, Señor Zapata. Here's my requisition order for the supplies we're buying, signed by me and Lieutenant Barkley. Please deliver it all to the quartermaster at Fort Joplin by tomorrow. He'll pay you in silver and give you a receipt."

"*Muy satisfactorio*," he said cheerfully, and we shook hands.

Next, we went to Emiliano Ortiz's shop, where we bought four more saddles and a dozen bridles. We also bought liniment, horse vitamins, equine antibiotics, and some other veterinary items that Corporal Bonham said would be useful for doctoring horses. I gave Señor Ortiz the necessary paperwork, and he promised to deliver our purchases to Fort Joplin by the end of the day.

Our little group rounded out our excursion by visiting several salvage yards that sold used tools and implements that had survived the rioting. We did not find mosquito repellant, but I bought wood-working tools and saws and arranged to have them delivered at Fort Joplin.

When we got back to the fort, an officer at the gate told me that General Mier wanted to see me right away. I went to his office in the university's old administration building, and he greeted me with a beaming smile.

"Mr. Burns," the general said, "I've got some good news for you. We found Colonel Merski's diapers!"

THE ARMY RAIDS THE HOUSTON FOOD BANK, AND GENERAL MIER TRAVELS TO BATON ROUGE

General Mier could hardly conceal his satisfaction as he told me how his people had found a cache of diapers in North Houston.

"After you left for Telephone Road this morning," Mier said, "Captain Lubbock recalled seeing diapers at the Houston Food Bank, which is a few miles north of here. I sent a squad up there this morning to check it out. And sure enough, they found a shit load of diapers!"

I was incredulous. I never thought I would fill Colonel Merski's diaper order. "Why didn't somebody steal them?" I asked.

"Well, the food bank *was* looted," General Mier replied, "along with almost every major building in Houston. But the looters were looking for food, not baby supplies. Someone scared off the rioters before they could burn the place down. I don't know who that was—the army maybe, or one of the neighborhood militias. In any event, the diapers are still in the warehouse along with a couple of dozen pallets of canned spinach. I guess the looters weren't hungry enough to eat spinach that day." The general chuckled. "I'll bet they're hungry enough to eat it now," he added ruefully.

"I'll have Captain Lubbock drive you there in a light truck tomorrow morning, and you can get what you need.

"Now I've got something else I want to talk with you about. When I saw Colonel Merski's requisition list, I realized that he was forming a cavalry unit. I hadn't thought that far ahead, but eventually Fort Joplin will need some horses too. Right now, we barely get enough fuel from the refinery in Pasadena to keep our light vehicles operating. We ration gasoline strictly, and require our soldiers to perform their duties on bikes when at all possible. Heavy armored vehicles are a thing of the past. Our tanks and armored personnel carriers are totally useless.

"I sent a message to Colonel Merski by Red Ball Express this morning, briefing him on the ambush on I-10 and your casualties. I also told him that I'm coming to visit him in Baton Rouge. I want to fill him in on some political developments in Texas.

"Mr. Burns, I propose that you travel back to Baton Rouge with me and Captain Lubbock tomorrow. We'll be driving a Honda Fit from the motor pool, which will be a little more comfortable than riding in a Red Ball 18-wheeler. At least my Honda has a windshield."

The next morning, Captain Lubbock showed up while I was eating breakfast. He had a truck waiting to take Lieutenant Barkley and me to the Houston Food Bank, and Lieutenant Barkley and I climbed aboard.

Four armed soldiers scrambled into the truck bed before we departed, which surprised me. *Surely we don't need six people to load diapers.*

We drove north on I-45, headed toward Dallas. We left the interstate on the far northside of Houston and drove into a rundown industrial district.

"Wow," I said as we pulled up in front of an enormous warehouse. "This place is huge. How many people got fed here?"

"About eight hundred thousand people a year back in the old days," Captain Lubbock said. "Of course, they didn't get fed on the premises. The food was distributed all over Houston and surrounding counties."

"Are you saying eight hundred thousand people didn't get enough to eat in the Houston region back when the economy was booming?"

"I guess not," Lubbock replied. "The politicians were crowing about a growing economy and record low unemployment, but more than three-quarters of a million people in the Houston area depended on free food, and that's in addition to the food stamps the government was giving out."

Captain Lubbock's remarks reminded me that the United States was in trouble long before our political leaders would admit it. A great many people were living on the edge of poverty, but no one noticed. Meanwhile, the federal government and millions of individual Americans were behaving in the same reckless manner—we were all borrowing money we couldn't pay back to enjoy a lifestyle we couldn't afford.

I put these thoughts aside as Captain Lubbock and I searched for a way to get inside the foodbank's warehouse. We walked past the metal rolling doors on the concrete loading dock and found them all chained shut. "Corporal," Captain Lubbock called out, "fetch the MOAB."

"MOAB?" I asked. "What's a MOAB?"

"Mother of all bolt cutters," Lubbock replied. "You would be surprised how often we need a big, friggin' bolt cutter these days. A bolt cutter is a lot more useful than an American Express card for opening doors."

A couple of minutes later, a soldier walked up with a huge bolt cutter—more than four feet long. It took him only a few seconds to snap the lock on one of the loading-bay doors, and then he rolled the door up high enough that we could enter without stooping.

We walked in and stood for a moment in the dim light until our eyes adjusted. The cavernous food bank was almost empty, but we found three pallets of disposable diapers in the back of the warehouse.

Lieutenant Barkley and I started loading the diapers in the truck. I had expected the soldiers to help us, but they didn't. After a while, I looked up and saw that they had spread out around the food bank warehouse with their rifles at the ready. They looked edgy.

"Captain Lubbock," I called out, trying to keep the anxiety out of my voice, "are we expecting trouble?"

"Maybe. Maybe not," he replied. "We're in North Houston now, only about forty miles from Huntsville and the old Huntsville prison."

"Is that a problem?" I asked.

"Could be. When the crunch came and law and order broke down, there were about two thousand male prisoners in the Huntsville prison, and there were more than two hundred prisoners locked up on death row. Nobody wanted to guard those guys, and nobody wanted to feed them. So the Texas Department of Corrections, in its wisdom, just unlocked the prison doors and set everybody free."

Now I was getting apprehensive. "Where are all those prisoners now?" I asked.

"I suppose some of them went home to their families, but most went back to their old trades: robbery, burglary, and rape. And since they couldn't get transportation, they're still hanging around this region, terrorizing the locals."

I started to ask Lubbock a question, but he shushed me with a hand gesture and began looking intently down a street lined with abandoned industrial buildings. Lieutenant Barkley looked in the same direction but said nothing. Several of the soldiers must have sensed some lurking danger because they, too, turned their eyes in the same direction. I saw a couple of them use their rifle scopes as binoculars to get a closer view.

No danger appeared, however. After a few minutes, I saw the soldiers relax a bit. I realized then that our little group was vulnerable to sniper fire coming from any one of a number of abandoned warehouses.

"I thought I heard something for a moment," Lubbock explained. "You started to ask a question?"

"What about the prisoners on death row?" I asked. "Did the corrections department release them too?"

"Oh no. You can say what you want about Texans, but nobody ever accused them of being soft-hearted when it comes to murderers and rapists. The Texas Department of Corrections organized a firing squad and shot every one of them.

"I suppose you could say that was a cruel thing to do, but most of them had been on death row for ten years or more. All of them had been convicted of serious crimes and all had been given the death sentence under Texas law.

"Most of these condemned men were just putting off their execution date by filing multiple appeals. I'm sure two or three of them were probably innocent and wrongly convicted. But these are hard times, and hard times call for hard decisions."

"Anything else out there I should be afraid of?" I asked.

"Oh, yeah," Captain Lubbock replied. "Besides the ex-cons from Huntsville, this part of Texas is infested with gangs of bandits and killers. We call these groups comancheros. Is that what people call them in Louisiana?"

"Yes, captain. That's what we call 'em. Lieutenant Barkley and I ran into some comancheros when we were taking the Red Ball to Houston a couple of days ago. They killed our driver and two passengers. Thank god Lieutenant Barkley and Sergeant Gomez were with us, or I think we would have all been killed."

"Did they get away with that?" Lubbock asked.

"We killed six of them," Lieutenant Barkley answered, "but we think maybe five or six more got away."

"Well, thank you for what you did," Lubbock said. "We're having a devil of a time with the comancheros in this part of Texas; the eastern part of the state is heavily wooded country where they can hide out.

"In fact, the comancheros have basically closed Interstate 45 between Houston and Dallas. It's not safe to drive that road without a military escort."

I could tell that our conversation about ex-cons and comancheros was making Captain Lubbock a little nervous. He began helping Lieutenant Barkley and me load diapers in the truck to get the job done faster.

"Are there any civilian communities in East Texas?" I asked. "Or did the comancheros drive everybody out?"

"A few small towns have organized community militias—Nacogdoches, in particular. And there are quite a few preppers north of here.

"Before the big crunch, a few people bought rural tracts in East Texas, built bunkers, and stocked up on food, guns, and ammo. Those folks are self-reliant, well-armed, and tough as hell. The comancheros don't mess much with the preppers."

"I've never met a hard-core prepper," I said. "What are they like?"

"Most of them are assholes," Lubbock replied. Then he thought a moment. "Correction: they're *all* assholes."

"What do you mean by that?" I asked.

"Think about it, Mr. Burns. The preppers have been preparing for doomsday for twenty years, and they finally got what they'd been waiting for. Now they can say, 'I told you so.'"

He tossed another packet of diapers into the truck bed. "But they're not happy. They're all paranoid about people stealing their shit—their food, their ammo, their assault rifles, their toilet paper, their whisky.

"So the preppers don't make friends with non-preppers. They won't invite non-preppers over for dinner because they're afraid their guests will see all their crap and ask for a can of beans, a bottle of bourbon, or maybe a few bullets. They're just hanging out in their concrete shelters, listening to Willie Nelson on their solar-powered CD players, playing cards, and waiting to die of old age. I don't like 'em."

This conversation made me want to wrap up our mission at the food bank and quickly get back to the safety of Fort Joplin. Lieutenant Barkley and I tried to haul off as many diapers as we could, so we crammed some in the truck cab and even stuffed some packages behind the truck's front bumper. Still, we had to leave half the diapers behind.

"I'm going to make an executive decision here, Mr. Burns," Captain Lubbock said as we got in the truck. "We'll send all these diapers back with you to Fort Sharpton, but we're going to keep the rest. We've got some families here that can use them.

"Fair enough," I responded. "I didn't think we'd find any diapers, and we wouldn't have found these without Fort Joplin's help."

"I hope Colonel Merski realizes that these may be the last disposable diapers in America," Lieutenant Barkley interjected. "People are going to have to go back to washing cloth diapers when these disposables are gone. Thank god my kids are old enough to wipe their own butts."

RUMINATIONS ON THE APOCALYPSE

I spent a second night in the BOQ, and the next morning I crammed myself into an olive-drab Honda Fit along with General Mier, Lieutenant Barkley, and Captain Lubbock. There was obviously not enough room for all of us and everyone's gear.

"This is not a Honda Fit," Lieutenant Barkley observed. "It's a Honda Tight Fit."

"This isn't going to work," General Mier admitted. "Captain Lubbock, I want you to ride in the Red Ball. Give 'em a little more security."

"Yes, sir," Lubbock replied. He unfolded himself from the backseat of the Fit. He showed no emotion, and I couldn't tell whether he was relieved to be out of the Honda, or unhappy about riding in the back of an open truck for twelve hours with a bunch of smelly civilians.

We pulled out of Houston shortly after dawn. Our Honda headed east on I-10 behind the Red Ball truck. It was reassuring to see Sergeant Gomez and her machine gun perched behind the cab of the truck up ahead—a truck loaded with diapers, cavalry gear, and Ernie Esperanza's ice-packed coffin.

In spite of Esperanza's death, I felt proud about my mission to Houston. I had helped fight off a gang of comancheros and even managed to kill one of them. And I got almost everything Colonel Merski asked for—even disposable diapers, which I had never expected to find.

A few civilian passengers had managed to buy a ride on the Red Ball, and they squatted in the open air on the back of the flatbed trailer. Captain Lubbock was sitting at the very back of the trailer, leaning against the porta-potty and cradling a rifle. He looked both bored and alert.

I was a little nervous about the long ride with General Mier. I was afraid he might have lost respect for me after I spoke up about Ernie Esperanza. But I was wrong.

"Mr. Burns," the general said as we passed by the burned-out Budweiser brewery, "you're a retired college professor. What's your take on what happened to America? How did we go from being a wealthy nation and the world's only superpower to the shit-show we're living in today?"

"General," I replied, "I don't have a good explanation for you. Sometimes I forget how much things have changed. I find myself planning a drive to the supermarket, then I realize I don't have a car and there are no supermarkets.

"But I think all our problems trace back to greed, arrogance, and stupidity.

"It was greed that sucked the vitality and wealth out of Middle America and sent it to the coastal elites. And of course, the people who impoverished the heartland despised the folks who lived there. Flyover Country—that's what those arrogant pricks called the whole Unites States between the East Coast and the West Coast."

I immediately regretted using the phrase "arrogant pricks," not wanting the general to think I meant him. I hurried on with my rant, hoping General Mier hadn't noticed.

"The American moneyed-class became globalists. The wealthiest Americans were getting rich in the global economy and didn't give a damn about working-class Americans. Year by year, American corporations sent jobs to China so that Americans didn't make anything anymore—not even blood-pressure medicine and antibiotics.

"And our universities drifted away from being centers of learning and became institutional vacuum cleaners for sucking up federal money. Even as the American economy was collapsing, I don't think most Americans grasped how corrupt our colleges and universities had become, or how many overpaid bureaucrats and administrators worked in them. And I don't think they realized that college degrees were becoming almost worthless."

"Surely, you're overstating things a bit," Mier protested. "I've read many times that college graduates earn significantly more than people who just have a high school diploma."

"Yeah," I admitted, "I guess I am. Most people who majored in engineering, chemistry, or the medical professions got good value for their tuition dollars. But the poor saps who majored in liberal arts, humanities, or social sciences racked up a lot of student-loan debt that didn't lead to good jobs.

"A lot of young people who got liberal arts degrees would have been better off going to a trade school and getting some technical skills. As the old times were winding down, pipefitters and welders were making more money than schoolteachers, and the people in tech jobs finished their training with a lot less debt."

I checked myself from talking any further about the shortcomings of American higher education. After all, the universities were all closed now, and I saw little point in discussing their faults. Instead, I shifted the discussion to the energy crisis that finally put an end to the old times.

"And of course, all this was happening as we were running out of the oil that we needed to fuel our consumer lifestyles and suburban living. The middle class was losing ground year by year, and our government tried to keep our Rube Goldberg economy running by printing money.

"Americans needed smart leaders, people who were civic-minded and could figure things out and turn our country around, but Americans elected crooks and thugs to Congress. I think everybody agrees on that."

"Do you think we can recover from all this?" General Mier asked. "Is there any way back to the old times?"

I could see it in his face; it wasn't a rhetorical question. General Mier genuinely wanted me to tell him how we could fix things.

"Well, let me answer that question by asking you a couple of questions: Do you think anyone is ever going to go to work again on the forty-fifth floor of one of those Houston skyscrapers? Will people go back to commuting three hours a day so they can work downtown and live in the suburbs?

"Petroleum for airplanes, cars, and army tanks is running out. Sure, we can build some electric cars that will allow people a certain degree of mobility, but we can only do that with wind turbines, nuclear power plants, and hydroelectric power. We'll never get that done in the new times, and we'll never have enough renewable energy to reconstruct our consumer culture."

"But maybe some good will come out of America's collapse," Mier ventured. "Maybe Americans will rediscover the value of honest toil."

"Maybe," I replied skeptically. "One thing is certain: We don't need financial advisors, videogame designers, and advertising executives any more. What we need is a lot more people growing food. That's basically what I'm doing; I'm a farmer. And I gotta say, I get a lot more satisfaction harvesting tomatoes than I got from directing dissertations.

"On the other hand," I added, a bit amused at the thought, "now that we've run out of toilet paper, all those dissertations sitting in university libraries might become useful."

I decided I had said enough about the collapse of American society. I was curious to know General Mier's perspective on the new times, so I began asking him questions.

"Tell me, General, how did Houston fare when the economy blew up? I know there was a lot of violence and mayhem in the big cities—LA, New York, and Chicago. Did it get that bad in Houston?"

"Yes, it did. I was here with an infantry brigade, and we saw some terrible things. A lot of people died from hunger, a lot died from disease, and a fair number were murdered.

"But here and there, decent people stepped up, and some Houstonians were able to protect their homes and neighborhoods. I'm sure that was also true in Los Angeles and Chicago."

"Which Houston neighborhoods fared the best, do you think?"

"Well, most Americans don't realize that Houston is one of the most culturally diverse cities in the country, and people here have generally gotten along with one another. We used to think of Los Angeles and New York as the nation's multicultural hubs, but those cities were no more diverse than Houston. We had a large Chinese community here, a Korean community, a big Vietnamese population.

"Before the bust," Mier added, "there were probably two million Hispanics living in Greater Houston—both legal and undocumented—mostly from Mexico and Central America. People from Eastern Europe, India, Pakistan—everybody just trying to make a living and take care of their families.

"People forget about Houston's innate friendliness and generosity. Remember Hurricane Katrina back in 2005? Houston absorbed 150,000 refugees from New Orleans, found schools for children, temporary housing, and helped people find jobs.

"Maybe I'm giving Houston too much credit." Mier conceded. "A lot of people believe that all American cities are basically alike, but I'm not sure about that. All I know is that when the deal went down in this town and we started seeing fires on the horizon, a lot of Houstonians banded together to save their city."

"So what did people do?" I asked.

"Houston is essentially a patchwork of ethnic neighborhoods, barrios, and middle-class homes. A lot of people had guns, and a lot of them knew their neighbors, so when things turned ugly, they formed their own militias and barricaded the streets to keep out the marauders.

"So did it get bad in Houston?" Mier asked rhetorically. "Yeah, it did, but it could have been a lot worse. Some residential housing was saved, although so many people died from hunger or disease over the past few years that there aren't many people living in them anymore."

Puttering along at twenty-five miles an hour, our little caravan took more than four hours to get to the Louisiana border. We stopped at the Texas Welcome Center for a bathroom break, and

General Mier chatted with the troops who were guarding the Sabine River bridge.

"Soldier," he said to a lean, young corporal, "explain to me why this post is flying a big Texas flag over a little American flag that's hanging upside down. Don't you understand basic flag protocol?"

"General, that's our way of saying that Texas is basically on its own," the soldier replied deferentially. "We're all soldiers here, and we've all sworn to defend the flag, but most of us feel that Texas has a better chance of surviving than the United States does."

"You may be right, Corporal," the general responded reflectively. "You just leave those flags the way they are."

We loaded back in our vehicles to drive the long, weary miles to Baton Rouge. We passed the spot on the causeway where the comancheros had ambushed us, and Lieutenant Barkley briefly told the general how we fought them off.

It was dusk when we pulled into Fort Sharpton, where Colonel Merski was waiting for us—jovial and glad to see his friend General Mier.

Spotting me, Colonel Merski called out. "Hey there, Willoughby. I hear you helped fight off the comancheros up on the causeway."

"I played a modest role," I said, because actually it was not only modest, but very reluctant and amateurish.

"Well, you shot three people this week," he replied, speaking in a low voice. "For a retired college professor, you're getting kinda lethal."

I noticed four Knights of Columbus, dressed in full regalia, waiting for Ernie Esperanza's body. They formed a small honor guard to take Ernie's remains to St. Joan of Arc Catholic Church. They managed to look both pathetic and noble at the same time as their hat plumes waved in the night breeze coming from the river.

I felt proud to have helped get Ernie's body back to Baton Rouge for a proper funeral mass. I was pleased to see his sturdy wooden coffin being reverently unloaded from the Red Ball truck—the coffin Sergeant Gomez had built to preserve the dignity of Ernie's remains. I shuttered at the thought of Ernie's corpse being dumped in a mass grave somewhere outside of Houston, or cremated among hundreds of other bodies in a gasoline-stoked fire. *How could I have explained that to his widow?*

I was saddened by Ernie's death, but I was also sad because I knew that men like Ernie were passing away, and no one would rise to replace them. Ernie was an old-time ethnic-American Catholic, one of the descendants of the European Catholics who immigrated to the United States by the millions in the nineteenth and early twentieth century. Irish Catholics, Italian Catholics, Polish Catholics, and German Catholics landed in New York, Boston, or other East Coast ports and began building new lives in a new country. And in South Louisiana, of course, the French Catholics were predominant.

Protestant Americans, whose ancestors had gotten to the New World first, despised the new immigrants, especially the Irish—despised their language, their culture, and their religion, which Protestants considered to be nothing more than superstitious gibberish. The public-school systems did their best to wean Catholic children from their parents' faith and turn them into good little Protestants.

So the Catholics built their own parochial school systems, founded their own colleges, and clung to their ancient faith. Decade after decade, these ethnic Catholic families clawed their way up the economic ladder, with each generation rising higher than the last.

Now, well past the middle of the twenty-first century, American Catholics had become assimilated into the larger, more secular population. For most Americans, religion wasn't so important anymore, even for the ones who still went to church on Sundays.

Ernie had been proud to be a Fourth Degree Knight of Columbus—the highest rank in the world's largest Catholic laymen's association. I doubted that his children would even attend Mass regularly or observe the Church's holy days of obligation. As American society became more materialistic and secular, young people began to see Sunday as purely a recreational day.

In my opinion, which I kept to myself, the Catholic Church was largely responsible for the dramatic decline in church-going Catholics. The child-abuse scandals among the clergy, which the bishops largely covered up, disillusioned a lot of lay Catholics—me included. And the Church's dogged refusal to allow divorced Catholics to receive communion caused millions of Catholics to drift away from the Church.

In fact, Ernie's son and daughter might grow up to marry lapsed Baptists or lapsed Methodists and forget that their family had ever been Catholic.

However, Colonel Merski's cheery greeting dispelled my melancholy reflections.

"General Mier," Colonel Merski called out in a hearty voice, "welcome to Fort Sharpton. Sergeant LeBlanc, our executive chef, prepared a special meal for you in the officer's mess. We have quite a few Cajuns at Fort Sharpton, and many of them are good cooks.

"Captain Lubbock, Lieutenant Barkley, and Willoughby, you're invited too."

A CAJUN DINNER AND
THE GHOST OF HUEY LONG

We walked toward the state capitol building, a towering art deco monstrosity that Governor Huey Long built as a phallic monument to himself. The sun was setting across the Mississippi River—brilliant splashes of reds, greys, and blues. We passed by a larger-than-life statue of Governor Long, looking forceful, earnest, and oddly honest.

As we strolled along, Colonel Merski assumed the role of tour guide. "Fort Sharpton occupies the grounds of the old Louisiana state capitol," Colonel Merski informed the group. "My offices are in the Pentagon Barracks," he added as he pointed in the direction of an old, five-sided structure near the river. "The army built those barracks before the Civil War.

"We store our ammunition in the historic arsenal that dates back to the early nineteenth century. It's as functional today as it was when it was built more than two hundred years ago.

"As you can see," Merski droned on, "the capitol itself is a magnificent structure that Governor Long built in the early 1930s. There's an observation deck on the twenty-seventh floor, where we post a lookout every day from dawn to dusk. We can monitor the river traffic from that deck, at least during daylight. After dark, you can't see a goddamn thing up there.

"Unfortunately," he continued, "most of this enormous building is utterly useless to us. We don't have enough electricity to run the elevators or operate the air conditioning. But we've turned the old coffee shop in the basement into our officer's mess."

I'll bet he's going to drag us over to the hallway where Huey Long was assassinated, I thought to myself. I had seen the spot dozens of times and had no desire to see it again.

Sure enough, Merski led us into the main lobby of the capitol building and assumed the tone of a museum curator.

"Before we go down to dinner," he intoned, "I want to show you the exact spot where Governor Long was assassinated in 1935. The state legislature was in session, and a local doctor shot Huey in the hallway—right here, as a matter of fact. Huey was surrounded by a pack of bodyguards who killed the assassin, but the shooting was so wild and reckless that no one knows for sure who killed Huey: the doctor, or one of his henchmen."

"I suppose that's a lesson for us all," General Mier observed. "If you ever need to hire a bodyguard, make sure you pick one that can shoot straight."

Without telling us where we were going, Colonel Merski led us down a dark stairwell into the capitol basement. "Are we exiting through the gift shop?" Mier asked. "I'd like to buy some souvenirs, maybe pick up a couple of T-shirts for my kids."

Merski ignored this gentle ribbing from a senior officer and ushered us into the officer's messroom where a formal dinner had been prepared for us. A candlelit table had been laid out with the gubernatorial China and silverware. The plates were embossed with the Louisiana state seal: a mother pelican feeding her young with meat torn from her breast.

Sergeant Leblanc, wearing a tall, starched chef's hat, came out of the kitchen as we seated ourselves and began announcing the evening's menu in a strong Cajun accent.

"Ladies and gentlemen, we have a dee-licious dinner prepared for you dis evenin'. First, we gonna serve you fried alligator as an appetizer, followed by a turtle soup dat's very fresh. Dat turtle come out of LSU lake dis very mornin'.

"Den, we serve the main course: roast venison covered with a Steen syrup and whiskey glaze. And dat will come with spinach madeleine and a pecan-covered sweet potato soufflé. And we finish off wid rum-soaked bread pudding."

"This meal would go great with a California cabernet," Colonel Merski commented as he turned toward General Mier. "I haven't sipped a good California cab in many years. And Louisiana wine is not an acceptable substitute, I assure you.

"But the locally brewed beer is good, and a few fellows are distilling some fine rum and whisky. In fact, the neighborhood hooch is better than I used to buy in the liquor store."

As if on signal, one of our Cajun waiters brought out large steins of Kölsch-style beer—ice cold. *Now I know how Colonel Merski is using his electricity*, I thought to myself. *He's keeping his beer cold.*

We began nibbling on our alligator appetizers, served with a locally concocted Asian peanut sauce. And we sipped our turtle soup, which Chef LeBlanc enhanced by adding a few drops of sherry to each bowl. *Where did that sherry come from?*

Then we dug into the main course: venison, sweet potatoes, and spinach madeleine. The venison was cut from the deer's backstrap and tasted like a filet mignon. The sweet potatoes, I knew, had come from Lâche Pas, as had the pecans.

About midway through dinner, General Mier set a somber tone for the evening's conversation. "Colonel Merski, as you know, I came to visit you here at Fort Sharpton because I want to brief you on the strategic picture in our part of the world.

"But let's save that discussion until tomorrow morning. Tonight, I would like to hear about the challenges you're facing in Louisiana. "Colonel Merski, what's the military situation in your sector?" Meir asked.

Merski wiped his mouth with his cloth napkin before answering, giving him a few seconds to form his response. "General, I've been at Fort Sharpton since before Hurricane Maxine, and our mission hasn't changed. My orders are to protect the remaining refineries along the Mississippi River, guard the major bridges—especially the

I-10 bridge in Baton Rouge, and keep river pirates and bandits from murdering our citizens.

"But as for the current situation, the army here faces two distinct threats. First, there are a couple of large paramilitary forces operating in the southeastern United States—the Nubian Nation and the New Rednecks.

"These two opposing forces are basically conventional armies fighting a race war. Because of their size and their logistical constraints, they are restricted from traveling off the roads. Most of the terrain east of us is heavily forested or swampy all the way to the Pearl River, so we don't expect them to come cross-country to threaten us.

"But we're closely watching the roads to the east—particularly Interstate 10 and Interstate 12. So far, neither the Nubians nor the New Rednecks have entered South Louisiana in force, but we've come across some of their small reconnaissance units along the Louisiana-Mississippi border.

"My biggest fear regarding the Nubians and the Redneckers is that they will attack Vicksburg, Mississippi to the north and capture the Mississippi River bridge there. If either group did that, they could head south along roads on both sides of the river and attack us in Baton Rouge."

"Do you have troops in Vicksburg?" General Mier asked.

Merski allowed himself a sip of Kölsch before answering, and General Mier used the interlude to signal to the waiters to bring out more beer.

"No, we don't," Merski replied. "Vicksburg is 150 miles from Baton Rouge, too far away for Fort Sharpton to provide support to a garrison in that town."

"Vicksburg," General Mier mused. "It was the fall of Vicksburg in 1863 that broke the Confederacy—that and the battle of Gettysburg, which happened at the same time. When Grant took Vicksburg, he split the Confederacy in two; and that was the beginning of the end for the Old South."

Merski could not resist displaying his own knowledge of the Civil War, even at the risk of offending his superior officer.

"Beg your pardon, General, but Vicksburg wasn't the last Confederate fort to fall on the Mississippi River. It was Port Hudson, which is located just twenty miles upriver from Baton Rouge. Vicksburg fell on July 4, 1863, as I'm sure you know. Port Hudson fell on July 9, five days later."

"I stand corrected," General Mier said stiffly. "Now please continue with your briefing."

"Now, where was I," Merski said, feigning confusion and probably wishing he'd kept his mouth shut about Port Hudson. "Oh yes, I've got a small force in Natchez that guards the Mississippi River bridge there and watches for hostile movements from the north. But the army has no presence north of Natchez.

"In fact, I'm thinking about extracting the garrison at Natchez and blowing the Natchez bridge. The force there is too small to fight off a sustained attack, and it's seventy miles from Fort Sharpton.

"Our second threat," Merski continued, "is more immediate. We're seeing more and more renegade gangs prowling around our neighborhood—heavily armed and highly aggressive. We call these groups comancheros.

"As best we can tell, the comanchero bands operate independently in small packs of one to two dozen people. They prey on isolated homesteads and travelers, looking for food, weapons, and gasoline.

"They not only commit murder, but they also rape their victims—men, women, even children—and sometimes torture them. Some of them practice cannibalism, and some are led by deranged sadists. They execute any prisoners they take and mutilate the bodies.

"The comancheros are bad dudes," Merski added darkly, "and we kill 'em if we find 'em."

"We've got a similar element in East Texas," Mier interjected. "And we call them by the same name—comancheros."

"It was a comanchero band that attacked the Red Ball truck a few days ago on the Atchafalaya Causeway," Merski explained. "This worries me. We've tried to keep them contained on the east side of the Mississippi River. Frankly, we don't have the troops to deal with the comancheros, let alone the Nubian Nation and the Redneckers. We're simply spread too thin.

"Nevertheless, in spite of these threats, the people of Louisiana are slowly rebuilding their society. The army provides protection to farm families who are growing crops on the east side of the Mississippi south of Baton Rouge. It's these farmers who provide the food for my troops and their families."

"Are these farmers using modern machinery?" Mier asked. "And if they are, where are they getting their fuel?"

"We've issued some gasoline and diesel fuel to farmers on a rationed basis so they can plow their fields and harvest their crops, and we've run an electricity line down to the farms. The power is not on twenty-four hours a day, but we provide enough juice for them to use their electric tools and charge Willoughby's bike.

"Slowly, season by season, the farmers are relying more on horse-powered agriculture, and they're finding or building horse-drawn farm machinery. But that transformation can't happen overnight. Draft horses are scarce, and the people who know how to farm with horses are even scarcer."

"I take it Fort Sharpton has some horses," Mier observed, "based on the saddles and horse supplies Mr. Burns purchased for you in Houston. Do you find them useful?"

"They're not that useful to us at the moment," Merski admitted. "Right now, they're just eating hay and making fertilizer. I think they'll be useful once we get saddles for all of them and teach our soldiers to ride 'em.

"But horses operate best in open terrain. Much of the country west of the river was farmland in the old times—land devoted to raising sugarcane, rice, and other crops. I think we can use horses effectively on the far side of the river.

"But horses are almost totally useless in the Atchafalaya Swamp and the brushy country east of the Mississippi. In the old days, the local deer hunters drove four-wheelers through that rough terrain, but of course, four-wheelers need gasoline."

I could tell that General Mier wanted to move the conversation along. "So Colonel Merski," Mier asked as a sort of wrap-up question, "what does the future hold for this region? Will the people who live around Fort Sharpton make a go of it?"

"I think this area is becoming basically self-sufficient and will soon be able to export food," Merski replied confidently. "But of course, the transportation grid for moving food stocks has almost completely broken down.

"Thanks to the farmers and stock raisers, South Louisiana can feed itself, but they will need to find some way to get their surplus crops to more distant markets. The farmers can't rely on the Red Ball Express to move fresh produce and meat products. Those trucks are too slow, and, of course, their cargo trailers aren't refrigerated."

General Mier then turned to Lieutenant Barkley. I noticed that she had not touched her mug of beer. She wanted to stay sharp, I supposed, when conversing with two superior officers.

Merski noticed the full mug and whispered loudly to her, "Lieutenant, if you're not going to drink that—" and she passed the mug over to him.

"Lieutenant, you're a combat soldier," Mier began. "What tactics are you using against the comancheros?"

"Well, General Mier," Lieutenant Barkley responded, "I've had a good bit of experience dealing with the comancheros, but we never know where they are until they raid a settlement or highjack a Red Ball truck.

"Colonel Merski has us organized into small units to hunt them down. We've got several local soldiers who are deer hunters—both men and women. Many of them have been hunting deer since they were twelve years old. They're excellent trackers and snipers and can move through the woods without making much noise.

"Our orders are to go into the field and not come back until we've found and destroyed any comanchero gang that attacks our citizens. We live off the land during these expeditions, just like the comancheros do.

"Fortunately, I suppose, the swamps are full of alligators, and alligator meat tastes like chicken. That's why the alligator appetizers tasted like chicken nuggets."

"I've heard that most wild meat tastes like chicken," General Mier observed. "Is that true?"

"Oh no," Lieutenant Barkley responded vehemently. "When we're in the field, we'll eat just about anything—raccoon, possum, nutria, armadillo, you name it. I can assure you that none of those animals taste like chicken."

"Colonel Merski told me about his horses," Mier said. "Do you chase the comancheros on horseback?"

"No, General Mier," Lieutenant Barkley replied. "As Colonel Merski just mentioned, horses are pretty near useless in the swamps around here. We use horses for routine patrols around Baton Rouge, but we mostly track down the comancheros on foot."

"What do you do with your prisoners?" General Mier queried. "Do you get any good intel out of them when you interrogate them?"

Of course, I knew the answer to that question. I had seen Lieutenant Barkley execute several comancheros who tried to surrender on the Atchafalaya Causeway. And I had killed a young comanchero who was begging me not to shoot him.

But I kept my mouth shut, and so did Lieutenant Barkley. After all, I didn't know what General Mier's stance was concerning prisoners. Maybe he ordered them shot as Colonel Merski did, or maybe he considered shooting prisoners to be a war crime.

Colonel Merski quickly interjected to answer General Mier's question. "So far," Merski said, "we haven't had the opportunity to capture any of the sons of bitches."

"How about you, Mr. Burns?" Mier asked, drawing me into the conversation. "You have a farm around here, I understand. How are civilians dealing with the comancheros?"

"General, I work a farm with a bunch of my relatives south of Baton Rouge. We have 160 acres where we grow food crops and run a few head of cattle. We also raise chickens and fatten a couple of hogs every year.

"Our homestead is on the grounds of the old Louisiana School for the Deaf, where several abandoned buildings are clustered. We fenced all the buildings into a compound, and we've installed steel shutters over the windows of the individual homes to help protect us from the comancheros. And all the adults carry weapons wherever they go."

"How many people live on your farm, Mr. Burns?" Mier asked.

"There are twenty-two of us—six married couples, three single adults, and seven children. We're all related either by blood or marriage. We teamed up when the food shortages started. We realized we would have to stick together if we were going to survive, and we concentrated on growing our own food."

"How many farms are there in your area?" General Mier asked.

"Our farm is one of about fifty small holdings on the east side of the Mississippi. We all know that we're vulnerable to comanchero raids, but the army's nearby and we've organized ourselves into a militia we can call up if we're attacked.

"So far at least, the comancheros have not threatened us, although we occasionally have to deal with individual thieves and pillagers. We call those people pickers."

I remembered Colonel Merski's advice, and I didn't mention the two pickers I shot on River Road a few days earlier.

"Let's talk about all this on a more formal basis tomorrow morning," General Mier said, signaling an end to our discussions. "If it's alright with you, Colonel, I'd like Mr. Burns to join us for a work session on the present state of affairs."

"I'm looking forward to it, General," Merski replied. "Will, why don't you spend the night at the fort? I'll send a courier down to Lâche Pas to let people know that you got back safely from Houston and will be spending tomorrow with us at Fort Sharpton."

At that point, Chef LeBlanc served the bread pudding, accompanied by a sweet dessert wine, which tasted like it might have been made from wild mustang grapes. *Not bad*, I thought to myself, but I didn't ask for a refill.

"But before the evening draws to a close," Merski said to the group, "Fort Sharpton's military band would like to treat you to some Louisiana music." At that moment, a three-piece band of Cajun soldiers stepped into the candlelight.

"I'll do the introductions," Colonel Merski told the diners. "That's Sergeant Benoit on the fiddle, Corporal Bourgeois on the guitar, and Corporal Gremillion on the accordion.

"And what will you soldiers be playing?" Merski asked the musicians.

Sergeant Benoit spoke up. "Tonight, we will perform 'You Are My Sunshine,' written by Governor Jimmy Davis; 'Jolie Blon,' the Cajun national anthem; and 'God Bless America,' which we will sing to you in Cajun French. Sing along if you know the words."

WILL TEXAS FORM A NEW NATION?

The next morning, I walked over to Colonel Merski's office in the old Pentagon Barracks, where I met General Mier, Captain Lubbock, and Lieutenant Barkley.

As I walked into the conference room, I smelled the gratifying aroma of fresh coffee.

"How about a cup of Community Coffee?" Merski called out. "We took about ten pounds of this caffeinated gold off a pirate boat we captured down near St. Gabriel last spring. I only have a couple of pounds left, so sip it slowly."

I quickly accepted Colonel Merski's invitation and savored the strong taste of Community Coffee. A pleasant sense of well-being swept over me, which I had not felt for a long time. *If I could just have one cup of Community Coffee every morning, I could handle whatever the day might bring—chaos, mayhem, terror, even the prospect of death itself. If only I could start the day with just one cup of Community Coffee . . .*

I could see, however, that General Mier was ready to start the meeting, so I set my cup down, reminding myself to finish my precious coffee before it got cold. I doubted whether Colonel Merski would offer me a refill.

With no preliminary remarks, the general got right down to business. First, he spread two maps on the conference table: a gas-station roadmap of the United States, and another roadmap of Texas.

"Let me start with the big picture: the United States no longer exists But you already knew that.

"As we all know, the entire Eastern Seaboard from Boston down to Washington, DC has been almost completely depopulated. Millions of people died from violence, disease, starvation, or radiation poisoning. New York, Boston, Baltimore, and Philadelphia are in ruins—as dead as ancient Carthage.

"Northern New England—Maine, Vermont, and New Hampshire—have established trading ties with Nova Scotia and the other maritime provinces and will probably be absorbed into what is left of Canada.

"The middle South and Deep South are experiencing a major civil war, with the two sides divided by race and organized into large armies. As we discussed last night, the Nubian Freedom Fighters, almost all African Americans, are fighting the New Rednecks, who are classic, old-school southern racists. I think the proper term for those folks is 'White Trash.'

"In the old times, the people of the urban and suburban South were as progressive and diverse as the people living in the northern cities. Unfortunately, most of the decent Southerners were killed in the Great American Apocalypse, and a racist element—the Redneckers—took control.

"Those people have a lot of guns and ammunition, and they're proficient with firearms. It didn't take long for the Redneckers to begin preying on the African American population.

"Frankly, I can't blame the African Americans for organizing their own paramilitary force. They did what they had to do to protect their families. Otherwise, they would have been the victims of genocide.

"In any event, the feds have abandoned this whole region, and aren't even trying to establish order there. The army has no idea what is going on in Atlanta, Nashville, and the other Southern cities. It's pure chaos now in the South.

"The upper Midwest," General Mier continued, "has been depopulated but the rural areas are fairly stable. Chicago, of course, is no more. The Great Lakes region may associate with Canada, but there is virtually no state or local government up there.

"Large-scale agriculture has stopped in the Great Plains states because there is no fuel for mechanized farming equipment—the big tractors, harvesters, and other farm machinery. The transportation infrastructure for hauling wheat, corn, cattle, and hogs has completely broken down, and there is a critical shortage of commercial fertilizer. In the old times, a lot of elderly people lived on the plains in small towns, but most of those people starved to death during the first winter of the new age."

General Mier paused to take a sip of coffee and then continued.

"California, as we all know, is a hellhole. It basically seceded from the Union, and the army has fallen back to a defensive position around Los Angeles and San Diego. For now, at least, Interstate 10 still connects the West Coast with the rest of the country—but that's a fragile thread.

"As for our southern border, that has dissolved. People can freely enter the United States illegally by wading the Bravo to get into Texas, or crossing the Sonoran Desert into New Mexico and Arizona."

I noticed that General Mier referred to the Rio Grande as the Bravo, which was the name the *Tejanos* of South Texas gave the river. General Mier, I deduced, was probably a Tejano. I knew that Ciudad Mier was a town on the Mexican side of the Rio Grande, where a famous battle between Anglo Texans and the Mexican Army had taken place during the days of the Texas Republic. Perhaps Mier's ancestors lived in that border town.

"In the old times," Mier talked on, "drug smugglers and human traffickers sneaked across the Rio Bravo, and the border patrol had a devil of a time trying to keep them out. But those days are over. Americans don't have money to buy drugs now, and the border states are as impoverished as Latin America, so fewer people want to come here.

"Now that we're in the new times, the army's not too worried about the international border. We have no troops down there. On the whole, our undocumented immigrants are more peaceful, more skilled, and more work-oriented than our homegrown Americans.

"Speaking personally," General Mier added, "I think we would have the violence under control in this country if we could swap our native-born arsonists, looters, and terrorists for hard-working Mexicans on a one-to-one basis.

"Now, you may be wondering how we manage to keep going. Well, the navy has something to do with that. A few military ships are nuclear powered—aircraft carriers and submarines mostly—but the navy needs fuel for its conventionally powered ships and aircraft.

"Colonel Merski commands the troops that defend the South Louisiana refineries, and my troops guard the refineries around Houston. Those refineries are producing fuel at sharply reduced capacity, and most of that fuel goes to the navy.

"Periodically, the USNS *Harvey Milk*, a navy tanker, shows up to get fuel, and the navy gives the army hard currency so we can pay the troops and maintain Forts Sharpton and Joplin. And the army gets to keep enough gasoline and diesel fuel to run a few trucks and jeeps."

So that's how it works. I had wondered where Colonel Merski was getting the silver he doled out to me to buy supplies and where he was getting his gasoline.

At this point, I broke into General Mier's briefing to ask a question that had long been on my mind.

"Tell me, General, who's in charge? Does the United States still have a democratic government, a president, a congress? Because the common sentiment among people I know is that we don't have a government anymore.

"We don't get newspapers now, and television disappeared long ago. We're completely ignorant about what's going on across the United States. In some respects, it's like we're living in the nineteenth century.

"In fact," I added, "we're even more ignorant about the world than Americans living in the nineteen hundreds. In those days, at least, even small towns could boast a daily newspaper.

General Mier glanced at Colonel Merski before answering. "Frankly, Mr. Burns, we don't know who's in charge.

"Every few weeks or so, the USNS *Harvey Milk* shows up to take on a load of fuel—gasoline, diesel fuel, and aviation gas. During these visits, Colonel Merski and I communicate with a single army officer, a mysterious fellow named Colonel Bernard Lawless. Colonel Lawless oversees the transfer of the fuel, and he gives us large bags of hard currency—silver and gold coins and bullion."

"Have you ever asked Colonel Lawless who he reports to or what he's doing with the oil?" I asked, trying not to sound impertinent.

Colonel Merski broke in. "Willoughby, I ask Colonel Lawless a bunch of questions every time I see him. All he will tell me is that he is attached to GULFCOM, which is the military command structure in charge of security for the Gulf-of-Mexico region."

"Have you asked him if the United States still has a congress or a president?"

"General Mier and I have asked those questions many, many times, and Colonel Lawless always gives us the same answer: 'That information is classified.'"

"But what do you think?" I asked both officers.

"In my view," General Mier replied, "the United States does not have a functioning government. In fact, I think it is a fantasy to speak of the United States of America as a nation. It's not a nation, and never will be again."

"And that's my view as well," Colonel Merski added.

"And this brings me to a development I want to discuss with you this morning," Mier said. "In Texas, political leaders are now talking openly about reorganizing the Lone Star State as a separate republic with its own national government, court system, and laws, unconnected in any way to the rest of the old USA.

"This movement is led by a charismatic fellow by the name of Cole Goodnight. Goodnight is a former trial attorney who practiced law in Austin but grew up out in West Texas. He owns a big ranch around San Angelo, and he and his family survived the meltdown by hunkering down on the Llano Estacado.

"Now he's back in Austin—or what's left of Austin—and he's organized a small group of Texans who want to make the state an independent nation."

"Interesting," I said. 'How does Mr. Goodnight plan to do that?"

"He and his supporters are going out to the surviving towns and settlements of Texas and asking people to elect delegates to a constitutional convention, which they plan to hold in Austin in October of next year.

"I think the plan is for the delegates to vote on a national constitution and some basic laws. Goodnight wants to scrap the old Texas Constitution—all eighty-five thousand words and more than five hundred amendments of it. And he wants to scrap all the federal statutes and state statutes and start over."

"A legal face lift," I said. "And what will the new constitution look like?" I asked.

"Maybe you'll get an opportunity to meet Goodnight and ask him yourself, but I gather he wants to adopt the US Constitution with all its amendments and no substantive changes.

"Goodnight's view is that the Constitution is a nigh perfect document. It's not the Constitution that failed the American people, I've heard him say. We screwed everything up by electing idiots to public office and allowing crooks to manipulate our financial institutions and drive the economy into the ground. And then there is that whole oil thing, the urban violence, and the epidemics."

General Mier's words startled me; I found them electrifying, almost breathtaking. Until that moment, it had not occurred to me that Americans could simply walk away from the moribund shell that the United States had become. I suddenly realized we could start over. We could wipe the slate clean of our corrupt politicians, our mountains of stultifying statutes and regulations, and our racial animosities—animosities that had grown more intense and vicious as the twenty-first century progressed. We could say goodbye to our soulless bureaucrats and the lazy professors who infested our public universities.

For years now, I had focused only on surviving and raising enough food to feed the people at Lâche Pas. It never occurred to me that the new times presented new opportunities, even the opportunity to construct a better nation.

I had a revelation. *Americans could craft something new and clean.* Maybe we could recover our people's once-generous spirit, our civic pride, and our decency. Perhaps we could restore the ideals that the nation's founders articulated in the Declaration of Independence and the US Constitution.

What an idea! Americans would become like the ancient Israelites, whom God forgave. "I'll remember your sins no more," Jehovah had said, and he gave the Israelites a fresh start.

And if there was anywhere across the continent where Americans could forge a new national identity, it was Texas—my native state. Texas had once been its own nation, and Texans had never completely lost their independent spirit.

I could see that spirit exemplified in the Lone Star Flag. Other states cluttered their flags with symbols, phrases, and icons; the Texas flag was simple: a single star on a field of blue, a single white stripe, and a single stripe of red. In addition to every other sentiment the flag evoked, it communicated this message: we are a unique people, and we stand alone.

Without thinking, I blurted out my allegiance to this radical scheme that I had heard for the first time from the lips of General Mier. "Well, let me be the first to say," I exclaimed, "that Mr. Goodnight has a great idea, and I'm for it."

I gave no thought to the fact that I had basically expounded treason before a group of US Army officers in a city governed by martial law. Somehow, I sensed that General Mier and Colonel Merski would indulge my indiscretion even if they didn't share my enthusiasm.

Having heard my incautious endorsement, General Mier turned to Colonel Merski. "What do you think about this, Colonel?" Mier asked. "Do you see Goodnight as an insurrectionist, or the father of a new country?"

"If the USA were a going concern," Merski said slowly, "I'd be worried about Mr. Goodnight's activities because he would be destabilizing our nation's democratic government. I suppose it would be my duty to track him down and hang him.

"But the USA is not a going concern. We're on our own here. As an army officer, I think it's my obligation to defend democratic government. If Goodnight's movement is a democratic movement, and it sounds like it is, then I'm fine with it."

Lieutenant Barkley spoke up. "I'm a combat soldier, and this fort has seen plenty of combat over the last few years.

"The warlords from the east—the Nubian Nation and the New Rednecks—are a constant threat, and I think they'll eventually try to destroy Fort Sharpton and capture the oil refineries."

I was surprised by Lieutenant Barkley's remarks. She was a junior officer, after all, and I glanced toward General Mier and Colonel Merski to see if they considered her observations inappropriate. But I could tell they were listening intently and respected her contribution to the discussion.

"Those armies need a lot of food," Barkley continued, "and I think they may try to overrun our farm communities. They might even enslave the farm families and make them raise food for the Nubians or the Rednecker troops."

"Oh, I'm sure you're right," General Mier responded. "Throughout the history of warfare, armies have captured and enslaved agricultural populations. That's basically what the Spanish did when they invaded the upper Rio Grande Valley in 1598. Juan de Oñate's cavalry patrols raided the Pueblo communities and stole their food, and then his troops and his Franciscan priests converted the Pueblo people to Catholicism and essentially reduced the natives to serfdom."

Turning to me, Mier added a dire prediction. "If these paramilitary forces get control of the lower Mississippi Valley, Will, you and your families will become slaves—raising food for their armies. Not a pretty picture, is it?"

I said nothing, but I realized immediately that the idyllic farmsteads spread along the river were a lot more vulnerable than I had assumed.

"I'll defer to my superiors, of course," Lieutenant Barkley continued, "but in my opinion, the garrison at Fort Sharpton isn't strong enough to defeat the Nubians or the Redneckers. In fact, we can't even neutralize the comanchero gangs that are raiding the Mississippi valley.

"The ruckus we had on the Atchafalaya Causeway a few days ago is the third time we've been attacked on the west side of the Mississippi. In my opinion, that's a bad sign."

"I think I catch your drift, Lieutenant," Merski responded. "You don't think the army is strong enough to handle the southern warlords alone. If I understand you correctly, you think people in this region need a strong civil government if they are going to defend themselves against the Redneckers and the Nubians."

"Yes, Colonel Merski. I guess that's what I was trying to say."

General Mier brought the meeting to a close. "Based on what I've heard from each of you this morning," he summarized, "I think the army should encourage the Texans to get organized to defend themselves, even if they break away from the United States—which is dead anyway."

"That's my view," Colonel Merski affirmed. "Anything that can be done to stabilize Texas and make it safer will benefit Louisiana too. Louisiana and Texas both have oil and gas reserves, and they both have refineries, so they face the same threats."

"Then, let's do what we can to support Cole Goodnight and the Texans," Mier concluded. "Now, Colonel Merski," Mier added, "can I have just one more cup of this delicious coffee?"

A NOSTALGIC RIDE TO AUSTIN
IN AN ARMY HUMVEE

A few days later, an army courier showed up at Lâche Pas with a packet for me from Colonel Merski. I was spreading cow manure on our garden plot at the time, making it ready for spring planting.

Colonel Merski's message was brief and direct:

To Willoughby Burns—

General Mier has arranged a meeting between you and Cole Goodnight in Austin, TX three days from now. Pack gear and provisions for seven days. General Mier will provide transportation and security from Houston to Austin. Report to Fort Sharpton tomorrow morning at 0500 to meet the Red Ball.

—Colonel Merski

So I had been summoned back to Texas, the country where I was born and raised. My thoughts turned to the Texas Panhandle, and to my father and my father's ranch. Suddenly, I remembered some of my father's trappings, which I had saved over the tumultuous years in a battered cedar chest. I opened the chest and peered inside. I saw a Stetson hatbox, which contained my father's Stetson hat. It was a silverbelly hat—silverbelly being the word that westerners gave to the distinctive color of Stetson and Resistol hats. Not white and not grey, a sort of off-grey color.

My father's hat was sweat-stained around the hatband, which marked it as a cowman's everyday working hat. It had a three-inch brim, narrower than the brims on the hats of the TV cowboys—not flashy, but serviceable.

Inside the crown, I noticed the classic silk lining of a Stetson, which displayed the famous "last drop" picture of a cowboy sharing his canteen with his horse and watering it from the crown of his Stetson. I put my father's hat on, and I found that it fit.

I also found my father's boots in the chest—elk hide Nocona boots, devoid of any ornamentation, and featuring a high curved heel designed to slip easily into a saddle stirrup. I had cleaned those boots with saddle soap shortly after my father died, and the leather was still supple. I had never worn them, but now I put them on, and the boots fit too.

My father was a real cattleman, not a windshield rancher, who was "all hat and no cattle," as the real cowmen might say. Typically, a windshield rancher was a wealthy, urban businessman with a few acres of land outside a Texas city where he and his family could spend long weekends grilling steaks on the porch of an aircondi- tioned board-and-batten ranch house.

Windshield ranchers wore expensive hand-tooled boots, extrav- agant cowboy hats with rolled brims, and starched Levi's; but they knew nothing about worming cows, castrating bull calves, or the searing smell of burning flesh when cattle were branded on a hot July day. They knew nothing about pulling a breached calf from its mother's womb, ratcheting it out with a fence stretcher or a lariat tied to the trailer hitch of a pickup truck. And they didn't know anything about searching for a newborn calf in a barren pasture during a January blue norther when the Texas Panhandle could be as cold as a winter day in central Alaska.

Texas cattlemen were all hard men, and my father was a hard man. You had to be hard to survive in the cattle business, buffeted by fluc- tuating cattle prices, beaten down by multi-year droughts, and running the daily risk of being trampled in a loading chute by a Brangus bull, or bucked off and stomped on by a half-broken quarter horse.

I believed as a youth that hardness was the mark of a real man—a man who was worthy of respect. And I knew when I was quite young that I could never measure up to my father. *Am I worthy to wear my father's Stetson and his Nocona boots?*

I did not know, but I sensed the coming days would challenge me in some way, would take my measure and test my grit. I decided to wear my father's hat and boots on my journey to Texas.

I arrived at the front gate of Fort Sharpton the next morning in accordance with Merski's instructions. A Red Ball truck idled in the parking lot as passengers and supplies were being loaded and unloaded—just like the last time I traveled the Red Ball the week before. The weather had gotten a bit cooler and a light fog from the Mississippi floated over the levee and into the fort. It felt like duck-hunting weather.

"Willoughby," Colonel Merski called out, "thanks for agreeing to go back to Texas. General Mier and I decided it'd be useful to get a civilian's perspective on Cole Goodnight, so that's why he set up a meeting. You and Goodnight are both from the same part of Texas, and you're both lawyers. We think you're the right person to check him out for us.

"I'm here to see you off, and I'm sending Lieutenant Barkley with you. She can help provide security, and will report directly to me to brief me on your meeting with Goodnight. Goodnight and his compadres say they are organizing a constitutional government, but if it's some kind of violent coup or a Nazi-style putsch, the army needs to know about it."

"I'm happy to do this, Colonel," I said. "I'm very curious about Cole Goodnight and the Texas Independence Movement. I'll learn all I can and report back to you."

We shook hands, and I climbed into the cab of an ancient Mack truck. A freckle-faced kid was behind the wheel. He introduced himself as McCarty, and offered me some snuff from his snuff tin. He wasn't wearing a pistol, but I noticed a double-barreled shotgun lying at his feet.

I noticed McCarty was wearing a vintage "Make America Great Again" hat—a bit of nostalgia from a bygone era.

"I see by your hat that you're a true believer," I said, merely by way of making conversation.

"Friggin' A, man," McCarty replied, and spat a big wad of snuff out the driver's side window.

"But you weren't even alive when Donald Trump was president. What makes you a MAGA guy?"

"My mom and pop were big Trumpsters," McCarty replied. "They thought he hung the moon."

"Yeah, what did your folks do for a living?"

"Pop was an assistant manager at Walmart, and my mom was a nurse's aide at the old folk's home in Alexandria."

"And what did President Trump ever do for your mom and dad?" I asked.

"Dunno. They were kinda vague on that."

Lieutenant Barkley climbed into the cab with us, along with her rifle and her Beretta. "Let's roll," she said to McCarty. With that, we departed once again for Houston.

After we had been on the road for an hour or so, I asked Lieutenant Barkley a question that had long been on my mind.

"Lieutenant," I asked, "why does the army still have forts named after people who have no connection with the military? Fort Janis Joplin, for example, and Fort Al Sharpton."

I was squeezed between McCarty and Barkley in the truck cab and drumming my fingers on the dashboard. "And wasn't there a Fort Saul Alinsky at one time? Naming a military installation after the guy who wrote *Rules for Radicals*—I mean, what the hell?"

I knew Lieutenant Barkley didn't want to talk to me because I was distracting her from watching the highway for danger signs. But I was bored and curious about the Lieutenant's political views, so I pressed the conversation forward.

"I remember long ago when the army renamed all the forts that had been named after Confederate war heroes—Fort Hood, Fort Bragg, Fort Pickett, and so on. I think most Americans understood why those fort names needed to be changed.

"But when Congress ordered forts to be named after rock singers and political radicals, I thought that was over the top. Now that the country's gone to hell and nobody can find Congress, why doesn't the army rename its forts after more appropriate people?"

"Well, Mr. Burns," she answered, slightly annoyed, "I don't think the army cares what its forts are named. In the end, the soldiers will do their duty no matter what people call their military installations. And anyway, like General Mier told you, there aren't many forts left.

"Fort Saul Alinsky, by the way, was wiped out four years ago. A bunch of punks from Chicago, led by some so-called community organizer, attacked it and killed everybody. They took no prisoners."

"I'm sure Mr. Alinsky would have been pleased," I said. "However, I do completely approve of naming a Texas fort after Janis Joplin. She was from Port Arthur after all.

"Did you ever hear her version of 'Me and Bobby McGee?'" I asked. "In my opinion, she should have gotten the Presidential Medal of Freedom just for singing that song."

I could see Lieutenant Barkley was not interested in Janis Joplin, so I asked her to name her favorite artist.

"John Philip Sousa," she answered, and that wrapped up our discussion.

I was sorry I'd been unable to engage the Lieutenant in a conversation about music, a topic I loved to talk about. I had grown up in the Texas Panhandle listening to all kinds of Texas music. I loved listening to Bob Wills and the Texas Playboys, and I often tried to imagine what it must have been like to dance in the old Texas dancehalls back in the 1930s when the Texas Playboys were in their heyday.

Bob Wills invented western swing, a new genre of American music that blended big band swing music with old-time country fiddle tunes. Western swing was the music of the working people during the Great Depression—oilfield roughnecks, refinery workers, soldiers stationed at the Texas military bases, cowboys, and factory girls.

Most Texans considered Bob Wills to be the king of Texas music. In my mind, his musical genius was a tribute to the culture of rural Texas—my culture. Wills grew up in the little town of Turkey in the heart of the West Texas cotton and ranching country, not so different from my hometown.

Wills was followed by an amazing list of country music artists who sprang out of small Texas towns: Lefty Frizzell, Ernest Tubb, Hank Thompson, Willie Nelson, and many more. As an adult, most of my friends had more sophisticated tastes in music than I did. But I never learned to appreciate other musical genres like jazz, the blues, hip hop—let alone opera and classical music. The music I loved was *Texas* music—the sound of the fiddle and the steel guitar, and guys with untrained voices singing songs of lost love with a Texas twang.

These thoughts brought an old Texas Playboy tune to mind: "Faded Love," Bob Wills's signature song. In an instant, "Faded Love" became an earworm, a short-term lyrical addiction that I couldn't banish from my mind.

"Faded Love" was still wafting around in my head when our Red Ball Express truck pulled into Fort Joplin around dusk. General Mier was waiting for us at the front gate and invited the Lieutenant and me to dinner at Mi Raza Su Raza on Richmond Street.

Mi Raza Sue Raza had been my favorite Mexican seafood restaurant back in the years I lived in Houston. Unfortunately, the restaurant had no seafood now, so we ate big plates of cheese enchiladas. The restaurant's famous margarita machine—which had laid me low on many occasions during my younger days—had broken down, so we drank bottles of local draft beer brewed like a Mexican lager.

The next morning, bright and early, a beefy NCO named Sergeant McLaglen drove up to the front gate in an up-armored Humvee, complete with bullet-proof windows, a turret, and a .50 caliber machine gun.

A lean teenage corporal named Buddy Frizzell was perched in the turret, vigorously chewing gum. He looked way too young to have his hands on a heavy machine gun, but I decided not to tell him so. It didn't seem wise to antagonize a guy manning a heavy weapon, even if he was just a kid.

"We're traveling in style today," Lieutenant Barkley remarked. I could see she was pleased to see that we weren't driving to Austin in a Honda Fit like last week. "Lots of legroom."

I was happy to be riding in a big vehicle, but I was mystified by the Humvee. "I wonder why General Mier drove us to Baton Rouge in a Honda, and today he puts us in this gas guzzler."

"The general knows you're meeting with Cole Goodnight," Lieutenant Barkley replied. "Maybe he wants to send a message to Mr. Goodnight that the army's still in charge."

"What kind of fuel mileage does this baby get?" I asked Sergeant McLaglen.

"About eight miles to the gallon on the highway, and four in town," he replied. "So enjoy the ride, because we'll be burning about fifty gallons of diesel."

We traveled west on I-10—sixteen lanes wide in the center of the city. Sergeant McLaglen drove the Humvee in the HOV lane, which was totally unnecessary because there were no other vehicles on the road.

We drove through the bleak landscape of suburban west Houston for more than an hour. Mile after mile, we passed by looted shopping strips, burned-out fast-food restaurants, and thousands of abandoned homes. Here and there we saw someone cultivating a garden or a group of kids playing in the streets.

Children always believe that the world they live in is normal. In the old times, kids carried cell phones and played video games. They ate McDonald's hamburgers and French fries, drank Cokes, and listened to toneless rap music. Until they were old enough to drive, their parents drove them around to a variety of enrichment activities: piano lessons, gymnastics, martial arts, soccer, and baseball practice. Then they got driver's licenses, and their parents gave them a car and a credit card to buy gas. That was the old normal.

The kids I watched from the window of the Humvee would never know that world. They would never play a video game or text their friends on a cell phone. Most of them would never own a car or carry a credit card. They were back to riding bicycles around their neighborhoods and playing sandlot baseball. That was the new normal.

I wasn't so sure that the kids I observed were being deprived of anything important. As long as they got enough to eat and were safe from violence, I figured kids in the new times would make their way in the world pretty much as young people had always done.

Boys and girls would find each other, get married, and have children. Some of them would be good parents, and a few—unfortunately—would be abusive. Some of them would stumble across good books from the crumbling libraries, read them, and be inspired with the love of learning. Some would discover that they had mechanical skills and adapt those skills to whatever needed to be constructed or fixed. Some would prosper in the barter economy of the new times, and some would be perpetually impoverished.

I also knew that some of the present generation of children would grow up to be unshakably cheerful, even in times of misfortune, while others would suffer from lifelong depression. A few children growing up now would be sustained all their lives by religious faith—but only a few. In the new times, most American children would grow up to be secularists.

I turned my attention back to the road ahead. I saw that Sergeant McLaglen had elected to drive us to Austin by the southern route—west on I-10 to Columbus, and then north on Highway 71.

I was pleased by the Sergeant's decision because the southern route would follow the Colorado River. We passed over the river several times, and it looked as cool and green and inviting as it did back in the old times.

I remembered fishing the Colorado a few times while I was in law school. My friends and I would hire a river guide who would float us down the slow-moving stream, and we would fish for bass—catch and release only. In those days, almost no one fished the lower Colorado, and I was always astonished and grateful to find the river so peaceful and pristine just a few miles from the high-rises and car-choked highways of metropolitan Austin.

I wondered now whether the rare Guadalupe bass still lurked in the river's shallow pools. I also wondered whether fishermen still released the fish they caught or kept them to eat. If subsistence fishing had replaced sport fishing on the Colorado River, the Guadalupe bass might well be extinct.

As we crept north up Highway 71, I spotted a familiar landmark: Weimar's Store and Gas Station. A roadside sign proclaimed: "Weimar's kolaches: Hell yes, we're open."

"Stop, Sergeant McLaglen," I said. "We've got to get some kolaches."

McLaglen seemed willing, and he pulled over without a murmur. The gas station I remembered from the old times had been trashed, but Weimar's store was open for business.

Inside, I saw an ancient, angular Anglo woman standing behind a glass display case. She was wearing an apron over a faded cotton dress, and carried a large revolver in a leather holster. The holster belt was too large for her, even though she had cinched it up to the last notch, and it had worked its way down below her waist and hung precariously on her bony hips.

"You have any kolaches?" I asked.

"Hell yes, we've got kolaches," she replied. "Didn't you read the sign?

"Old Man Weimar practically invented the kolache," she added. "In fact, he *did* invent the kolache—right here in this store. All that stuff about Bohemia is just bullshit."

"Well, do you have any sausage-and-cheese kolaches?" I asked.

"We ain't got any sausage-and-cheese kolaches today," she answered, "and we ain't got any chorizo kolaches neither. So don't ask for 'em. But we've got apricot kolaches and we've got peach kolaches."

"How about coffee? You got any coffee?"

"We've got a little Folgers—kinda stale and kinda expensive. Will that do?" I said yes and ordered four cups.

"I'm surprised you still have coffee," I said. "It's virtually disappeared in Louisiana."

"Well, Old Man Weimar—bless his soul—was kind of a prepper," the woman replied. "Or maybe you'd call him a hoarder. He knew the economy was going to shit, and he got ready for it.

"He didn't stock up on guns or ammunition or even food. He stocked up on coffee. We had six hundred pounds of Folgers in the store when the stock market crashed."

"I remember Old Man Weimar. I used to come by here during the old times," I told the woman, "back when I was in law school in Austin. I never drove down Highway 71 without stopping here and getting a kolache and a cup of coffee."

"And what good did that law degree do you," she replied sourly, "now that we ain't got no law, no cops, and no courts?"

"Well," I said defensively, "I became a college professor."

"Then you were part of the problem, weren't you?" she said reproachfully. "Slick lawyers and numbskull professors is what got us into this world of shit."

I silently agreed with her, but I decided to change the topic. "That's a big revolver you're wearing," I commented. "Is that a .44 magnum?"

She sized me up for a few seconds before she answered. "Yes, it is. Are you gonna ask me if it's loaded?"

I didn't answer her question, but I continued trying to chat her up. "I only shot a .44 magnum a few times, and that was a long time ago," I said. "I found I couldn't control the recoil and I couldn't hit a damn thing with it. Isn't that a little too much gun for you?"

"My brother-in-law tried to give me his .380," she replied. "It's a lot smaller and a lot lighter than this cannon I'm carrying. But a .380 ain't got no stopping power.

"You might as well spit on a comanchero as shoot him with a .380. All you'd do is piss him off, and I don't need no pissed-off comanchero."

I could tell that this woman knew a lot more about guns than I did, and I should have ended the conversation right there, but I asked one more question. "Is it hard to get bullets for your .44 magnum?" I asked. "I don't see many of them around."

"Listen, mister," the woman snapped back, "I don't like guns, and I don't like talking about 'em. A lot of folks around here carry pistols now, but most people don't know how to use 'em.

"I know how to use this thing, but I miss the days when only the police carried guns. Remember back in the old times when people wanted to defund the police? I wonder what they're thinking now. I'll bet they wish we had the cops back. I know I do."

I started to tell her my own views about defunding the police, but the woman cut me off in mid-sentence.

"I'm only talking with you about this because you must be one of the good guys. You show up here with three soldiers and you bought 'em all a cup of coffee.

"But, like I said, I don't like talking about guns, and I don't like talking about politics neither. And you'd be smart if you kept your mouth shut on both subjects."

She was right, of course. I ordered four peach kolaches and four apricot kolaches to share with my military escort. My ill-tempered server poured out four cups of hot coffee into ceramic mugs and set them on the counter.

"You have any cream for the coffee?" I asked, thinking of Lieutenant Barkley, who might not like to drink her coffee black.

"Sure, we got cream," the woman retorted. "You know how to milk a cow?"

I didn't answer. I silently paid for my purchases and headed for the door.

"Bring back those mugs when you're finished with 'em," the woman called out. "They ain't Styrofoam."

I handed out coffee and pastries to my companions. Lieutenant Barkley and Sergeant McLaglen stood beside the Humvee while they drank their coffee, but Corporal Frizzell remained at his post behind the machine gun. I noticed that he was constantly scanning the landscape around the store—a grassy savannah dotted with live oak trees, where Brahman cows grazed contentedly.

I was glad to see that Frizzell was vigilant. *The kid may be young but he seems to know his job.*

I decided to go back inside the store and browse around the store's souvenir section, which I remembered from long ago. Most of the Texas souvenirs from the old days had been picked over or looted: the Lone Star coffee cups, the cheap bluebonnet landscape paintings, the straw cowboy hats, and the Texas-themed tea towels.

All I found were some children's "Don't mess with Texas" T-shirts and some beer koozies bearing a quote from Davy Crockett when he lost his Tennessee bid for Congress: "You may all go to hell, and I will go to Texas."

Davy can rest easy because Congress did in fact go to hell.

But then again, so did Texas.

I MEET COLE GOODNIGHT
AND VISIT THE CANNON LADY

Sergeant McLaglen drove us into Austin as the sun dropped low over the rugged hills of the Edwards Plateau, its rays lingering for a moment on the University of Texas library tower where Charles Whitman kicked off the mass-shooter era so long ago, shooting college students like deer with his high-powered rifle from the tower's observation deck. There were no police SWAT teams in those days, and an off-duty cop climbed all the way up the tower and shot the son of a bitch with a revolver.

Lieutenant Barkley and Sergeant McLaglen found quarters at Camp Mabry, where the Texas National Guard maintained a small presence. Sergeant McLaglen promised to have Lieutenant Barkley back at the capitol in time for my meeting with Cole Goodnight.

I checked in to a so-called bed-and-breakfast on Lamar Street—lumpy bed, no breakfast, and no coffee in the morning. Fortunately, I still had one kolache, and I made myself a cup of herbal tea in the B&B's kitchen—vile stuff, and non-caffeinated. I then walked over to the Texas state capitol, where I was scheduled to meet Cole Goodnight in the Texas Secretary of State's office. Lieutenant Barkley was waiting for me outside the main entrance.

As we walked in the front door of the capitol building, I could see that all was just as it had once been. Like St. Joseph's Cathedral in Baton Rouge, the Texas capitol had been defended by armed civilians during the riots and was never looted. The stately, pink-granite edifice was undamaged, soaring a few feet taller than the old national Capitol. The Goddess of Liberty still stood on top of the capitol's dome, holding a sword in one hand and a five-pointed star in the other.

I walked over the capitol's highly polished floor with the names of famous Texas battles embedded in the tiles: Goliad, the Alamo, San Jacinto, and several more. Portraits of all the past Texas governors hung in the rotunda, including painted images of Ma and Pa Ferguson, who outdid Huey Long in cornpone populism back in the 1920s and 1930s.

Cole Goodnight rose to greet me as I came into the Secretary of State's office. He looked to be in his early fifties, and he was dressed in blue jeans, a chambray shirt, and wearing polished, hand-crafted western boots. He looked like a cattleman, but he carried himself like a really good trial lawyer—which is what he had once been— with confidence and a certain modest dignity.

"So Mr. Burns," Goodnight said without any preliminary chit-chat, "I hear you want to know about the Texas Independence Movement. And since you came here in an army vehicle and you have an army officer with you, I'm guessing the army sent you to find out if I'm a revolutionary. Am I right?"

"That's right, Mr. Goodnight. And before we begin, may I ask if you are a descendant of Charlie Goodnight?"

"Yes, I am, Mr. Burns. I'm a direct descendant. He was my father's great-grandfather. Do you know anything about Charlie Goodnight?"

"I know a little: the Goodnight-Loving Trail, Palo Duro Canyon, the Texas Rangers, the rescue of Cynthia Parker . . . I grew up in the Panhandle, and we covered Charlie Goodnight in my high school Texas History class. As I recall, we spent the rest of the semester talking about the Alamo."

"I wish we had Charlie with us today," Goodnight replied. "Charlie would know what to do, and I think he would agree with what we *are* doing.

"So I'll tell you briefly about the Texas Independence Movement. Our goal is to hold a constitutional convention in Austin, Texas, to declare Texas as a sovereign nation and adopt a national constitution.

"Right now, my compadres and I are traveling across Texas, holding meetings in all of the state's 254 counties. We are asking people to elect constitutional delegates to meet in Austin twelve months from now."

"I'm impressed," I said, "but how do you manage that? I mean, I've traveled recently in a worn-out Red Ball truck, a Humvee, and a Honda Fit. How are your people getting around the state? Where do you get the gasoline?"

"Natural gas, Mr. Burns. Our vehicles are powered by compressed natural gas. I assume you know that cars and trucks can run on natural gas."

"Yeah, I guess I knew that. My father had an NG-fueled pickup truck back when I was a kid. But I forgot about that."

"Well, there are still natural-gas reserves out in West Texas, and we're using compressed gas to power our vehicles. In fact, our caravan is leaving tomorrow for Wise County. We've got a rally scheduled in front of the old courthouse in Decatur.

"Do want to come along? I can tell you more about the Texas Independence Movement, and you can tell me what's going on in Louisiana."

"Sure," I said. "I'd love to join you. Can Lieutenant Barkley come along as well?" She had been sitting quietly in a corner with her service rifle resting on her knees.

"Of course. It's always good to have someone around who knows how to shoot a rifle. Now, here is a person I would like you to meet."

Just then, a woman walked into the room. She was in her mid-forties, I guessed, brunette, thin, and fit. She might have been a University of Texas cheerleader back in her college days, and she was wearing a 9 mm pistol with two spare magazines clipped to her holster.

"I'm Adina Morales," she said by way of introduction. "I'm chief of the Texas Rangers."

I was caught off guard. "The Texas Rangers? Do mean the 'one riot, one ranger' Texas Rangers, or the baseball team?"

"The 'one riot, one ranger,' Texas Rangers," she answered dryly. "Did I hear someone say that you and Lieutenant Barkley are traveling with us to Decatur tomorrow?" I nodded. "That's good," she answered. "I want to know more about the security situation in Louisiana. We've had a couple of incidents on the Texas border over near Shreveport by an outfit called the Redneckers."

"We're familiar with them," Lieutenant Barkley said.

"Vicious sonsabitches," Morales declared. "I hate to admit it, but it took more than one ranger to put 'em down."

"Meet us at seven o'clock sharp tomorrow in front of the State House," Goodnight instructed us. "We have a rally scheduled in Decatur at four in the afternoon."

I bid Goodnight and Morales goodbye, and realized I had the rest of the day to myself. I decided to explore the capitol grounds to see which statues and monuments had survived the nationwide purge that had raged across the United States back in the early twenty-first century.

To my surprise, three statues commemorating the Confederacy still stood on the capitol lawn, and none had been defaced or molested. One statue was dedicated to Terry's Texas Rangers, another to John Bell Hood's Texas Brigade.

And one very large statue was dedicated to the entire Confederate military. Four figures stood on the corners of a granite pedestal, representing the Confederate infantry, cavalry, artillery, and navy. And above them all stood a patriarchal image of Jefferson Davis, president of the Confederacy.

As I wandered about the Texas capitol grounds, I saw other monuments commemorating nearly every aspect of Texas heritage. There was a bronze memorial to Texas children, a statue honoring pioneer women, and statuary salutes to Texas cowboys and volunteer firemen. I also saw a tribute to disabled war veterans and a miniature version of the Statue of Liberty.

But the largest and most impressive statues were dedicated to the African Americans of Texas and the Tejanos. The African American statue was more than thirty feet long and twenty-five feet high. Dozens of figures were sculpted in bronze, including an image of a Buffalo soldier, a tribute to the African American cavalrymen who fought the Apache out in the Big Bend country in the nineteenth century.

The Tejano Monument was also enormous. Ten bronze figures were placed on a mammoth granite base. Statues honored the early Spanish explorers, the Tejano settlers in Spanish Texas, and the *vaqueros*.

Altogether, I saw more than twenty statues and memorials on the capitol grounds. As far as I could tell, not a single one had been vandalized or removed. Even the Ten Commandments, graven on a stone tablet, stood under the capitol elms, having survived a legal fight that went all the way to the US Supreme Court.

It was midmorning now and a sunny day, so I decided to walk south down Congress Avenue toward the Colorado River. Austin's skyscrapers still lined the street, but they were empty and dilapidated. Rioters had broken the windows on the lower floors, and spray-painted racist epithets desecrated the walls. Those gleaming office towers hadn't survived the new times as well as Jefferson Davis.

As I trod along Congress Avenue, I came across another statue right in the middle of the sidewalk, one I had forgotten about—the Cannon Lady!

Austinites erected the Cannon Lady Statue to honor Angelina Eberly, who is credited with saving the city as the Texas Republic's capital. In December 1842, so the story goes, President Sam Houston dispatched some Texas Rangers to remove the records in the Texas General Land Office, which was located in Austin, and transfer them to Washington-on-the-Brazos. By moving the land records, Houston hoped to annul Austin's status as the Texas capital and move the capital somewhere to the east . . . maybe the little town of Houston, Sam's namesake.

But Angelina Eberly heard the commotion and raised the alarm. A loaded cannon stood on Congress Avenue as protection against a Mexican army that had invaded Texas earlier in the year. Eberly fired it directly at the land office. Her quick action alerted the townsfolks, who retrieved the land records. Sam Houston's scheme was foiled.

So many statues and monuments! Which should be preserved, I asked myself, *and which should be taken down or destroyed?*

A lot of Confederate monuments had been removed all over the South during the last years of the petroleum age—condemned as racist tributes to a slave culture. Was Texas a retrograde society for not removing the three Confederate statues on the capitol grounds?

Maybe. But on the other hand, I felt sure that most people approved of the bronze tributes to African Americans and Tejanos—and to Texas children.

But perhaps those statues should come down too. The Tejanos settled land along the Rio Grande that had once belonged to Native Americans. The Buffalo soldiers fought the Apache. Did that make them lackeys working in service to a racist white culture?

Maybe even the statues of Texas children should come down. Their very presence is an endorsement of American civilization—a racist project that Christopher Columbus launched.

But who would remove the statue of the Cannon Lady—even though she played a small part in the rise of Anglo Texas and all that it represents?

Not me.

I decided that the Texans had taken the right approach. Instead of tearing down statues, they just erected more: a statue to pioneer women, Texas cowboys, Tejanos, the state's African Americans, and the Cannon Lady.

I concluded these ruminations as I reached the Congress Avenue Bridge over Lady Bird Lake. Lady Bird—champion of Texas wildflowers, and a First Lady of great dignity. How many statues had been erected of President Lyndon Baines Johnson over the years, and how many had been erected to honor his spouse?

But I decided I had thought enough about statues without coming to any firm conclusion. Switching the focus of my thoughts, I wondered whether Austin's famous Mexican free-tailed bats still lodged under the Congress Avenue bridge.

I crawled down the bank of Lady Bird Lake and looked up into the bridge's grey, concrete underbelly. I saw a few bats, but not as many as I had expected.

A young bicycle rider saw me scrambling out from under the bridge. He was wearing a vintage "Keep Austin Weird" T-shirt and spandex bike-riding shorts.

"Hey old guy," the bike rider called out. "Are you looking for the bats?"

I said that I was but hadn't found many.

"The bats split for Mexico in the fall," he explained, "but they'll be back next spring to eat our mosquitos."

"So the bats are doing fine, then?"

"Oh yeah," the biker replied. "There's more than a million of them under that bridge in the summer. And why not? They eat bugs, and we'll always have bugs in Austin.

"Unlike us humanoids, the bats never got hooked on gasoline."

DANCING ON A PONY KEG

The next morning, I met Cole Goodnight, Chief Ranger Morales, and Lieutenant Barkley in front of the Texas State House. A small caravan of vehicles was parked in the circular drive: a vintage black Cadillac Escalade pickup truck in mint condition and fitted with an LPG tank in the pickup bed, an old Amazon delivery van, an LPG truck, and a Texas Highway Patrol car.

Morales had her hair pulled back in a ponytail. She was wearing a Stetson, a tan skirt and blouse, and western boots. She also sported a shoulder holster, which made her look like a cross between a rodeo performer and a Bronx police detective.

"Everything's as it should be," Chief Morales observed. "Two women and two men, and only the women are carrying guns.

"Or maybe I'm wrong about that," Morales added. "Cole, are you packin'?"

"No, Chief Morales," Goodnight replied in a formal tone. "I'm unarmed because I have complete confidence in your ability to keep me safe."

"How about you, Mr. Burns. Are you carrying a gun?"

"No, Chief Morales. Colonel Merski gave me a strict order when I left Baton Rouge not to take a weapon to Texas. He said there were already too many Texans carrying guns, and I'd only get myself in trouble."

"Very well," Morales replied. "Saddle up!"

Morales slid behind the wheel of the Escalade—a top-of-the-line model that smelled of leather. A small Texas flag flew from each of the two front fenders, which made the car look something like a diplomat's vehicle. Lieutenant Barkley rode shotgun in the front seat, and Goodnight and I settled into the vehicle's back seat—as comfortable as an expensive couch.

In only a moment, Morales headed the car north on I-35, and then she hit the gas pedal. By the time we passed the ruins of Georgetown, we were barreling down the highway doing seventy-five miles an hour. Our support vehicles—the delivery van and the LPG truck—couldn't keep up and slipped out of sight behind us. The officer driving the Texas Highway Patrol car must have decided to stay with the slower vehicles.

Steering the Escalade with one hand, Morales fumbled among some CDs in a hand-tooled leather carrying case until she found the one she was looking for. She jammed it into the car's CD player, and suddenly we were listening to "Miles and Miles of Texas."

Ah, some Texas music, I thought, not realizing that Morales's CD contained nothing but songs about Texas. As we sped up I-35, I heard "Waltz Across Texas" by Ernest Tubb, "Bob Wills is Still the King," by Waylon Jennings, "Texas Cookin'" by Guy Clark, and several more songs about Texas. She even had Kinky Friedman's "Asshole from El Paso" in her CD collection, along with Ray Wylie Hubbard's "Screw You, We're from Texas."

When "Deep in the Heart of Texas" started, Morales sang along and beat one hand on the steering wheel during the part of the lyrics when listeners traditionally clap their hands.

I wouldn't say Morales was driving dangerously, but the Escalade weaved a bit when she took one hand off the steering wheel. And there were potholes on the highway, which hadn't been maintained for years. Morales missed most of them, but not all of them. Goodnight's Escalade was taking a beating.

I was only a guest on this expedition, and I didn't think I should tell a Texas Ranger how to drive a car, but I could see that Goodnight was growing concerned as the Escalade wandered in and out of its lane.

Finally, he spoke up. "With all due respect, Chief Morales, maybe we've heard enough Texas songs for a while." As if to support his point, a song by the Austin Lounge Lizards came up on the CD: "Just Another Stupid Texas Song."

"Well, maybe you're right, Cole. How about some Johnny Cash?"

She selected another CD from her collection, and soon we were listening to Johnny Cash and June Carter sing "Jackson."

"I really like this song," Morales said to no one in particular, "but I don't understand some of the lyrics—like when June sings that she'll be dancing on a pony keg. Have ya'll ever seen a pony keg? They're too small to dance on."

No one had a response to that observation, and in almost no time at all, we were hurdling through burned-out Waco, which was one hundred miles north of Austin. As we crossed the Brazos River doing seventy, Chief Morales called our attention to another musicological conundrum.

"That reminds me. Y'all know that song 'Cross the Brazos at Waco' that Billy Walker sang? You know that part where he sings that he can cross the Brazos River and then ride his horse to San Antonio in one night? That doesn't make sense either. I mean it's 180 miles from Waco to San Antonio. No one can ride a horse from Waco to San Antonio in one night. It would probably take six or seven days. Am I right about that, Cole?"

Goodnight didn't seem to want to join this discussion, but he agreed with her. "You're right, Chief Morales. It's 180 miles from Waco to San Antonio. No one can ride a horse from Waco to San Antonio in one night."

I figured, *What the hell*, and I decided to do my part to keep the conversation going. "My guess is that whoever wrote that song didn't care how far it is between San Antonio and Waco and just wrote the lyrics so they would rhyme."

"Maybe, but it's not geographically accurate," Morales insisted. "I think songs about Texas should be geographically accurate."

I began to suspect that Ranger Chief Morales was just another eccentric, jingoist Texan, and I wondered how she managed to become head of the vaunted Texas Rangers. But then I remembered that I had known a lot of eccentric Texans over the years, and most of them were pretty cool and professional in a crisis. This proved to be true of Chief Morales.

When we reached the interchange south of Dallas where I-35 crosses I-20, Morales pulled the Escalade onto the shoulder and waited for the van and the LPG truck to catch up. In a few minutes, they emerged from the south and pulled up behind our vehicle. The rangers in the patrol car pulled up as well, but they stood by their vehicle watching the road for any danger that might arise. I noticed that one of the patrol-car rangers was an African American woman.

Two rangers got out of the van and two more got out of the LPG truck, all donning their Stetsons as they walked toward our vehicle. I noted that all four were Hispanic. They spoke to each other in Spanish as they approached Chief Morales.

Morales greeted them in Spanish—perhaps to remind them she could understand them when they were not speaking English. And then she was all business.

"All right, rangers, here's what we got. Interstate 35 is blocked in downtown Dallas, but of course, that's been true for years. They never got all those burned-out vehicles off the road. So we will swing around to the east on I-635.

"Now here's the problem: we've received reports about a sniper on I-635 somewhere around the old High Five Interchange.

"So this is what we're going to do: Ranger Almaráz and I are going to drive that route all away around Dallas to check things out. If we draw sniper fire or run into trouble, we'll have to go to plan B. So one of you fellers get out a map and figure us an alternate route to Decatur. Almaráz, you better bring your rifle."

Almaráz walked back to the delivery van and returned with a hard-plastic gun case, which presumably held a scoped sniper rifle.

"Everybody hangs tight till we get back," Morales instructed us. "We should be back here in about an hour." Morales and Almaráz then drove away in the Escalade.

It was late morning now, a pleasant autumn day with a slight breeze blowing out of the southwest. One of the rangers brought out a vintage YETI ice chest and distributed brisket sandwiches. Another ranger poured out cups of sweet, iced tea from a five-gallon insulated water cooler.

My brisket sandwich was delicious, and I was instantly refreshed when that familiar, ice-cold, caffeinated super-sweet tea went down my throat. Goodnight and Morales were good company, and I had an army lieutenant and a half-dozen armed Texas Rangers standing watch. Life looked good as the sun shined down on us, highlighting Texas sunflowers that were swaying in a nearby field. Mourning doves darted around the field because mourning doves love sunflower seeds.

"Ah, sweet tea," I said, feeling a welcome jolt from the caffeine and sugar.

Ranger Rodríguez agreed with me. "Yep. Sweet tea is pretty damn good." He pronounced sweet tea as if it were one word: sweettae.

I looked at Rodríguez more closely. He was another one of those extraordinary Tejanos who spoke flawless Spanish and yet spoke English with a broad West Texas twang. He could move back and forth between two cultures effortlessly, and I envied him.

"Where are you from, Ranger Rodríguez?" Goodnight asked.

"I'm from Laredo, down on the Bravo."

"I've been in Laredo a few times. I used to go dove hunting down in South Texas. White-winged doves, not mourning doves like we have up in this part of Texas."

"Well, you don't have to go to South Texas anymore to hunt white-winged doves," Rodriguez responded. "They've extended their range into Central Texas. In fact, that's one flying over us right now."

"Maybe that's a good sign," I said. "Doves are a symbol of peace and the Holy Spirit."

"Maybe," Rodríguez said doubtfully. "I suppose it is good that white-winged doves are moving north. But what about the armadillos, the nutria, and the fire ants? And the alligators? They're moving north, too, and I don't think they're a symbol of peace."

"And feral hogs are on the move," Goodnight added. "There's more than two million of them in Texas now, or so the experts tell us. They're tearing up the farmland, and the big ones are dangerous. It's getting so people have to carry a gun if they go walking in the woods."

"How about deer?" I asked. "Years ago, the deer population was out of control in the Texas Hill Country. Is that population still growing?"

"No, Will, the deer population is under control," Goodnight replied. "Now that Texas has no hunting season, people shoot them all year around. And they're not looking for that trophy buck anymore. People are killing deer strictly to get something to eat."

A few minutes later, Ranger Morales drove up, churning up a great cloud of dust as she fishtailed across the weedy median from the south-bound lane at a pretty good speed. She and Ranger Almaráz both looked drawn and anxious.

"Well, boys and girls, there *was* a sniper up on I-635. Some cabrón with a 30.06 on the roof of the old Hilton. Almaráz shot him, so we never learned his political affiliation. He was just standing on the roof, offering Almaráz an easy shot. I guess the dumbass didn't figure we'd have our own sniper. Almaráz recovered the rifle.

"Cole, I'm sorry to tell you this, but there's a bullet hole in the side of your classic Escalade. Gives it a kind of rakish look, don't you agree? I think the sniper was aiming for your LPG tank, but he hit the driver's-side passenger door. No harm done."

COLE GOODNIGHT RALLIES
WISE COUNTY

Minutes after Morales and Almaráz returned from neutralizing the sniper, our cavalcade was on the road again. This time all four vehicles stayed together as we looped around Dallas on the I-635 bypass at sixty miles an hour. No country music blasted out of the CD player. No one talked as Chief Morales and Lieutenant Barkley scanned the road ahead looking for signs of trouble.

North of Dallas, we joined I-35 East and sped through the towns of Farmers Branch, Lewisville, and Denton. The road took us past the University of North Texas campus. Much like the University of Houston, the buildings were abandoned but intact, and the empty football stadium looked like a postmodern Roman coliseum.

When we reached the outskirts of Denton, our caravan left I-35 and headed west on Highway 380. Soon we entered the eastern boundary of the Texas Cross Timbers—a rolling country dotted with groves of blackjack and oak trees. Just a little to the west, I knew, the trees disappeared, and the Texas plains began.

We arrived in Decatur about half an hour before the town meeting was scheduled to begin. "Good," said Goodnight. "We're on time. One of the important lessons of politics, Willoughby, is to keep your promises. People expect us to be here at 4:00 p.m., and we're here."

We drove into Decatur and parked our vehicles about a block from the Wise County courthouse. And what a courthouse! A magnificent neo-Romanesque structure stood in the center of the courthouse square—a massive edifice made of granite with whimsical turrets, a clock tower, and little balconies tucked into the walls.

Goodnight gazed at the courthouse for a moment and then turned to me.

"That courthouse, Willoughby, was built in 1896. The county financed the project with bond money, and it took the people of Wise County almost fifty years to pay off the debt.

"It's one of the many great county courthouses of Texas—an architectural gem. The Texans of that day believed in democratic government, and the people of Wise County obviously wanted their courthouse to symbolize their commitment to it. That's where they kept the land records, marriage certificates, and death certificates. That's where people voted, and that's where people went to seek justice.

"I'm glad it's still standing and undamaged."

A crowd had gathered, and I looked it over as Goodnight and Morales conferred. I figured about three hundred or four hundred people were assembled. Almost everyone was wearing a broad-brimmed hat as protection against the Texas sun, and a few women wore old-fashioned bonnets. I saw a young couple with two small children, and all four family members were wearing safari-style pith helmets which made them look like cartoonish African explorers.

A stage had been erected in front of the courthouse, and a fiddle trio was playing "San Antonio Rose," a classic Bob Wills tune. Some couples were dancing the Texas two-step on the sidewalks—old folks mainly, who still remembered how to dance.

I wiggled my way through the crowd and found a place to stand close to the speaker's platform. Lieutenant Barkley was right behind me with her M4; the crowd gave us plenty of breathing room.

At 3:59 p.m., Goodnight mounted the stage, followed by Chief Morales.

At precisely 4:00 p.m., Goodnight started speaking. There was no microphone, but Goodnight spoke loudly and clearly, and his voice carried through the courthouse square.

"I'm Cole Goodnight from Austin, Texas. I grew up on a ranch near San Angelo out in West Texas. With me here today is Chief Ranger Adina Morales, head of the Texas Rangers. She will speak to you in just a few minutes."

Goodnight paused for a couple of seconds and then began again.

"Texans," he said, "it is time to face the crisis of our time and organize ourselves into a free and sovereign nation—the Republic of Texas, completely independent of the old United States of America."

It was clear that his audience had been expecting this message. With the exception of a young man in the back of the crowd who howled out a tepid rendition of the Rebel Yell, no one said anything. His attentive listeners remained silent.

"The United States as we knew it in the old times is no more. It has fallen and will never rise again. We have no Congress, no courts, no mail service, no schools, and no president. If we do still have a president, no one can find her.

"We're on our own. We are confronting an organized and well-armed terrorist threat on our eastern border. Chief Morales will tell you about that in a few minutes. There is only one army unit in the state—a small garrison in Houston. State and local police forces have dissolved with the exception of the Texas Rangers, and there are not enough rangers to fight off the invasion that is coming from the east.

"We've got to get organized. We've got to re-establish our civil government and put together a defense force. We've got to re-open our schools and our courts, and get the mail service going again. That's the job of government, and currently, we have no government.

"Now, this is what I and my patriotic colleagues have done: we've scheduled a constitutional convention for next October to take place in Austin, where delegates will consider ratifying a declaration of independence and a national constitution.

"At this convention, I hope delegates will approve the United States Constitution as the Constitution for the Republic of Texas with only a few alterations, along with the same Bill of Rights. I also hope the delegates will elect a provisional president with the power to appoint a cabinet, including a secretary of defense and a secretary of state.

"This is what I hope to accomplish today: I hope to persuade you to hold a county-wide election to select two Wise County delegates and two alternate delegates to represent you at the convention. We've brought printed blank ballots that we will leave with you. People can write in the name of the individuals they want to represent Wise County.

"You should appoint a small election committee of honest citizens to organize the election and count the ballots. When the election is decided, the committee should prepare an affidavit naming your Wise County delegates and your alternative delegates, signed by at least three committee members.

"That affidavit will be your delegates' ticket for admission at the constitutional convention next fall. Ideally, we will have two delegates from all 254 counties.

"At that convention, I am confident that Texas will declare itself a free and sovereign nation among the nations of the world."

The speech was short and sweet.

I looked at the crowd around me. They were clearly riveted by Goodnight's brief oration and perhaps a little surprised by its brevity and simplicity. I glanced at Chief Morales, who must have heard this speech or something like it many times before. And yet I could see that she, too, was moved by Goodnight's words— her eyes were locked on his face.

"Now," Goodnight continued, "I would like to introduce Chief Ranger Adina Morales, head of the Texas Rangers. She's going to tell you about the security situation in Texas."

Morales took off her Stetson and stepped forward.

"Thank you, Mr. Goodnight," she said as her eyes swept the gathering.

"Texans, I am a Texas Ranger, not a politician; and I'm not making a political speech. I am here today to alert you to the threat of terrorism from the east and to ask you to help defend our Texas soil.

"Less than a month ago, a band of about fifty terrorists, well-armed and disciplined, crossed the Mississippi River at Vicksburg, where they attacked and wiped out a volunteer militia group that was guarding the Vicksburg bridge. We've identified them as Redneckers—a white supremacist, terrorist group with a vicious record of violence.

"They headed west along I-20, killing, raping, and looting along the way, and then they crossed into Texas near the town of Waskom.

"A ranger detachment—about twenty officers—confronted these terrorists near the Sabine River. I was with them. Although we were outnumbered, we managed to disperse the group, killing some of them and driving the survivors back into Louisiana.

"In my opinion, this gang was a reconnaissance unit that was preparing the way for a large Rednecker army, which intends to invade our state very soon. I think the Redneckers' aim is to enslave the civilian population and force it to provide them with the food and supplies they need to conquer the entire state and prosecute a race war against the Nubians—an African American paramilitary force. They want to set up a white aristocracy to bring back the antebellum South."

Now this got the Wise County folks' attention. Certainly, she got my attention. I think the immediate reaction from most people listening to Morales was shock and fear.

"I'm here today to urge you to participate in the constitutional convention next October and to begin organizing yourselves into militias that can respond quickly if the Redneckers enter Texas again—which I'm sure they will."

And that was all Morales had to say.

At this point, Goodnight spoke again.

"We brought a couple of guests with us from Louisiana. Willoughby Burns, would you stand up? And we also have Lieutenant Wilhelmina Barkley of the United States Army, who is stationed at Fort Sharpton in Baton Rouge. Would either of you like to say a few words?"

I was completely unprepared for this, but Goodnight and Morales had stirred my blood with their brief speeches. They'd made a true believer out of me in only a few short minutes. So I walked up on the stage and started talking—just winging it.

"I'm Willoughby Burns. People call me Will. I grew up in the Texas Panhandle, not far from Shamrock. My father was a cattle rancher. I went to law school in Austin and practiced law in Houston in my younger days. I was a professor in Louisiana for many years before the new times.

"But I still consider myself a Texan. And I can tell you that Louisiana is confronting armed groups pushing west from the southern states—Alabama, Mississippi, Tennessee, and Georgia.

"I fully support the Texas Independence Movement," I told the crowd, "and will do everything I can to get Louisiana to cooperate with you."

Figuring I had said enough, I stopped speaking. Then to my surprise, Lieutenant Barkley spoke up.

"I'm Lieutenant Barkley," she told the crowd. "I'm an infantry officer at Fort Sharpton in Louisiana. I am not a politician. I'm a soldier assigned by my commanding officer to learn more about the political and military developments in Texas.

"I can say, however, that Chief Morales is right about the Redneckers. Our forces have spotted small units of Redneckers east of the Mississippi River, and we've fought terrorist gangs several times west of the river. As a soldier, I hope you will carefully consider what Mr. Goodnight and Chief Morales have told you, because Texas faces a mortal threat from the east."

Lieutenant Barkley made a huge impression on the crowd. The fact that she was a middle-aged woman dressed in combat fatigues and carrying a rifle gave her extemporaneous speech a dramatic quality, and she clearly conveyed that she was speaking from her heart.

Goodnight and Morales glanced at each other as Barkley finished speaking, and I could see that they were surprised. They hadn't expected my bodyguard to speak up at a public rally about Texas independence, and they certainly hadn't expected a US Army officer to basically endorse their messages. By speaking at the Decatur rally, Lieutenant Barkley was signaling that the army was not opposed to the Texas Independence Movement.

At this point, Goodnight stepped forward to close out the rally. "Chief Morales and our ranger escort will be headed back to Austin in a few minutes," Goodnight told the audience. "We've set up a table with plenty of sample ballots. We're also giving out copies of the United States Constitution and the Bill of Rights and copies of *Robert's Rules of Order*. Feel free to take what you need."

So that was what the delivery van contained: ballots, copies of the Constitution, and administrative rule books—a nation-starter kit!

"We've got a few minutes," Chief Morales added. "Mr. Goodnight and I will take some questions."

A man, who appeared to be in his late fifties , raised his hand. He wore a threadbare sports coat and tie, which distinguished him from the rest of the crowd—mostly people who were dressed like farmers or people who worked with their hands. Unlike most of the people around him, he was hatless, and I saw sweat dripping from his bald head onto his florid face.

"I don't understand why each Texas county only gets two delegates," the man complained. "Some counties are practically uninhabited, and others are in big cities. It doesn't seem fair for Deaf Smith County, where almost no one lives, to have an equal vote with Houston's Harris County."

"That's a very good question," Goodnight replied. "As we all know, Texas was an urban state during the old times. More than half the state's population lived in six cities: Austin, Houston, El Paso, San Antonio, Fort Worth, and Dallas.

"But we only have a vague idea now about how many people survived the plagues, the famine, and the violence. Our best guess is that about 15 percent of the pre-crisis population is still alive. Major Texas cities are depopulated. Most of the survivors moved out into the countryside where they can grow food or at least be closer to their food supplies.

"We are going to conduct a census to find out just how many Texans are still alive in the state. One of the reasons we asked the counties to select alternate delegates is to be able to adjust the delegate representation if it turns out some counties have very large populations. That's the best we can do for now."

A woman wearing a hand-braided, straw cowboy hat raised her hand and began speaking in a strong, accusatory voice.

"Texas has a long history of racial violence and racism," she began. "Texas was a slave state that fought for the Confederacy during the Civil War. Then it enacted Jim Crow laws to keep African Americans down.

"Your own law school, Mr. Goodnight, wouldn't admit African Americans until the US Supreme Court forced it to. The state also made homosexuality a criminal offense until the Supreme Court struck down the law as unconstitutional.

"Are you doing anything to make sure that African Americans, Latinos, gays, and lesbians will have their voices heard at this convention you're holding?"

Chief Morales fielded this question.

"Well as you know, I'm a Texas Ranger, and the rangers have some blots on their record as far as race is concerned. Historians have shown us that the rangers committed atrocities against Mexican civilians during the Mexican War, and they were pretty rough on the Tejanos and Mexicans along the Rio Bravo for a long time. Texas as a whole has a legacy of African American slavery and bigotry toward gays.

"But a new day dawned on Texas during the civil rights movement of the 1960s. Today, we are a multicultural society, and this new reality is reflected in the makeup of the rangers. There are six rangers with me today—four are Hispanic, and one is an African American woman. I don't think we have any Asian rangers with us this afternoon, but we have several Vietnamese officers in the field.

"This is my point: Texas has come a long way toward racial justice, and I think it's time to put old animosities and grievances aside and band together as Texans."

"Let me add a few words," Goodnight interjected. "You mentioned discrimination against gays, and you are right. The Supreme Court struck down the Texas sodomy laws in the *Lawrence* decision back in 2003. Personally, I don't give a damn about anyone's sexual orientation, and I don't think the people of Wise County give a damn either.

"If we spend our time squabbling over ethnic, racial, sexual, and religious representation at the convention, we will never get anywhere. I think it is time to put all that behind us. Texans aren't flavors of Blue Bell ice cream; we're one people who share some basic human values and a common culture, and we're facing a perilous future."

I thought the crowd was finished asking questions, but I was wrong. "Mr. Goodnight," someone called out, "will the new constitution protect our right to carry firearms?"

Searching with my eyes, I found the questioner in the audience: a frail, old man with grey, wispy hair, wearing suspenders to hold up his baggy pants and a dirty trucker's cap that advertised Bob's Cattle Truck Wash.

Goodnight laughed good-naturedly. "Sir," he said, "that's a question I always like to answer. The Second Amendment in the US Constitution will certainly be enshrined in the new Constitution of the Texas Republic."

Goodnight spread his arms expansively to take in the entire audience. "I'm guessing everyone here today is carrying a gun.

"Well, maybe not everybody," he conceded. "That little boy on a tricycle's probably not packing.

"Let's remember," he continued, "that in the old times, there were thirty million Texans, and collectively, they owned more than thirty-five million guns. Now there are only 3.5 million Texans, but there are still thirty-five million firearms. That means the State has ten guns for every Texan. Clearly, Texans have enough guns to protect themselves."

Goodnight carried on after a pause. "But here's what you need to be thinking about: *ammunition.* You all need to stockpile enough ammo to fight off the bad guys that Ranger Morales and Lieutenant Barkley told you about. And you need to organize yourselves into a local militia so you can defend your families and your communities."

On that somber note, Decatur's independence rally came to an end. I sensed that the entire audience was receptive to the message that Goodnight and Morales had delivered. Not a single person spoke up to argue for continued allegiance to the United States of America. Everyone knew that the once-great American republic was dead.

As the four of us left the courthouse square, I heard the fiddle trio striking up another Bob Wills song—"Roly Poly," a song about a little boy who eats too much. I thought it was a curious choice to play to a bunch of people who are just barely getting enough to eat, but it's a great swing tune. People can dance to it, and that's what people were doing as we prepared to leave Decatur.

ADINA MORALES AND THE FIGHT TO SAVE SAM HOUSTON'S STATUE

When we reached the Escalade and its escort vehicles, Chief Morales asked Goodnight to drive us home.

"I'm beat, Cole. I've been up since four o'clock. I'm going to have the rangers drive me back, maybe get a little sleep on the road. Why don't you drive the Escalade and just follow the ranger vehicles? You've got Lieutenant Barkley with you for security."

So Goodnight slid behind the wheel, and I took the passenger seat next to him. Lieutenant Barkley climbed into the backseat and quickly dozed off, but we felt pretty safe following a caravan of Texas Rangers.

"So you grew up in the Panhandle," Goodnight said as we cruised east on Highway 380. "What was that like?"

"It was okay. My dad raised wheat and stocker cattle in Wheeler County, not far from Shamrock."

"Do you still have family in the Panhandle?"

"Not many. Wheeler County was in the Dust Bowl during the First Great Depression, and a lot of my great-grandfather's relatives packed up and headed for California during the 1930s. The Texas Burnes and the California Burnes have completely lost touch with one another.

"My family still has relatives in western Oklahoma—farm families doing the same thing my parents did, raising wheat and cattle.

"We used to visit our Oklahoma relatives when I was a kid. I remember driving east on Route 66 to visit my aunts, uncles, and cousins; we called them Okies. I used to feel sorry for them—I don't know why.

"There's not a dime's worth of difference between the Texas Panhandle and western Oklahoma, but I felt grateful to be living in Texas. I remember I always got a little thrill of pride when my family returned home from Oklahoma, and I saw that Lone Star flag blowing in the breeze when we crossed the border on old Route 66."

"Where did you go to college?"

"I went to West Texas University in Canyon—majored in English."

"And then you went to law school, right? Where did you get your law degree?"

"Fortunately, I got into the law school at the University of Texas. That changed my life.

"When I got to law school, I was surrounded by hundreds of very smart people. The law professors were brilliant, and the students were also very bright. Most of them were far better educated than me. A lot of students were the sons and daughters of lawyers, so they knew what to expect when they got to law school. I had no idea what to expect and I had to study seven days a week just to keep up."

Goodnight nodded in sympathy. "I remember my first year of law school," he said. "That was a tough year." I felt a bond growing between us, knowing that we both had experienced the stark terror of being questioned in a first-year law class by a crusty, Harvard-trained law professor.

"By the end of my first year at UT School of Law," I continued, "I discovered that I liked the law—it made sense to me. I did well in law school, and I graduated with honors. Then I got a job with one of the big Texas mega-firms and practiced labor law in Houston.

"I was a pretty good lawyer, but I found it very stressful. I know you are a renowned trial lawyer, but I hated being in the courtroom.

"After a few years, I took it into my head that I wanted to be a professor. I gave up my law practice, got an advanced degree, and began my teaching career. I worked at several universities, including Louisiana State University. I met my wife there and retired in Baton Rouge."

"How did you like being a college professor after having practiced law?" Goodnight asked.

"I was disappointed. I was surprised to find so much soulless bureaucracy in the universities, so much mediocrity and incompetence. People can say what they want about lawyers, but at least they're in the problem-solving business. College professors and administrators don't want to solve problems; they just want to get paid to talk about them."

"Well, we are in a different world now, Will. We will not survive unless we start solving problems and making better decisions than our former national leaders did.

"And your wife," Goodnight asked, changing the subject, "is she back in Baton Rouge now?"

"No, I'm a widower. My wife and kids died in Hurricane Maxine."

"I'm sorry to hear that," Goodnight said. "Do you mind if I ask you how they died?"

"Well, Anne Marie was from a big Louisiana family—a big Catholic family. We lived in Baton Rouge, but she had a married niece with two kids who lived in the Ninth Ward in New Orleans.

"Hurricane Maxine was out in the Gulf, and the weather forecasters predicted it would make landfall near Pensacola as a Category 2 and wouldn't threaten New Orleans. But Maxine was a freak storm. Contrary to all the predictions, it shifted west and picked up speed.

"One of Anne Marie's uncles lived in Livingston Parish in a flood zone near the Amite River. He was quite elderly and needed a walker to get around his home.

"We decided I would drive to Livingston Parish and bring Anne Marie's uncle to our home in Baton Rouge to weather the storm. It made sense for me to go because I was best able to help get her uncle in and out of our car. Anne Marie would go to New Orleans to get our niece's family because our niece and her husband didn't own a vehicle.

"So that's what we did. We knew a hurricane was coming, but we didn't think it posed a major threat to New Orleans. We thought we were playing it safe and that Anne Marie had plenty of time to pick up our niece's family before the hurricane made land.

"We didn't have a babysitter, so Anne Marie took our kids with her. It was going to be an adventure.

"That was a mistake," I said. "No, I made a mistake. If the storm was dangerous enough to evacuate Anne Marie's niece and family from New Orleans, it was too dangerous for Anne Marie and our kids to go there. If anyone should have gone to New Orleans when a hurricane was out in the Gulf, it should have been me.

"Well, as I said, Maxine shifted west, grew to a Category 5 hurricane, and plowed right into New Orleans. The levees were overtopped, and the city was basically wiped out.

"Anne Marie, our two kids, and our niece's family were in our car—we had one of those big Ford Expeditions—and they were headed west on I-10 toward Baton Rouge. The state police had contraflow going, and both sides of the highway were jammed with cars headed west.

"Somewhere on the Bonnet Carre Causeway, a tour bus loaded with nursing home patients hit an SUV, and that triggered a two-hundred-car pileup that totally blocked the road.

"Anne Marie and the family were about a half-mile back from the first collision, but their car smashed into the car in front of them, and another car hit them from behind. So they were basically wedged into a big parking lot of wrecked vehicles with no way to get off the causeway.

"Anne Marie and I talked to one another on our cellphones, and I spoke with my children until Anne Marie's phone went dead. We always kept bottled water and snacks in the car, so I wasn't worried about them getting hungry or dehydrated. We didn't say goodbye because we didn't know what was going to happen next.

"About six hours after the big pileup, Hurricane Maxine made landfall at 160 miles an hour with a huge storm surge. Almost everyone trapped on the causeway was killed, including Anne Marie, our kids, and our niece's family—seven people.

"As you remember, government infrastructure and services were already breaking down. No one could get to the pileup for more than a week. The Cajun navy came in and picked up a few survivors, and someone notified me that my entire family was dead."

"My heart is in the coffin with you," Goodnight said.

"Pardon?"

"My heart is in the coffin with you. It's something my grandmother used to say. It was her way of expressing her deepest sorrow and sympathy."

We were both silent for a moment.

"I've never experienced a loss like that," Goodnight ventured. "I'm told that you never get over it."

"No, Cole, you never get over it. My mind has gone back more than a thousand times to a vision of my family trapped on the Bonnet Carre Causeway, just waiting to die. Waiting to die while I was sitting at home watching the Weather Channel on television."

It seemed like a good time to change the subject.

"Cole, I just have to ask you this: do you realize how dangerous it is for you to be heading up a Texas Independence Movement? The US experienced dozens of political assassinations over the years as the old times wound down. You're liable to get yourself shot or blown up by a car bomb."

"I've thought about that, Will, but Adina is in charge of the Texas Rangers, and she has promised to assign a couple of rangers to protect me for as long as necessary.

"Besides, the Texas Independence Movement is a cause worth dying for. I value my life as much as the next person, but I can't hunker down out in West Texas and watch the state return to the stone age.

"Besides, I hope to have grandchildren someday. I want them to live in a decent world. I want them to have enough to eat. I don't want my granddaughters to get raped or my grandsons to get gutted by some psychopathic gang like the ones roaming around Alabama and Mississippi."

"Okay, Cole, I get that. But do you think the Texans have enough courage to shake loose from the old USA?"

"Oh, yes," Cole answered. "I have no worries in that regard.

"As you know," he continued, "Texas was its own nation once before—from 1836 until 1846. And the challenges Texans faced in those years were as daunting as the ones we face today. On its own, with no help from Uncle Sam, Texas defended its southern border with Mexico and the Comanche frontier. No, I have no worries about Texas courage."

Totally satisfied with Goodnight's answer, I changed the subject again. "Tell me about Adina Morales, Cole. She's an impressive person. How did she manage to become chief of the Texas Rangers?"

"Adina is an interesting woman, Will. She comes from one of the big ranching families down in South Texas. They got rich in oil and raised cattle. Her family has a ski chalet in Breckenridge—or did have, I should say—and I think they owned a home in Provence. Very wealthy.

"Naturally, Adina went to school at UT where she joined a sorority and majored in interior design—totally frivolous.

"She was in school during that whole Defund-the-Police period, which kept escalating for several years. You may remember that time when twenty-five cops were assassinated over one weekend."

"I remember," I replied. "Crime was spiraling out of control and our society turned on the police. It was insane."

"Well, all that turmoil radicalized Adina. She transferred from UT to Sam Houston State University in Huntsville and changed her major to criminal justice. While she was in school, she did an internship at the Huntsville Prison, and she made quite an impression on the warden.

"Law and order were breaking down all over Texas when Adina was in college. The cities were laying off cops because they couldn't afford to pay them, and there were very few jobs in law enforcement."

I could tell that Goodnight was settling into a protracted narrative about Adina Morales, but he kept both hands on the steering wheel as we drove south on I-35 and remained attentive to his driving. Unlike Morales, Goodnight missed most of the potholes on the road.

"After Adina graduated," Goodnight continued, "the Huntsville warden offered her a job as a corrections officer, and she accepted. Huntsville is a men's prison, but she didn't interact directly with the prison population. She had some kind of administrative job in a rehabilitation unit, but she got certified to carry a firearm.

"You remember those times, Willoughby? Banks were closing, people were losing their jobs, and universities were shutting down because they couldn't attract enough students to pay the bills."

"Yeah, I remember those times, Cole. Most of the universities were so desperate for tuition-paying students that they threw out all admission requirements and enrolled anyone who had a pulse."

"That's right, Willoughby. And that woke-culture thing was going around college campuses like a virus in those days. College students weren't learning anything, and they knew there were no jobs when they graduated. So what did they do? They tore down statues and monuments."

We continued driving down I-35 as Cole talked and Lieutenant Barkley slept in the Escalade's backseat. We drove by the ruins of the little town of West—a Czech community that had once supported several kolache bakeries.

In fact, I remembered, West had been named the home of the Texas Legislature's official kolache. I wondered idly what the gun-toting lady at Weimar's Store would say about that. I knew I wouldn't be the one to break the news to her.

"You've seen that huge statue of Sam Houston in Huntsville, haven't you, Willoughby?" Goodnight asked. "The one out on I-45?"

"Oh yeah. That thing is huge. It must be forty feet tall."

"No, Willoughby. Sam's statue is sixty-seven feet tall, and it stands on a pedestal that's ten feet high. It's not the biggest statue in the United States, but it is pretty darn big.

"Well, some college students from the University of Houston with too much time on their hands decided that Sam Houston was a white racist who abused the Native Americans when he was president of the Texas Republic.

"I think they got Houston mixed up with Mirabeau Lamar, the second president of the Texas Republic. He is the one who kicked the Native Americans out of Texas, not Sam Houston.

"Houston, however, had a Cherokee girlfriend when he lived up in Oklahoma Territory. That's before he came to Texas. I think her name was Talihina. Anyway, he dumped her when he left Oklahoma and later married a white woman about half his age. So maybe the UH students were mad at Sam for ditching Talihina.

"In any event, about forty student protesters drove to Huntsville bent on tearing Sam's statue down. They knew it was going to be a big job, so they rented a front-end loader, which they were going to use to knock it over.

"The citizens of Huntsville saw what was going on and called the cops. But the town of Huntsville had disbanded the police. So someone called the warden at the Huntsville Prison, a guy by the name of Tucker Belton.

"Have you ever met a Texas prison warden, Will?"

"No, Cole, I've never had that honor."

"Well, I've met a few, and they're all sonsabitches. You can't be a prison warden in this state unless you are devoid of all compassion.

"And Warden Belton was no exception. When he heard that a bunch of good-for-nothing college kids were vandalizing Sam Houston's statue, he got hopping mad. And he ordered some corrections officers to go out to I-45 and restore order. I don't think Warden Belton was bothered by the fact that Texas corrections officers don't have the legal authority to arrest anyone. I doubt that he even thought about that.

"Well, Adina was one of the officers who went out to protect Sam Houston's statue. When she arrived on the scene, she saw a college kid trying to knock the statue down by ramming it with the bucket of the rented front-end loader."

Goodnight was warming to his narrative now, and I was listening intently. I began to envision a youthful Adina Morales in a corrections-officer uniform defending a monster-size statue of Sam Houston, father of the Texas Republic. I was interpreting the tale as a comedy, but I could tell that Goodnight understood his story as a primal battle between good and evil.

"So Adina took charge," Goodnight continued in a serious voice. "She told the college students that it was a felony to deface a public monument and to go back to Houston, or they'd all be arrested.

"Well, the students didn't pay any attention. I think they suspected she didn't have jurisdiction over them, or maybe she just didn't look mean enough to scare them. Meanwhile, the kid driving the front-end loader kept banging away on Sam Houston's statue.

"So Adina put herself between the front-end loader and the statue and ordered the kid to turn off the machine and go home or she would lock him up.

"Now there was a time when an armed Texas law enforcement officer could order someone to cease and desist, and that person would comply. Everybody knew what a Texas Highway Patrolman was capable of, and nobody wanted to wind up in some small-town Texas jail where they might lose a few teeth and get their nose rearranged.

"But those days were over, and the kid on the front-end loader paid Adina no mind. He headed right toward her without slowing down.

"Incidentally, you may be wondering how I can be giving you all this detail since I obviously didn't see any of this. Well, most of the students had cell phones, and at least a dozen of them posted videos on Facebook. You remember Facebook, don't you?"

"Sure, I remember Facebook," I replied. "In my opinion, Facebook helped bring the country down. Millions of people became Facebook addicts and spent their days gossiping online with their friends instead of doing their jobs."

"Yes, that's about right," Goodnight responded.

"Anyway," Goodnight continued, "I watched the episode on Facebook. I quizzed Adina about the incident after I got to know her, and she said she didn't think the son of a bitch would actually run her down, so she didn't move.

"But he did run her down—knocked her down with the steel bucket of the loader and cracked a few of her ribs. She had to scramble out of the way to keep from getting crushed.

"Still, Adina gave the guy one more chance. She drew her weapon, told him he was under arrest and to shut down his machine.

"Did he respond to that?" Goodnight asked rhetorically. "No, he did not. He tried to run her down a second time.

"So Adina shot him—shot him one time in the chest. And she killed him.

"Well, as it turned out, the kid she killed was one Walter Waffleburger who was from a prominent Houston family. His parents raised a big ruckus, tried to get Adina indicted for first-degree murder, and filed a civil suit against her.

"But the Walker County DA refused to indict her. In fact, the DA charged the parents with negligent supervision. He said this never would have happened if they had raised their son to respect authority."

"But, Cole," I protested. "This Waffleburger kid must have been an adult. Under Texas law, a parent isn't legally responsible for supervising an adult child."

"I know that, Will, and you know that. The Walker County DA probably knew that too. But I think he was trying to make a point: don't sue the police for trying to do their duty in stressful situations.

"And a federal judge threw out the family's civil suit against Adina," Goodnight added, "and assessed costs against the Waffleburger family. In Texas, anyway, no one is going to get away with suing an attractive, brunette law enforcement officer for shooting a dumbass who's trying to deface a statue of Sam Houston."

"I remember hearing about that," I said. "It was all over the news. So that was Adina Morales!"

"Yes, that was Adina Morales. The affair made her famous— kind of like Charles Lindbergh crossing the Atlantic in the *Spirit of St. Louis*. The rangers heard about it, were impressed, and hired her on as a Texas Ranger.

"After that, she rose through the ranks of the rangers. She was in some firefights with the drug cartels down on the Mexican border— got wounded a couple of times—and that's how she became chief ranger."

GOODNIGHT INVITES ME TO JOIN THE TEXAS INDEPENDENCE MOVEMENT

Goodnight got us back to Austin around midnight—he didn't drive as fast as Chief Morales. As we drove up the circular driveway to the Texas Statehouse, he asked me to meet him in the Secretary of State's office early the next day.

I spent another night at the no-breakfast B&B. Early the next morning, Sergeant McLaglen picked me up in the Humvee and dropped me off in front of the capitol building.

I enjoyed being seen getting out of an armored vehicle that sported a heavy machine gun. I could see that people figured I must be important. I was wearing my father's Stetson hat and his Nocona boots; I suppose that gave me added allure.

Lieutenant Barkley, my rifle-carrying bodyguard, accompanied me. She was wearing her helmet and her Kevlar vest. She eyed onlookers like she was on the lookout for an assassin, and I found that I liked the idea of having personal security.

Goodnight asked me to sit down as soon as I walked in and got right to the business at hand.

"Will, I've been thinking about what you said in Decatur last night. It made an impression on me. You obviously grasp the importance of what we're doing. You spoke sincerely, and I could see that you connected with the people of Wise County. Why don't you come to Texas and help Adina and me organize the Texas Constitutional Convention? Adina and I can't visit every Texas county in the time we've got. We've covered most of central Texas, but we have to canvass the Rio Grande Valley, the Trans-Pecos, West Texas, and the Panhandle. We could use your help."

I didn't hesitate for a second. "Count me in, Cole."

"Good. Then put your affairs in order. I'm going to loan you a truck to drive back to Louisiana. Say your goodbyes and get back to Austin as quick as you can."

Within a half-hour, Lieutenant Barkley and I were headed back to Baton Rouge in a vintage LPG-fitted crew-cab truck. It was a Dodge Ram 2500 with running boards and huge chrome tailpipes— the very acme of aggressive Texas masculinity.

Other than the ancient 18-wheeler that Lieutenant Barkley ordered me to drive after the ambush on the Atchafalaya Causeway, I hadn't driven a motor vehicle in many years. At first, I felt awkward behind the wheel; but then that old muscle memory kicked in, and we were cruising down Highway 71 at sixty miles an hour.

Soon, we were back on I-10 and headed east toward Baton Rouge. Someone had tossed a case of bottled water in the truck, and Lieutenant Barkley rummaged through a couple of boxes of MREs she'd gotten at Camp Mabry, looking for something for us to eat.

"Bad news, Mr. Burns. Your luncheon choices today are cold spaghetti and meatballs or cold spaghetti and meatballs. Which will it be?"

"You know, Lieutenant, I'm not that hungry. Is there a candy bar in that MRE?"

She picked through the MRE boxes and found a candy bar and a packet of crackers. "Remember the old days, Mr. Burns? Back when the diet companies advertised special meals to help people lose weight? If Americans had just switched to eating MREs, the whole country would have gotten a lot thinner."

I laughed and agreed with her.

As I drove east, I began to feel a keen sense of urgency about getting back to Baton Rouge. *Did Colonel Merski know that*

Redneckers had crossed into north Louisiana, I wondered, *and were the Redneckers still there?*

"We better stop at Fort Joplin, Mr. Burns," Barkley said as we reached the outskirts of Houston. "General Mier needs to know about the Rednecker activity in northeast Texas."

I agreed. We drove into Houston and made our way to Fort Joplin. I parked the truck outside the front gate, and General Mier saw us immediately.

Lieutenant Barkley assumed her military visage as we walked into Mier's office, and she reported to Mier in a clipped and crisp voice.

"General Mier," she said, "as you know, Colonel Merski ordered me to accompany Mr. Burns to Texas to assess the political situation. We met Cole Goodnight in Austin, and he invited us to go to Decatur with him, where he held an independence rally. Adina Morales, Chief of the Texas Rangers, joined us on that trip."

"I've never met Chief Morales," Mier said, "but I know her by reputation."

"Chief Morales told us that an armed body of Redneckers overwhelmed the local militia at Vicksburg, Mississippi, and captured the Vicksburg Bridge.

"After that, the Redneckers crossed the Louisiana border and committed atrocities along I-20, raping and murdering people, and looting and burning the towns. Then they invaded Texas west of Shreveport."

Lieutenant Barkley paused for a few seconds to allow General Mier to absorb this news.

"Chief Morales and the Texas Rangers stopped the Redneckers at the Sabine River, killed a bunch of them, and drove the survivors back into Louisiana.

"Morales believes this group was a reconnaissance team for an army of Redneckers. She thinks the Redneckers will cross the Mississippi River in force and mean to conquer parts of Texas and Louisiana."

"This is serious," Mier said. "You need to get on the road immediately and report this information to Colonel Merski. The Redneckers might move south and attack Fort Sharpton.

"Mr. Burns, we're going to load your pickup truck with explosives. Colonel Merski may decide to destroy some of the bridges around Fort Sharpton to hinder the Redneckers, but I don't know if he has enough explosives to do that. I'm going to send him enough Semtex to do the job."

We got back on the road immediately after leaving Fort Joplin. We stopped at the army checkpoint on the Louisiana border, and Lieutenant Barkley produced her pass signed by General Mier.

A lanky corporal looked over our documents and spied the explosives in the back of the Dodge.

"Christmas came early this year," the corporal exclaimed. "And it looks like Santa brought me just what I was wishing for—stuff to make bombs!"

"Hands off the ordnance, soldier," Lieutenant Barkley snapped. "This stuff is for Fort Sharpton. Anyway, you look too young to be messing around with fireworks."

GOOD COP, BAD COP

Lieutenant Barkley and I arrived at Fort Sharpton after nightfall. I drove over to the Pentagon Barracks, where I found Colonel Merski relaxing in his personal quarters. He had a drink in his hand and greeted us with a mellow look that told me he had been sipping the locally distilled whiskey.

This was the first time I had seen Merski out of uniform, but I noticed that even his sleepwear appeared to be military grade. Merski was wearing camouflage pajamas and olive drab bedroom slippers. I observed his sidearm lying on the coffee table, and I felt sure the gun was loaded.

"Hello, cowboy. How did you make out among the Texicans?"

Before I could answer, he spied the Dodge truck I was driving. "Sweet!" he exclaimed. "Where did you get the wheels?"

"It's a loaner," I explained. "My Porsche is in the shop."

Merski set his drink down when Lieutenant Barkley began her report. "Redneckers crossed the Mississippi River at Vicksburg," she told him, "and a small force of terrorists made their way to Texas on I-20."

She quickly reiterated what she had told General Mier earlier in the day, and she told Merski that the general had loaded my truck with explosives. I could see that Merski had shaken off the effects of the whisky and was processing Barkley's information in his mind while she talked.

"Good report, Lieutenant. Good report.

"This fits with the intelligence I received yesterday. One of our patrols questioned a couple of pickers coming down Highway 61 from Vicksburg. They told us that an armed force had captured the Vicksburg Bridge. That must have been the Redneckers.

"Apparently, a scratch force of local farmers tried to prevent the attackers from crossing the river, but the bridge defenders were all killed. The pickers didn't have any more information. I didn't know that some of the Redneckers had made it all the way to Texas.

"I sent a scouting force up the river last night to get more information. We rounded up some boats and gasoline and launched a patrol from Natchez. I told the squad leader not to engage with the enemy but to capture some prisoners to interrogate if she could do that without being detected by the Redneckers.

"Will," Merski said as he turned to me, "the army is taking your truck. I've got a unit guarding the Natchez Bridge commanded by Captain Dickinson. We need your truck to haul explosives up to him. Depending on how things develop with the Redneckers, I may order Dickinson to destroy the Natchez Bridge.

"You've got two choices: you can drive your truck up to Natchez tomorrow morning to deliver the explosives, or I can get someone else to drive it. What do you want to do?"

Of course, what I really wanted to do was get Merski to pour me a drink, and then I wanted to go to bed and sleep in tomorrow. But I could never say no to Colonel Merski, and I didn't want to look like a coward in front of Lieutenant Barkley.

"I'll drive the truck to Natchez for you," I said, trying to sound nonchalant.

Lieutenant Barkley and I left Baton Rouge before daylight the next morning headed for Natchez. We had two young soldiers with us who sat in the backseat of the crew-cab Dodge. They said they were demolition experts and looked over the stuff General Mier gave us.

"This will do the job," one of them said.

"Try not to hit any bumps," the other soldier added.

We arrived in Natchez at about nine in the morning. From a distance, we could see soldiers piling up sandbags on the bridge. They looked nervous when they saw the Dodge.

Lieutenant Barkley told me to stop the truck while she identified us to the troops. She walked down the highway with her hands in the air, shouting "Captain Dickinson, Captain Dickinson! It's me—Lieutenant Barkley."

I saw her huddle with the officer in charge—evidently, Captain Dickinson—and then she waved me forward. Soldiers quickly unpacked the truck, and I turned it around to head back to Baton Rouge. I had a keen sense that things were about to get dicey.

And then I heard a commotion coming from the riverbank. The recon patrol had arrived back from its mission upriver to Vicksburg. I could see that soldiers had bagged a couple of prisoners—two bedraggled-looking guys with their hands secured behind their backs by plastic handcuffs. Enlisted men wearing camouflage were frog-marching their captives up the steep riverbank.

Lieutenant Barkley conferred a few minutes with Captain Dickerson and then filled me in on the new developments. "We're taking two prisoners back to Baton Rouge, Mr. Burns, and we're also taking the mission leader. She has some important news for Colonel Merski."

I was surprised to see Sergeant Gomez, the machine gunner who had been with us on the Atchafalaya Causeway; it seemed like a lifetime ago. She was wearing camouflage paint on her face. I hardly recognized her. She told us she hadn't slept in a couple of days, and she looked exhausted.

We loaded the prisoners in the back of the truck and drove south to Baton Rouge on Highway 61. I asked Sergeant Gomez what she learned in Vicksburg, but she said she couldn't talk about it.

Colonel Merski was delighted to see Sergeant Gomez back at the fort and even more delighted to see the prisoners. He allowed me to remain in the Pentagon Barracks' conference room while Sergeant Gomez gave her report.

"We traveled up the Mississippi during the night," she said, "and landed in south Vicksburg—about a mile below the I-20 bridge. We got close enough to the bridge to confirm that the Redneckers are in control. We couldn't get a firm fix on the numbers, but I estimate about four or five hundred people. Maybe more."

"Any vehicles?" Merski asked.

"Yes, they have some trucks and buses. I saw six trucks driving back and forth across the bridge."

"What kind of weapons were they carrying? Any tactical?"

"They've got at least two heavy machine guns, which are mounted on trucks. The foot soldiers are carrying all kinds of weapons—hunting rifles, shotguns, and a few military-style rifles."

"Did you get any sense of where these numbskulls are headed?" Merski asked. "Are they marching on Texas, or do you think they're headed downriver toward us?"

"Colonel, it looked to me like they're getting organized on the west side of the Mississippi, and from what we saw, I think they are headed south on the Louisiana side of the river."

"Okay, okay," Merski mused, as if Sergeant Gomez's report confirmed his own suspicions.

"Sergeant Gomez, get some rest while we interrogate the prisoners. We're going to good cop-bad cop 'em just liked they used to do on television—back when we had television.

"Will, you used to be a lawyer. I imagine you've had quite a bit of experience taking depositions, cross-examining hostile witnesses, and whatnot. You take a crack at 'em. Do that old 'ah shucks' thing you're so good at. That'll make you the good cop.

"If you can't get anything out of 'em, we'll have to go to plan B because we don't have any bad cops.

"I suppose we could waterboard 'em like we did in the old days," Merski mused nostalgically. "Would you like us to torture these guys a little before you interrogate them, Willoughby? Would that make your job easier?"

"No, Colonel," I replied. "I think that would make me the bad cop."

"Have it your own way then," Merski said. "Which prisoner do you want to question first?"

"I'll start with the younger one." I replied.

A couple of minutes later, two soldiers brought a young man into the conference room and stood by with their rifles at the ready. Colonel Merski had departed, and it was just me, the prisoner, and the two guards in the room. The Rednecker was wearing an old University of Mississippi T-shirt and dirty brown cargo pants.

I learned a long time ago—back when I practiced law—not to make threats that I didn't intend to carry out. People can usually tell when you're bluffing. I decided to be as candid as I could with the prisoner without giving away anything important.

"Okay, buddy, what's your name?"

"Jerry. My name's Jerry. Jerry McGoogan."

"Jerry, we're going to cut the handcuffs off you while we talk. But the soldiers will put cuffs on you again after our meeting is over. Don't try to escape because these guys *will* shoot you.

"I've got some good news and some bad news for you, Jerry. First, the good news. Number one: the army captured you instead of shooting you in Vicksburg. As a rule, the army doesn't take prisoners. No place to put them and not enough food. They're kind of like the Russians during World War II.

"Number two: the army isn't going to torture you." I realized as soon as I had said this that Merski had mentioned waterboarding only a few minutes ago, but I hoped he had abandoned that idea.

"Now the bad news: the army considers you a terrorist. You will probably be tried before a military tribunal. You *will* be found guilty, and they'll shoot you.

"In the old days, the army might have sent you to Guantanamo, but that's not an option anymore.

"On the other hand, if you cooperate with us and tell us the truth, we'll parole you after this ruckus is over and send you back to where you came from. Where did you come from, by the way?"

"I'm from Meridian, Mississippi, but we're from all over the South—mostly men, but quite a few women. We got organized in Alabama, but a lot of us are from Mississippi, Georgia . . . all over."

I could see that Jerry was listening attentively to my bullshit, and although he tried to maintain an air of surly defiance, I saw him relax a little bit just knowing nothing bad was going to happen to him immediately.

I decided to adopt my old lawyer's deposition-taking style and ask the easy questions first.

"You were carrying a shotgun when the army picked you up—at Weatherby, I believe— and they found fifty rounds of buckshot in your gear. What are your comrades carrying?"

"A bunch of different kinds of guns: shotguns, deer rifles, some assault rifles. All calibers: 30-30, .270, 30.06—you name it."

"Any bigger weapons? Machine guns, mortars, rocket launchers, that kind of stuff?"

"We've got two .50 caliber machine guns that we mounted on pickup trucks. I think we got those out of a National Guard Armory in Georgia.

"And we've got ammo for those guns," he added helpfully.

I realized then that this prisoner didn't have any strong ideological convictions because he appeared to be answering my questions candidly and without reservation. In Jerry's mind, I concluded, the conflict between the Rednecks and the army was over. I think he just wanted to get a hot meal and head back to Mississippi.

Also, I think Jerry felt relaxed talking to me because I was obviously a civilian. He conversed with me as if he were chatting with a neighbor about a mildly interesting recent event—like a ballgame between LSU and Ole Miss. His team lost, but he had no hard feelings.

Based on Jerry's surprising helpfulness, I dropped all pretense to guile and just chatted amiably with him. "Where are you getting your gasoline?" I asked.

He shrugged. "Don't know, but we've got a tanker truck full of gas."

And now the big question. "Where are you folks going?"

"We're headed south for Baton Rouge. Our leaders want to capture those farms you have down here and take over the refineries."

"We heard you were headed for Texas."

"Nah, that's just what you call a feint. We sent a few people to East Texas to make you think we were going that way, but we're headed south down the river."

"East side of the river, west side, or both sides?"

"West side. The plan is to surprise you. We didn't think you would be looking for us on the west side of the Mississippi."

Next, I questioned the older prisoner. Somewhere I had read that old guys are easier to interrogate than young guys. They are too wizened to buy into that name-rank-and-serial-number crap. And old men are almost never gung ho to get themselves killed or tortured for the motherland . . . or the fatherland, for that matter.

The older man's name was Jedediah Raines, and he was originally from Georgia. He basically corroborated everything McGoogan said, but he offered up a few more details.

"I heard our company commander say that there are 525 of us," he volunteered.

"How are you fixed for ammo?" I asked.

"We've got plenty of ammo. A lot of us were preppers back in the old days, so we were getting ready for this. I have three thousand rounds of .223 ammo for my rifle, and most of the guys have at least a couple of thousand rounds. You know ammunition used to be real cheap. I bought it online and just kept it in my garage."

Although I hadn't asked him any detailed questions about the hunting rifles, Raines told me that many of the rifles had scopes and that a lot of the Redneckers had been deer hunters in the old times and were pretty good snipers.

I figured I had gotten everything I could out of this poor old guy, so I wrapped up my interrogation. And then—just as the soldiers were putting the cuffs back on him, he gave me one more important tidbit.

"I could tell you something else," he said slyly, "but you probably wouldn't believe me."

"Try me."

"The Redneckers have teamed up with the Nubian Nation. They're working together now."

Raines was right. I didn't believe him. "Bullshit!" I said. "Everyone knows the Redneckers are big-time racists. They'd never make peace with the Nubians."

"I told you that you wouldn't believe me. I'm just sayin' that the Redneckers and the Nubians are allies. Both sides want to capture the South Louisiana refineries and the generals realize they can't do that if the Nubians and the Redneckers are fighting each other.

"The Rednecker army in Vicksburg is just a small force. The Nubians and most of the Redneckers are going to attack you from the south. They want those refineries down in South Louisiana, and they've got to knock out the Baton Rouge garrison to do that."

"Why are you telling me this, Walter? If what you're saying is true, you're betraying your friends."

"I'll tell you why I'm tipping you off: I hate the Nubians. I signed up with the Redneckers to kill 'em. I ain't never going to fight side by side with them sonsabitches."

COLONEL MERSKI CALLS
OUT THE MILITIA

After I finished my interrogation of the two Rednecker prisoners, I reported to Colonel Merski, who was still in his office conferring with his junior officers. He didn't seem surprised when I told him that the Redneckers and the Nubians had formed an alliance. "Do you think he's telling the truth?" I asked.

"Probably. It's that old line that the enemy of my enemy is my friend. Military history is full of these unholy alliances. Remember Hitler signed a nonaggression pact with the Russians just before he stabbed them in the back and invaded in 1941.

"Of course, the Nubians and the Rednecks will eventually turn on each other. But that won't happen in time to do us any good."

And then Merski started issuing orders.

"Lieutenant Barkley, the Nubians and the Redneckers may be headed our way from the east. Take a vehicle and a couple of soldiers and check out I-10 and I-12 and look for any sign of those people.

"Get back here by dawn tomorrow. If you see any sign of a significant force, be prepared to take a demolition team to destroy the Amite River bridges, beginning with the one over I-12. That'll slow up the hostiles if they're in our neighborhood.

"Now, what should we do about the Redneckers west of the river?" he asked himself, and then answered his own question.

"Here is how we are going to handle those bad boys. We are going to fuel up our vehicles with the fuel we've been hoarding and head up Highway 61 to Vicksburg. We'll cross the river on the I-20 bridge and attack the Redneckers from behind.

"We'll alert Captain Dickinson on the Natchez Bridge, and if we're lucky, we'll trap the sonsabitches between two forces on the west side of the river and wipe 'em out."

I had a funny feeling that Colonel Merski was going to draw me into his scheme, and I was right.

"Will, you need to alert the farmers along the east side of the Mississippi that there are Nubians and Redneckers in the area. Tell all your noncombatants to bring some food and come to Fort Sharpton to shelter until we get this resolved.

"And get your militia organized to help defend Baton Rouge. Your brother-in-law is the militia leader, right? Tell him to have his people grab all their weapons and ammunition and come to the fort.

"They need to get here damn quick. I'm taking most of our forces north to Vicksburg. We'll need your people to help provide security for Fort Sharpton until we get back.

"Now, what can we do with those goddamned horses we've been feeding all these months?" Merski asked me.

I didn't have an answer, but Merski supplied an answer of his own.

"Will, you're in the militia, right? And you can ride a horse? Round up some militia people who can ride and have weapons, and you guys patrol the river to the south of us. It's possible the Nubians and the Rednecks might attack us from downriver.

"Don't engage them. Just send word as fast as you can if you see the enemy headed our way."

I wanted to explain to Merski that I did not have a combat role with the militia. In fact, Gordon, my brother-in-law, was the militia commander, and he strictly forbade me to carry a gun at our militia drills.

"I want you to be my consigliere," Gordon had told me face-tiously, "like Robert Duvall in *The Godfather*. Robert Duvall didn't shoot anybody; he just gave advice and handled legal problems."

Of course, what Gordon was really telling me was that he didn't want me in the militia, which was fine with me. After all, I knew very little about guns.

Somehow it didn't seem the right time to tell Colonel Merski that I was the militia's consigliere. And so I went down to Fort Sharpton's stables and saddled a horse.

I picked a pinto mare for myself and saddled a roan gelding for Gordon. Then I rode south down to Lâche Pas, where I found Gordon overhauling a tractor. I told him that I had brought him a horse and briefed him on developments.

Without saying anything, Gordon wiped the grease off his hands and went to the family's gun safe where we kept our firearms. He retrieved his Glock and mine and checked to make sure they were both loaded. Then he tossed me a couple of fifteen-round magazines and took two for himself.

"Okay," he said. "Let's alert the farmsteads downriver and tell people to go to Fort Sharpton and bring all the food they can carry. There's no sense in a bunch of us prowling around downriver, and we only have horses for you and me. I'll tell the militia to head to the Fort, and you and I will ride south along the levee and see what we find."

So that's what we did. As we rode southward, we alerted the farm families that Redneckers were in the area. Soon we saw families streaming toward Fort Sharpton with bundles of food and bedding. Several farmers had tractors and were pulling trailer loads of refugees upriver to Fort Sharpton.

The further downriver we rode, the fewer people we encountered, and then we saw Sonny Savoie, one of the farmers, galloping toward us on horseback with a shotgun slung behind him. He was riding a gray Quarter Horse stallion. "Wait up," he shouted. "I'm goin' with you."

Gordon told Savoie to turn back. "Will and I can handle this, Sonny. You should help your family get moved into the fort."

But Savoie insisted on going with us. "I'm not afraid of trouble, me," he said in a strong Cajun accent.

After a few miles of riding, we saw the L'Auberge Casino ahead, sitting right next to the riverbank. We could see a crowd of people milling around the casino grounds, and I knew they weren't there to play the slots.

Gordon had a good pair of binoculars, and he scanned the scene ahead.

"Redneckers," he said, "and they're armed." He gazed through the binoculars a few seconds longer. "And the Nubians are with them."

"Le' me see 'em," Savoie said, reaching for Gordon's binoculars. And at that instant, Savoie jerked back in his saddle and slid to the ground. He had been shot in the head.

Savoie's right boot got tangled in a stirrup and the weight of his body pulled his saddle under the stallion's belly. The horse panicked and began bucking and kicking in a frantic effort to get free of Savoie's corpse and the saddle.

"Let's get out of here," Gordon said. More bullets whizzed by us; we didn't try to retrieve Savoie's body.

We kicked our horses into a fast gallop and rode into the timber along the riverbank, hoping to find cover from the Redneckers' rifle fire. Horses like to stay together when they're scared, and Savoie's mount tried to keep up with us.

But the stallion had gone mad. It had caught a bullet in its flanks and was still dragging Savoie's body. The other horses began to share its terror. Gordon and I were losing control of them.

Even though we were still being shot at, Gordon reined in his horse and dismounted. He grabbed the stallion by its bridle and spoke soothingly to it until it stopped bucking. Then he pulled his belt knife out of its scabbard and cut the saddle's cinch strap.

Sonny's body and the stallion's saddle fell to the ground in a heap. Gordon retrieved Sonny's shotgun and ammunition bag. Then he remounted and we rode on.

When we had gotten around a bend in the river and were out of sight of the attackers, we set our horses to loping upriver along the levee, headed toward Fort Sharpton.

We didn't know if anyone was following us or whether the Redneckers had a vehicle they could use to pursue us. We decided to ride between the levee and the river, hoping the levee would conceal us from anyone looking for us on the river road.

Before long, our horses were winded and lathered with sweat.

"We can't keep pushing the horses, Gordon," I said, "or we'll kill them. Let's get them some water and then walk them back to Fort Sharpton."

We led our mounts to the riverbank and let them drink to their hearts' content. I was thirsty myself, but I wasn't desperate enough to drink Mississippi River water.

Gordon was thirsty too. "What I wouldn't give for a suitcase of Miller Lite," he said as he watched our horses drink.

As we passed by the Lâche Pas compound, I asked Gordon if we should stop and get our ammunition and the rest of our weapons. "No," he said. "Sam will gather up the guns and ammo, and he'll take them to the fort."

"Do you think the Redneckers will burn our farms?" I asked.

"Maybe not," Gordon replied. "I think they want to enslave us and make us grow their food. But they'll loot our houses and steal all our provisions."

THEY EAT HORSES, DON'T THEY?

We walked our horses through downtown Baton Rouge and remounted just before we reached the gate at Fort Sharpton. We saw our militia members sitting together on the capitol lawn near Huey Long's statue. They all had their weapons, and their backpacks were full of ammunition. Most were men, but there were a couple of women in the group.

"The hostiles are on the river," Gordon told the farmers. "Will and I saw Redneckers and Nubians at the L'Auberge Casino. They shot at us. If they've got vehicles, they could be here in half an hour."

At first, I thought Gordon had understated what had happened to us. After all, Sonny Savoie had been killed by a sniper. But then I realized that we hadn't told Sonny's wife yet that she was a widow, and I understood why he said nothing about Sonny's death.

At that moment, an army officer walked up in full combat gear. He introduced himself as Major Ken Weatherford and told us that Colonel Merski had pulled out for Vicksburg with most of Fort Sharpton's troops. Weatherford said Merski had appointed him as the fort's commander until the colonel returned.

I had never seen Major Weatherford before and neither had the other farmers. He must have sensed our initial reluctance to take orders from him.

"Thank you all for coming," he told the farmers. "We need you.

"I know I am new to you all, but I just transferred into Fort Sharpton, and I happen to be the senior officer here while Colonel Merski is away. I'd be grateful for any information you might share that would help me defend the fort and the farm families."

Weatherford's humility and his subtle reminder that the militia would be defending their own families seemed to win everyone over to him. I sensed an attitude of goodwill emanating from the farmers.

After his brief introduction, Weatherford pulled Gordon and me aside and lowered his voice.

"What did you see downriver?" he asked, almost in a whisper.

"We saw some people with guns at the L'Auberge Casino," Gordon replied. "We got shot at, and one of our farmers was killed. From what we could see, the Nubians and the Redneckers have joined forces."

"How many?"

"Don't know. After the Redneckers began shooting at us, we turned around and headed back to Baton Rouge."

"How many people in your militia?" Weatherford asked.

"There're about sixty of us."

"We have 120 soldiers here at Fort Sharpton," Weatherford said in a worried voice, which told me he didn't think he had enough troops to defend the fort.

"We've also got around four hundred noncombatant dependents at Fort Sharpton: spouses, children, and elderly family members. They all live in Spanish Town, which is inside the fort's perimeter.

"And by my rough count, about three hundred people from the farms came into the fort this afternoon. We've quartered them in Spanish Town with our army families."

"Based on what Will and I saw, I think the Redneckers are using the casino as a staging ground for an attack on the fort," Gordon said. "Do you think we can hold 'em off until Merski gets back?"

"It'll be tough," Weatherford admitted. "As you can see, the perimeter is nothing more than a chain-link fence we topped with razor wire. But that fence won't stop a concerted attack, and it's a big area to defend."

"How about those structures?" Gordon asked, pointing toward a cluster of office buildings on the south edge of the state capitol grounds. "Are they inside your perimeter?"

"No," Weatherford replied. "Those are all state government buildings. It's amazing how many bureaucrats it took to run Louisiana in the old times."

"They all look to be eight or nine stories tall," Gordon observed. "Snipers could get on the roofs of those buildings, and they'd have your whole fort within rifle range."

"That's a weak spot for us," Weatherford acknowledged. "Spanish Town worries me too. It's a warren of old wooden homes and narrow streets. If the Redneckers breach the perimeter in Spanish Town, it'll be very hard to drive them out."

Gordon and I stood silently, waiting for Major Weatherford to tell us what to do. After pondering the situation for a couple of minutes, he seemed to have made up his mind.

"Here's what we are going to do," Weatherford told us in a calm voice. "I'm going to send a patrol out after dark and see if we can determine how big the Redneck army is and how it's disposed.

"We'll let the civilians spend the night in Spanish Town and decide tomorrow morning whether to move them. I'll post a strong guard around the perimeter, and we'll put a double guard on the capitol building's observation deck at dawn tomorrow. You can see a lot from up there, and the bastards won't be able to sneak up on us—at least not during daylight hours.

"Gordon, I want your people to guard the north side of the capitol. We're protected a bit there by Capitol Lake and by the river to the west. I'll send a sergeant to show you what to do."

I could tell by looking at Gordon's face that he had confidence in Major Weatherford, in spite of the fact that Gordon had only known him for a few minutes. I had confidence in him too. I think

Gordon and I were won over by Weatherford's decisiveness, and we were both ready to do anything he asked.

"I think you and Will should both get some rest," Weatherford continued. "It's not every day that you get shot at.

"Your militiamen can spend the night with their families, but I want you two close by. Why don't you bed down in that office building north of the Pentagon Barracks, and I'll brief you tomorrow morning when the night patrol reports in."

We walked over to an ugly structure that looked like it had been designed by and for a pack of Louisiana bureaucrats. The building had been trashed during the riots, but I figured no one had bothered to steal the furniture. "Let's check out the Executive Suite," I said. "I'll bet there are a couple of couches there we can sleep on."

And there were. I ripped the curtains off the windows to use as blankets. Gordon and I were both caked in horse sweat, but we agreed that horse sweat didn't smell too bad. In a few minutes, we were fast asleep.

At about four in the morning, a soldier shook me awake. "Major Weatherford wants you right now," the soldier said. "Lieutenant Barkley got back from her patrol, and the night patrol is back too. They both have news about the Redneckers."

Gordon and I felt our way through the darkness to the Pentagon Barracks. Several soldiers were sitting or standing in Colonel Merski's conference room drinking the last of the colonel's Community Coffee. I quickly walked over to the coffee pot, which I tipped on its side, and managed to drain off about half a cup of the dregs, which I shared with Gordon.

I saw Lieutenant Barkley standing with other soldiers. Her combat fatigues were caked with mud, and she looked tired.

"Hey, soldier boy," she greeted me. "I heard you got shot at down by the casino yesterday. We're going to have to put you in for a Combat Infantryman Badge."

Lieutenant Barkley was teasing me, but she was also paying me a compliment. She was acknowledging that I had performed a military task when Gordon and I went riding down River Road looking for Redneckers.

But I couldn't get Sonny Savoie's bloody corpse out of my mind. "Yeah, Sonny Savoie was killed," I replied in a tone that let Barkley know I was in no mood for banter.

"I'm sorry," she responded. "I shouldn't have been joking. I didn't know that one of your friends got shot."

"That's okay, Lieutenant. I'm very glad to see you. I'm glad you're safe."

Major Weatherford asked Lieutenant Barkley to tell us what she found out about the Redneckers.

"The Redneckers came up Interstate 10 from the east," she reported. "They left the interstate at the Sunshine Bridge exit and traveled up River Road to the L'Auberge Casino. The Nubians are with them."

"How many?" Weatherford asked.

"I would say about a thousand. They're traveling in a hodge-podge of vehicles—school buses, vans, trucks. We sneaked up and got as close as we could without being seen. They're definitely looking for trouble; they're all armed."

"Any tactical weapons?" Major Weatherford asked.

"They've got at least one heavy machine gun, and they may have more tactical weapons. There were some trucks parked between the casino and the casino hotel, but we didn't get a good look at them."

Sergeant Gomez spoke up. Evidently, she had led the patrol that left the fort in the early night hours.

"We patrolled south through downtown and then followed Highland Road toward LSU. Someone shot at us a couple of blocks north of the university. We probed around the campus after that, and we could see a bunch of vehicles and people around the student union. I think they plan to attack the fort."

"I'm sure you're right," Weatherford said. "They've already moved from the casino to LSU. That's only about four miles from the capitol."

As he talked, I could see that Major Weatherford was coming to a decision. "We can't defend the entire perimeter of Fort Sharpton against a thousand combatants with the forces we have. We'll have to fort up in the state capitol.

"Once we are inside the capitol, we'll be protected to the north and west by the river and Capitol Lake. Gordon, I want your militia to keep guarding that area. My troops will fortify the capitol building.

"Mr. Burns, I'm putting you in charge of the civilians. Go over to Spanish Town, wake everybody up and move them into the state capitol. Tell them to take their bedding and all the food they have on hand. They also need to bring some containers that can hold water and any weapons and ammunition they have.

"Tell them not to panic, but to hurry. We could be attacked at any time. Tell them they'll be safe once they're tucked inside the capitol. I'll send a couple of soldiers with you to show the folks you are giving orders, not making suggestions.

"We'll put the civilians in the upper floors, and we'll fortify the lower floors and barricade the doors. I expect we'll be under siege until Colonel Merski's force gets back from Vicksburg."

Before he dismissed us, Weatherford issued another order. "Gordon, have your people build a makeshift corral in the parking lot on the north side of the capitol. I want you to put the fort's horses in there for the duration, so move all the horse feed to that spot.

"I know the horses will need water," Weatherford added, "but I figure the militia can get water for them from Capitol Lake."

"Horses?" Gordon asked. "What are we going to do with horses?"

"Well, if we get besieged here at Fort Sharpton and Colonel Merski doesn't get back soon, we're going to eat them."

THE GOOD GUYS ARE BESIEGED

I left the Pentagon Barracks and hurried over to Spanish Town. It was not yet daylight, and most people were asleep when the soldiers and I started banging on doors.

Nobody panicked. Parents woke their kids and got them dressed. Older people started clearing the kitchen pantries and rolling up blankets. Soon the civilians were moving toward the capitol. Some people were pulling children's wagons or pushing baby strollers loaded with food.

I saw Sonny Savoie's wife Clotilde herding her kids along. I realized we hadn't told her that Sonny was dead.

"Have you seen Sonny?" she called out in a worried voice.

"I don't have time to talk to you now, Clotilde," I replied. "I'll find you later. I need you to go to the capitol lobby and direct the families up the stairs. Tell them not to settle in until they're on the seventh floor. The army needs the lower floors."

I saw soldiers and civilians moving ammunition out of the old arsenal and storing it in the capitol basement. Other soldiers were stacking sandbags around the doors and making machine gun emplacements.

I wasn't scared. I was relieved that Major Weatherford had given me something useful to do, and it felt good seeing all the activity

I had stirred up in Spanish Town. No one looked frightened, and parents, in particular, tried to appear calm—even jolly. I think they wanted their kids to believe we were on some spur-of-the-moment field trip.

If the Redneckers had attacked us that morning, they would have wiped us out. Clearly, the army hadn't prepared for a siege, and soldiers and civilians were completely exposed to gunfire as they fortified the capitol building.

Hour by hour, we started getting our situation under control. By around ten in the morning, all the civilians were inside the capitol, and all entrances were guarded. Soldiers kept working to fill sandbags and barricade the building.

Major Weatherford spotted me as he hurryied by. "Mr. Burns," he said, "have the civilians fill up every bucket, every trash can, every empty coke bottle and container with water. We've got water now, but the first thing the Redneckers will probably do is shut off our water supply.

"And put all the food in the basement and inventory it for me. I want a full report on the food situation by the end of the day."

I spent the afternoon organizing our food supplies. A couple of army wives helped me, and we agreed that we had enough food for about a week. The Redneckers would probably eat better than we would because they had probably grabbed up everything edible at the farms by now.

Fortunately, the Redneckers didn't attack us that day. I don't think they knew what to do after we consolidated our position in the capitol building.

On the second day of the siege, we saw Rednecker patrols slinking around outside the capitol, looking for weak spots in our defenses. Several snipers appeared on the roofs of the government buildings and began firing at the soldiers.

"Those snipers are a damned nuisance," Weatherford said after a bullet ripped past his head. He called for Lieutenant Barkley, who appeared almost immediately with a bolt-action sniper rifle fitted with an oversize scope. Sergeant Gomez was with her.

"Lieutenant Barkley, clear out those snipers," Weatherford ordered.

In a few minutes, Barkley and Gomez were climbing up a stairwell to the upper floors of the capitol tower. They didn't stop until they were high enough to look down on the Redneckers who were shooting at us. I went along to help them tote their gear, and two stoic enlisted men obligingly toted a couple of sandbags up the stairs.

Looking out from the twenty-fifth floor of the capitol tower, we could see Redneck sharpshooters firing from the roof and upper stories of the Iberville Building and the Bienville Building—both about nine stories tall. We couldn't hear the sound of their rifle fire, but we saw their upper bodies jerk slightly from the recoil every time they pulled the trigger.

Lieutenant Barkley and Sergeant Gomez went to work in a businesslike manner. First, they broke out a window and put the sandbags in place to make a shooting pad for the sniper rifle. Then they took their helmets off and put on noise-protection headphones. Without their helmets, I could see that Barkley had her greying auburn hair pinned up in a bun, and Gomez's raven-colored hair was tied in a short ponytail. This killing project was a purely feminine enterprise.

Soon Barkley fired slowly and methodically down on the Redneckers, with Gomez serving as her spotter. Through her binoculars, Gomez could see where the bullets were falling, and she reported this information to Barkley.

Neither soldier seemed in a hurry. I heard them discussing windage, velocity, and distances as if they were working out an algebra problem.

With Sergeant Gomez's guidance, Lieutenant Barkley kept adjusting her aim, and soon she began hitting her targets. If a sniper appeared to be only wounded, she shot him a second time to make sure the guy was dead.

After Barkley had killed five or six snipers, the Redneckers stopped firing and dragged their dead off the roofs. "We control the high ground," Sergeant Gomez exclaimed triumphantly. "Thank you, Huey, for putting an ugly tower on your capitol building."

As we clamored back down the tower stairs, I asked the Lieutenant where she had learned to shoot so well.

"My father was a cop back in eastern Pennsylvania," she told me, "so I grew up around guns. Pop was a big-time deer hunter, and he taught me how to shoot a rifle.

"I joined the army right out of high school. That's where I met my husband, Frank, and when I discovered that I'm a pretty good sharpshooter."

On the evening of the siege's third day, Weatherford called a meeting with his junior officers. Gordon attended as the militia commander, and Weatherford invited me to report on how the civilians were doing.

"Assuming Colonel Merski's forces are intact," Weatherford told the group, "the Redneckers are running out of time. They've got to wipe us out before Merski's troops get back, or his forces will destroy them. I'm sure they know that Merski takes no prisoners.

"On the other hand, the Redneckers may know more about Colonel Merski's fate than we do. If his force was destroyed or pinned down upriver, the Redneckers can just wait us out. They know we've got children in the building, and we'll be out of food soon.

"I think they'll attack us from Spanish Town. They've got good cover there, and they can concentrate their forces in that concrete parking garage on the east side of the capitol. From there, it's less than a hundred yards to the east entrance.

"I'm guessing they'll hit us tomorrow morning. If you've seen the John Wayne movies—and I know you have—you know that the bad guys always attack at dawn. But who knows? The Redneckers may sleep in and show up around lunchtime."

Then Weatherford turned to me. "Mr. Burns, how are the civilians holding up?"

"Very well, Major. I've appointed a captain for each floor, and I told them their job is to keep the hallways and stairwells cleared and the bathrooms clean. The toilets are still flushing, so we don't have any sanitation issues yet. Each floor sends a couple of people down to the basement to get food twice a day, and no one is complaining."

But that night, the Redneckers shut off the water, and the toilets stopped working. We started rationing all the water that we had stored, and I could feel the civilians getting anxious.

A few minutes before dawn on the fourth day of the siege, the Redneckers attacked us just as Major Weatherford predicted. Looking like the extras from a long-ago episode of *The Walking Dead*, dirty and bedraggled men and women boiled out of the parking garage and sprinted toward the east entrance of the capitol, firing at us with rifles and shotguns.

A pickup truck with a machine gun mounted in the pickup bed drove up to the top level of the parking garage, and soon the Redneckers were firing at us with a .50 caliber machine gun. But the truck was not armored, and the army's snipers soon killed the machine-gun crew.

Weatherford had instructed me to stay with the civilians if we were attacked, and I had a good view of the action from the eighth floor. Army machine guns opened up on the charging Redneckers, and in just a few seconds, about forty of them lay on the capitol lawn, either dead or wounded. The survivors scurried back to the shelter of Spanish Town.

About an hour later, a Rednecker emerged from the parking garage waving a white flag. He was an emaciated guy in his early thirties, and he was wearing camouflage pants and a camouflage jacket that made him look very much like the soldiers he was fighting.

"I propose a one-hour truce," the man shouted, "so we can pick up our dead and wounded."

Almost immediately a shot rang out from the capitol building, and the guy with the white flag slumped over dead. About a minute later, our soldiers fired down on the wounded Redneckers lying in the open, and soon they were all dead too.

There was no more fighting that day. I went downstairs in the evening for what was becoming the daily briefing. I learned that no one in the capitol had been injured in the attack.

"How's it going upstairs, Mr. Burns?" Weatherford asked. "Everyone holding up?"

"The civilians are holding up well under the strain, Major. They're all doing their part, and they were relieved to learn that our side suffered no casualties in today's attack.

"But, as you know, the toilets aren't flushing anymore. I searched the building until I located all the custodians' storerooms. I found plastic trashcan bags, a couple of cases of air freshener, and some cleaning supplies.

"I told people to piss in the sink and crap in the trashcans. When the trashcan bags are full, we're tying them closed and replacing them with new trash bags. And people are spraying the air freshener whenever they go into the restrooms, which are starting to stink.

"With your permission," I added, "I'd like to throw the bagged shit out the windows."

"Of course," Weatherford replied. "But be careful where you throw it. I don't want any shitbags falling on my troops. Bad for morale."

MAJOR WEATHERFORD SENDS ME TO FORT JOPLIN TO GET HELP

For the next two days, nothing happened. More than a thousand people hunkered down in the capitol, which became more unsanitary with each passing day. We were running out of food and water, and we saw no sign of Colonel Merski or his troops.

On the seventh day of the siege, the Redneckers and the Nubians attacked again. This time, they charged us in school buses. Apparently, they had spent the previous two days bolting metal plates on their buses, attempting to make them into ersatz armored personnel carriers.

Although the soldiers fired with every gun they had, two buses made it through the fusillade, and their drivers rammed the buses up against the barricaded door of the east entrance. Redneckers and Nubians swarmed out of the vehicles and started throwing Molotov cocktails into the sandbagged, machine-gun emplacements.

I saw flames erupting at the barricades and soon our troops stopped firing. I couldn't see what was going on from my vantage point in the tower, but I figured the Redneckers were huddled against the walls of the capitol and throwing gasoline bombs inside.

This is bad, I thought to myself. If the soldiers weren't firing back at the Redneckers, the enemy would soon be inside the building. And once inside the capitol, everyone in the tower would be trapped. I knew the Redneckers would show us no mercy; after all, we had shown them no mercy.

But Major Weatherford's soldiers were still in action. I saw them appear on the roof of the main building, which was only about four stories high. From there they began throwing hand grenades down on the attackers. Some of the Redneckers bolted back toward Spanish Town and were shot in the back while running. Some went around to the north side of the building hoping they could get away from the hand grenades.

But Gordon's militia was waiting for them and shot the Redneckers down as they came around the corner of the building. In a few minutes, the gunfire stopped completely, and all was quiet with the exception of the sound of the crackling gasoline fires.

Black smoke drifted upward to the upper stories of the capitol tower, and I heard two loud blasts when the buses' gas tanks exploded.

And then there were two more quiet days. On the tenth day, one of the militiamen shot a horse, and the farmers butchered it. But one horse can't feed a thousand people, so the farmers shot two more.

At the evening meeting, Weatherford addressed the fact that there were forty or fifty bodies rotting just outside the building. The smell was almost unbearable.

"In retrospect," Weatherford admitted, "I probably should have let the Redneckers collect their dead and wounded. Now we have to do something about the corpses.

"Let's wait until nightfall, and I'll send a team out to collect the bodies and put them in a pile for burning. We'll lob some smoke grenades in that direction to give the troops some protection from snipers."

He turned to me then. "Mr. Burns, make sure the moms don't let their kids look out the east windows while we're burning the bodies. We don't want to traumatize the little tykes."

On the evening of the siege's eleventh day, Weatherford met again with his officers. "We've got to assume Colonel Merski's force was defeated somewhere up north," he told us. "We can't expect Merski to rescue us.

"We'll be running out of water in a couple of days. We're low on food, and we've shot most of the horses.

"I'm going to send a messenger to Fort Joplin in Houston to ask General Mier to come to our aid. Willoughby, I'm giving you that assignment."

I admit I was so anxious about our situation that I was only half-listening to Major Weatherford, and he startled me when he spoke my name.

"I realize you're a civilian," Weatherford explained, "and I'm asking you to do a soldier's job, but you're the best man for this mission.

"You know General Mier, you have a truck that can make it to Houston, and you've also made contact with Adina Morales and the Texas Rangers. If you run into the rangers, you've got to beg them to help us.

"I'm sending Lieutenant Barkley with you. She'll deliver my written plea for help."

I didn't say anything, but I had lots of questions. First of all, where *was* my Dodge truck? I assumed that Colonel Merski had commandeered it and that it was somewhere in Mississippi. I hadn't expected to see it again.

Second, how did Weatherford expect me to break out from the siege? We were surrounded on all sides.

And finally, how would Lieutenant Barkley and I get across the Mississippi River?

But I kept my questions to myself and waited for Weatherford to lay out his plan.

"Willoughby, your truck is down in the governor's parking garage, and you've got enough LPG to make it to Houston. The Rednecks are concentrated in Spanish Town and downtown Baton Rouge. They've only got a light guard on the north side of the capitol.

"From the capitol's observation deck, we can clearly see the I-10 bridge. The Redneckers control it, and it would be damned diffi-cult—probably impossible—for you to cross the river over I-10.

"But the old Huey Long bridge is still intact and only lightly guarded. If you and Lieutenant Barkley can wiggle your way through North Baton Rouge, I think you've got a good chance of getting over the river on the old bridge."

"Okay, Major. When do we leave?"

"I want you to leave tonight around 0100 hours. I would send more soldiers to go with you, but I can't spare them. It'll just be you and Lieutenant Barkley."

I looked at Barkley, and she seemed completely at ease. From her expression, you would think Major Weatherford had asked her to go to the grocery store and pick up a quart of milk.

"Willoughby," Weatherford continued, "I advise you to get some sleep because you'll be driving through the night. We'll get the truck ready to go and wake you around midnight."

I was too tired to walk up ten flights of stairs to my quarters in the tower, so I made myself a makeshift bed in the Senate Chamber. The chamber was dark, quiet, and empty; I went to sleep almost immediately.

A soldier woke me at the appointed hour and led me down to the governor's parking garage. Lieutenant Barkley was already there. She had her rifle, a light machine gun, and plenty of ammunition. She was wearing her Kevlar vest, and she gave one to me.

The soldiers must have sensed that I was anxious. "Don't worry, Mr. Burns," one of the troopers said reassuringly, "Lieutenant Barkley is a crackerjack with an M240. It's her signature weapon. If she can't get you safe to Houston, nobody can."

Just before leaving, Gordon showed up to wish me good luck. "I asked to go with you," he said, "but Major Weatherford said no. But here's a little going-away present. I'm sorry I didn't have time to wrap it."

Gordon handed me one of those personal-protection shot-guns—a nasty-looking weapon that has a pistol grip instead of a traditional rifle stock. It was a short gun, designed for use at very close range.

He also handed me two boxes of buckshot—fifty rounds.

"How thoughtful! I'll think of you every time I shoot someone with it."

"Seriously, Will, I think a shotgun might be more useful to you than your Glock if you get waylaid on the road before you get to Houston. Just remember which end that the buckshot comes out of."

"Thanks, Gordon. I'll leave my Glock with you. I don't think I can handle more than one gun at a time."

As I slid behind the wheel, I noticed a case of bottled water in the backseat of the crew-cab truck, which I had forgotten about. I also saw the two boxes of MREs that Lieutenant Barkley had rifled when we were driving from Austin to Houston. I had had very little to eat over the past few days, and those packets of cold spaghetti and meatballs looked appealing.

I removed six of the water bottles and gave the rest to Gordon. I handed him the MRE rations. "Give these to the kids."

But Gordon turned me down. "Two foil packets of spaghetti aren't going to do anything for the civilians upstairs. You and Lieutenant Barkley take these boxes with you. You don't know when you'll find something to eat.

"Besides," he added, "if you don't get through, ain't none of us going to eat."

Someone lifted the steel door of the parking garage, and Lieutenant Barkley scrambled into the pickup bed. "I can shoot better from the back of the truck," she told me. "I'll ride back here until we get over the bridge."

I started the truck, stomped on the gas pedal, and we shot out of the parking garage. A few Redneckers started shooting at us almost immediately—night pickets, I supposed.

But we had good covering fire. Gordon's militia began shooting at the Redneckers' gun flashes, and Weatherford's soldiers poured rifle fire into the darkness from the upper floors of the capitol build-ing. Barkley shot her machine gun. It was a grand sendoff.

I thought fleetingly about something Winston Churchill had said: "There is nothing quite so thrilling as to be shot at to no effect."

In a few seconds, we were beyond the Redneckers' sentries, and we threaded our way through the surface streets of North Baton Rouge. Almost completely burned down, charred buildings stood everywhere. I drove with the headlights turned off. I was afraid we might bump into a Rednecker patrol, but we didn't see a soul.

Several streets were blocked by collapsed buildings, downed trees, or abandoned cars; it took us almost an hour to get to the on-ramp of the Huey Long Bridge.

The highway over the bridge sloped gently upward to the middle of the river and then sloped down to the west bank. I couldn't see what was ahead over the crest of the bridge, so I drove slowly—about thirty-five miles an hour.

We surprised a couple of sentries standing in the middle of the bridge. They were smoking a joint, and their rifles were leaning against the guard rail.

Lieutenant Barkley cut them both down with her machine gun. One sentry fell off the bridge and plunged into the river—just like in the movies. Coming down the west side of the bridge, we saw a few more Redneckers, but Barkley's machine-gun fire seemed to rattle them. I heard a shot or two, but no bullets hit the truck.

We had gotten away.

IS THE CAVALRY COMING?

When we had gotten safely over the Huey Long Bridge, I pulled over and Lieutenant Barkley climbed into the passenger seat next to me.

I headed west on old Highway 190, driving a steady forty-five miles per hour. Time was of the essence. I knew that, but I didn't want to take the risk of running over some debris in the night and getting a flat tire.

We drove through several burned-out Cajun towns: Krotz Spring, Livonia, and Port Barre. "Krotz Spring used to have a famous speed trap," I told Barkley as we drove through the hamlet. "If you came over the Atchafalaya River Bridge at one mile over the forty-five miles-per-hour speed limit, your chance of getting pulled over was 100 percent.

"But tonight," I said, "I'm going to flirt with danger," and I sped through Krotz Springs doing seventy. It felt great!

Lieutenant Barkley pulled out two foil packets of cold spaghetti and meatballs from their MRE boxes—the same rations that we had disdained when we were driving through Texas only two weeks before.

We were on the verge of starvation and the MRE entrees tasted delicious. "I like them better cold than warm, don't you?" Lieutenant Barkley asked me jokingly.

"I suppose," I answered, "but we could use some Tabasco sauce."

We saw no one on the highway when we rejoined I-10 in Lafayette, and I turned the driving over to the lieutenant. "Get some sleep," she told me. "Who knows what will happen tomorrow?"

Around six in the morning, we crossed the Sabine River where General Mier's soldiers were still maintaining a roadblock. Lieutenant Barkley showed the sentry Major Weatherford's message to General Mier.

The soldier read it and waved us on. "*Via con Dios*," he called out and threw two candy bars through Barkley's open window. Before we pulled out on the highway, Lieutenant Barkley and I switched places again. "Try to get some rest," I told her. "Don't worry. I know the way to Fort Joplin."

I drove into the fort about four hours later and immediately asked to see General Mier. As I walked to his office, I saw three black suburbans parked outside the gate—sinister-looking SUVs with tinted glass. All three were marked as Texas Ranger vehicles.

And then I saw Chief Ranger Adina Morales. "Hey Burnsie!" she called out. "What brings you back to God's country?"

I briefly explained why Lieutenant Barkley and I were in Houston, and Morales asked if she could join us when we met with General Mier.

"I've got fourteen rangers with me," she explained. "We're headed to Laredo to deal with a gang of terrorists that are shooting up the town, but maybe General Mier could use our help."

General Mier was sitting at his desk when we walked into his office, and he knew before we said anything that we were bringing urgent news. He silently read Major Weatherford's message, and then he read it aloud—presumably for Ranger Morales's benefit.

General Mier—

Twelve days ago, the New Rednecks and the Nubian Nation joined forces to attack the garrison at Fort Sharpton. We are besieged in the Louisiana state capitol by approximately one thousand hostiles. I have 120 troops under my command plus sixty members of the local militia. Approximately seven hundred noncombatants are sheltering with the troops, including almost two hundred children.

*Casualties have been light, and we have plenty of ammunition. We are, however, critically short on food and water. **If we are not relieved within the next forty-eight hours, we will be forced to surrender. We expect no quarter from the enemy.***

Please send a strong relief force to our aid as soon as possible.

—Major Weatherford

"Captain Lubbock," Mier shouted, "come to my office."

Lubbock appeared immediately, and General Mier began issuing orders. "Notify all troops to prepare for a combat mission," he said. "Then round up every vehicle you can find—military or nonmilitary—and fuel them up for a run to Baton Rouge.

"Put the armored Humvee in the lead, followed by army vehicles, with the civilian vehicles bringing up the rear. I don't want the Redneckers to see our Honda Fit until they're heard from our machine guns.

"We'll be relieving the garrison at Fort Sharpton," General Mier told Captain Lubbock. "Let's get the combat force rolling by 2200. We'll leave a skeleton force here at Fort Joplin. Have those people organize a relief column with food and water for twelve hundred people—enough to last them a week." Lubbock was out the door in an instant, and Ranger Morales spoke up.

"General Mier, I would like to offer you the assistance of fifteen Texas Rangers. We're combat-ready with ammunition and Kevlar vests, and we're driving three armored SUVs. We would be honored to serve under your command."

General Mier replied immediately. "Thanks, Ranger Morales. I accept your offer. Have your people ready to roll by 2200."

For the next several hours, Fort Joplin's troops worked feverishly to prepare for their rescue mission. I tried to make myself useful by helping to load cases of food and water into various relief vehicles.

By 10:00 p.m., the convoy was organized—a ragtag assortment of military trucks and civilian trucks, buses, and cars. The armored Humvee was the lead vehicle, and I recognized Corporal Frizzell standing in the machine-gun turret. He was energetically chewing gum just like the last time I had seen him.

General Mier was going over last-minute instructions with his officers when he spied me standing around and feeling useless.

"Mr. Burns, we're putting you in the lead vehicle. You know Baton Rouge better than any of us, and you can direct the convoy to Fort Sharpton when we get inside the city."

I was holding the pistol-grip shotgun that Gordon had given me, which General Mier immediately confiscated. "We've got plenty of guns for this expedition, Mr. Burns. I think we'll all be a little safer if you turn that shotgun over to me."

I was relieved to give it to him and remembered to tell him the shotgun was loaded.

It went without saying that Lieutenant Barkley would stick with me, and we both crawled into the Humvee. Sergeant McLaglen was driving. General Mier sat up front in the shotgun seat.

"¡Ándale!" Mier shouted out the Humvee's window. "¡Ándale!"

Sergeant McLaglen put the Humvee in gear, and our caravan of assorted vehicles streamed out Fort Joplin's gate and headed east toward Louisiana.

A group of civilians was clustered around the fort's front gate—spouses and children of the departing soldiers. Many of them waved goodbye to their loved ones, and some saluted.

"TEXANS, I WILL LEAD THIS CHARGE!"

I was exhausted as we lumbered east in the Humvee. I desperately wanted to sleep, but I didn't want to appear like some doddering old codger who nods off in church.

"General Mier," I said, "Lieutenant Barkley and I were up all last night driving from Baton Rouge to Houston. Is it alright with you if we rest our eyes for a bit? Wake me if you need me for anything."

General Mier gave me the thumbs-up sign, and I immediately fell into a deep slumber. Lieutenant Barkley fell asleep, too, and I felt her head lolling about on my shoulder.

Neither of us had bathed during the siege of the capitol building; we couldn't spare the water. I washed my face and cleaned myself as much as I could while I was waiting for the army to mobilize at Fort Joplin. But I hadn't changed my clothes, which were beyond grimy. I planned to burn them as soon as I got some new threads.

I came half-awake when I felt the Lieutenant's breath on me as she slept, and I sensed she was clean. She must have found time to shower while we were at Fort Joplin. She had on clean fatigues as well. Someone at the fort must have given them to her.

As she lay with her head on my shoulder, I smelled soap—military-issue soap. Not French-milled scented soap, but pleasantly fragrant, nonetheless.

It had been years since I had felt a woman's touch, even a touch as impersonal as I was feeling now. It brought me back to my wife's touch and the touch of my children—the warmth, the softness, the trust.

I had no romantic feelings toward Lieutenant Barkley. I was long past that time in my life, and Lieutenant Barkley was probably long past it too. But it moved me that she was clean. She was going into battle and might be killed in the coming hours, but she had taken time to wash her hair.

We both woke up after a couple of hours, and General Mier began peppering us with questions.

"How are the Redneckers positioned?" he asked.

Lieutenant Barkley fielded that question. "Most of them are besieging the capitol building, but some are either guarding the Mississippi River bridges or looting the town. We think their biggest force is concentrated in the Spanish Town neighborhood, where they have good cover from our sniper fire."

"Are you sure that the Redneckers and Nubians have become allies?" Mier queried.

"Oh yeah," Barkley replied. "We're definitely fighting a racially diverse coalition."

General Mier then turned to me. "Is the militia reliable? And are the farmers proficient with firearms?"

"I think you can count on the militia, General," I replied. "Gordon McIlhenny is the militia commander. He's my brother-in-law, and I can attest that he is a steady man under pressure.

"And all the farmers are deer hunters, so they have good rifles with scopes. They've been shooting deer since they were twelve years old."

"Yes," General Mier replied, "but it's one thing to shoot a deer at a distance of three hundred yards. It's another thing to kill a human being who is trying to kill you. How do you think they'll perform in close combat?"

"All I can say, General, is that these guys are called ragin' Cajuns for a reason. Most of them have been carrying pistols for years, and they're all mighty handy with a skinning knife.

"Don't forget, these guys are defending their families. If it comes down to hand-to-hand combat, the Cajuns will stay in the fight as long as they have breath in their bodies."

Our motley caravan arrived at the outskirts of Baton Rouge just after dawn. We could see the I-10 bridge in the distance. Its curving span over the river was high enough to accommodate large ships, and people occasionally jumped off it to commit suicide.

General Mier signaled for the convoy to pull over. He got out of the Humvee and glassed the bridge for several minutes with his binoculars. "I can see people on the bridge," he said to no one in particular, "and some kind of barricade. But I can't make out exactly what we are dealing with."

Ranger Morales walked up beside Mier, and she, too, scanned the bridge through her own binoculars. "Those are hostiles," she remarked, "but I can't tell how many or how they're armed."

"Captain Lubbock," Mier called out, "take a light truck forward and get as close as you can to the bridge without drawing fire. Give me an estimate of how many bad guys are on the bridge and what that barricade is made of."

Meanwhile, Ranger Morales needed a bathroom break. "Hey, boys and girls," she called out, "now's the time to pee if you need to. Ladies, you go in the woods on the right side of the road. Gents, you pee on the left side."

Hundreds of soldiers and rangers scrambled into the woods, and I could see that General Mier was mildly irritated by Morales's unauthorized order to his troops.

"Who's in command here, Ranger Morales?" he asked sharply.

"I'm sorry, General. But when you gotta pee, you gotta pee."

By the time everyone got back from relieving themselves, ten minutes had passed. Still, Captain Lubbock had not returned from his reconnaissance. Mier waited patiently, but Morales was becoming agitated.

"General," Morales said to Mier, "we've got to get moving, or we're going to lose the element of surprise."

Mier didn't acknowledge Morales's observation and continued to wait for Captain Lubbock to return from his reconnaissance.

"Fuck it," Morales said under her breath and waved her rangers forward. Within seconds, three black, armored SUVs were lined up on the shoulder of the highway just a few feet behind Mier's Humvee.

Morales huddled with her rangers for a few minutes, but I couldn't hear what she was saying. Then she shouted out, "Texans, I will lead this charge!"

The rangers ran to their vehicles. I heard SUV doors slamming, engines starting, and the sound of rangers chambering their rifles.

"Burnsie," she called out, "you're riding with me."

Morales didn't invite Lieutenant Barkley to accompany the rangers, but my bodyguard joined me in the backseat of the lead SUV. I could tell that General Mier clearly disapproved, but he didn't order Lieutenant Barkley to stand down, and he didn't ask Morales what the hell she was up to.

"¡Vámonos, muchachos!" Morales yelled. Ranger Almaráz—whom I vaguely remembered from my trip to Decatur—was behind the wheel, and he stomped down on the gas pedal.

Three black SUVs raced toward the bridge going sixty miles per hour. Our vehicle was in the lead. Almaráz rolled all the windows down, and the wind made a terrific racket.

Morales poked an M4 out her window, and Lieutenant Barkley did the same. The Redneckers shot at us, and the rangers shot back.

The wind caught the brim of Morales's Stetson, pushing it up against the hat's crown. She looked a bit like a demented cowboy in an old western movie.

"Don't slow down, don't slow down!" she shouted at Almaráz. "Ram that barricade!"

I had just enough time to cinch my shoulder belt tighter. Less than a hundred feet from the Redneckers' barricade—mostly old cars parked two deep—Almaráz lost his nerve and slammed on the brakes. Our SUV weaved violently from side to side. I smelled burning rubber, and then we hit the center of the barricade doing about forty miles an hour.

The barricade hardly budged. The SUV's airbags went off, which stunned everyone in our vehicle. Almaráz must have hit his head against the windshield because blood streamed down his face.

Lieutenant Barkley was clearly dazed, but she kept firing her rifle. I'd surrendered my shotgun to General Mier and didn't have a weapon.

Just as well, I thought. I was wedged in between Barkley and a burly Texas Ranger, and everyone who had a window seat was shooting. I was showered with shell cases and quite content to stay where I was.

"Keep ramming that goddamned barricade," Morales ordered. Almaráz put the SUV in reverse, then put it in drive and lurched forward to ram the barricade again. At first, the barricade didn't move, but after a few tries he had pounded out a small opening just wide enough for our vehicles to get through.

Incredibly, our suburban was still mobile. None of the rangers had gotten out of their vehicles, and Morales yelled for us to keep moving. The three SUVs bolted through the barricade like rabbits on the run, and a few seconds later, we were over the bridge.

"Okay, Burnsie," Morales said as she slipped a loaded magazine into her rifle. "What's the quickest way to the action?"

I guided us to Fourth Street, where we could see the state capitol building straight ahead. We were doing sixty in downtown Baton Rouge, ignoring the stop signs and speeding through the intersections.

When we came to the capitol grounds, the other two SUVs pulled up beside our vehicle, and we charged three abreast over the lawn past Huey Long's statue. We didn't stop until we reached the steps of the capitol building.

"Where are the goddamned Rednecks?" Morales asked me.

"Over there," I replied, pointing toward Spanish Town.

Within a minute, all three SUVs were prowling through the narrow streets of the Spanish Town district, and rangers shot at everyone they saw.

We were outnumbered by about fifty to one. I began preparing myself for imminent death. But we caught the Rednecks and the Nubians by surprise, and they began fleeing toward downtown Baton Rouge.

Inside the capitol building, Major Weatherford must have realized that reinforcements had arrived because I saw his soldiers streaming over the barricades, apparently acting under Weatherford's orders. They were grey-faced, hungry, dehydrated, and haggard; but they rallied at the sight of the rangers and swarmed into Spanish Town to join the Texans.

Soon, Weatherford's troops were joined by General Mier's reinforcements, who arrived on the scene a few minutes after the rangers. "So glad you decided to join us," a ranger called out sarcastically to one of Mier's soldiers. The soldier just grinned at the ranger and flipped him off.

Gordon's militia tried to join the fray, but Weatherford said no. "You guys are dressed as civilians, and you might get mistaken for Redneckers. I want you to stay in the capitol and protect the civilians."

Weatherford's soldiers brought hand grenades, which they lobbed into any house where they thought a Rednecker might be sheltering. I heard gunfire, explosions, shouting, and pleas from Redneckers begging to surrender.

Soon, Spanish Town was on fire. All the rangers in my suburban had jumped out of the vehicle and were chasing down Redneckers on foot. I sat in the SUV as long as I could, hoping someone would return and tell me what to do. Lieutenant Barkley was with Morales and off somewhere in the fighting. *Where the hell is my bodyguard?*

I was almost completely blinded by the smoke, and the heat of the fire forced me out of the SUV. Armed Redneckers and Nubians ran by me from time to time, but they apparently mistook me for a comrade because none of them shot at me. Soldiers trotted up and down the streets looking for someone to shoot, their faces blackened by soot.

Then I saw a soldier run by who looked familiar. It was Colonel Merski.

"Hey, old-timer!" he called out cheerfully. "I should have known you'd be here. Did you start all this commotion? I hope you've got liability insurance!"

"Colonel Merski, I'm glad to see you," I croaked, and could think of nothing else to say. Tears were streaming down both our faces, which I credited to the smoke.

"We had a hell of a time in Vicksburg," he told me hurriedly. "IEDs knocked out almost half of our forces, and then we got pinned down in downtown Vicksburg. I'm sorry we're late."

FATHERS AND SONS

Soldiers and rangers roamed through Spanish Town for about an hour, hunting down Redneckers and their Nubian allies. Redneckers who weren't killed retreated into downtown Baton Rouge, hoping to hide themselves in the ruins. A few tried to escape by jumping into the Mississippi but were swept away by the current and drowned.

I groped my way out of the conflagration and went to check on the civilians. Some were looking down from the upper-story windows of the capitol tower and watching as the fire consumed their homes. They were dirty, hungry, and dehydrated. The children clearly suffered from trauma and looked at me with unblinking, deathlike stares.

All the civilians were in extreme distress, not knowing whether their loved ones would survive the fighting. I reassured the army dependents that casualties among the soldiers were light—even though I had no idea whether that was true. I told the farm families that Major Weatherford had ordered the militia not to go into Spanish Town, so none of the militia members had been injured—which was true.

I learned from various soldiers that the army took no prisoners during the first frenzy of the fighting. Fort Sharpton's troopers shot every Rednecker or Nubian they saw, even those who threw down their weapons.

But as the day wore on, the soldiers wearied of the carnage, and they began allowing their attackers to give themselves up. The Texas Rangers also took prisoners, which they turned over to the army, and Adina Morales told me later that no ranger shot anyone who offered to surrender.

By the end of the day, the army and the rangers had captured almost three hundred prisoners, which they herded into two pens. The biggest group—about two hundred combatants—were marched to the courtyard of the Pentagon Barracks. Another hundred were driven into the horse corral the militia had built near the capitol building at the beginning of the siege. Merski ordered Gordon's farmers to guard these prisoners and to shoot anyone who tried to escape.

It was Merski's policy to execute anyone who attacked Fort Sharpton or its soldiers. Thus, by the evening of the Spanish Town battle, about three hundred men were under a sentence of death. Merski ordered firing squads to execute all male prisoners at dawn on the following day.

In the late afternoon, an army patrol discovered around fifty Rednecker children and adolescents who had sheltered on the LSU campus during the fighting. Merski told his troops not to shoot the kids.

Meanwhile, Spanish Town burned to the ground, and a black plume of smoke wafted toward the capitol building and drifted over the river.

That evening, I saw Colonel Merski sitting on the capitol steps eating a cold MRE. All the steps were chiseled with a state's name. Merski was squatting on New Jersey. He looked weary and despondent.

"War is always hell," he told me. "I've seen a lot of it, but this has been the worst day of my life.

"In the Middle East, Afghanistan, and even in California, the fighting was vicious, but I knew I'd get good medical care if I was wounded. I could at least look forward to a hot meal, a hot shower, and a cold beer every now and then—even in a war zone.

"But today felt more like the Thirty Years War of the seventeenth century than a modern battle. We weren't fighting for our country. We were fighting for our families. If we'd lost this battle, all of us would have been killed—even the children."

"But, Colonel," I said, "you beat the Redneckers and the Nubians. You must feel good about that."

"Yeah, but you know what Wellington said about war: 'The only thing worse than a battle won is a battle lost.'

"Look at us, Will. Soldiers have been fighting all day without food or water. Our quarters in the capitol reek with the smell of human filth, and the civilians have been traumatized by the violence. Spanish Town, where our families lived, has been destroyed. Who knows how long it will be before we can restore some sense of normalcy?

"Yes, we defeated the Rednecks today. But the enemy probably burned the farms south of here and stole all the food—the food we need to survive the winter. We have hard times ahead of us."

I decided to turn the conversation to a less depressing subject. "Colonel Merski, what did you decide to do about the Natchez Bridge? Did your people blow it up?"

This question immediately lightened Merski's mood. "Oh yeah," he said enthusiastically. "We blew the hell out of it. The Natchez Bridge is a massive structure, and it gave me a real charge to see that bridge crash into the Mississippi. I wish we still had cell phones and YouTube. If I could've posted a video of the explosion on YouTube, I'd have gotten a million hits."

"How about the other bridges over the Mississippi? Will the army blow them up too?"

"General Mier and I discussed that with Ranger Morales about an hour ago. She wants the army to destroy every bridge over the Mississippi from New Orleans to Minnesota—with the exception of the two bridges in Baton Rouge, of course. After all, Fort Sharpton is on the east side of the river. Those bridges would be our only retreat routes to the west if we're ever forced to evacuate."

"So are you going to do that?"

"Well, of course, it would be a lot of fun. Nothing warms the heart of a soldier like destroying some infrastructure. But General Mier and I decided against it. If we demolish all the bridges, we would be splitting the USA in half—maybe forever. Those bridges would never be rebuilt, at least not in my lifetime."

Merski rose and we walked together up the capitol steps into the once-elegant main lobby. The marble-lined walls were marred by bullet holes, and shell casings and blood littered the polished Italian lava floors. The statue of Jean Baptiste Sieur de Bienville, founder of New Orleans, lay toppled and headless, and the place smelled of sweat and feces.

"Hmm," Merski said as he sniffed the stench. "Brings back fond memories of San Francisco! All we're missing is the drug paraphernalia."

At that moment, as I took in the destruction and the foul odor wafting around the capitol building lobby, I was filled with despair. After the siege began, I didn't think about our farms being burned or our food being stolen. But Merski had reminded me that our homes and all our provisions had probably been destroyed by the Redneckers. How would the farm families survive the next few days without food and shelter, much less the coming winter?

As often happens, however, our situation looked brighter in the morning. Army engineers worked through the night to restore the water system, and the toilets started flushing again. Civilians brewed great pots of hot, black tea, which they served at dawn in China cups they found in the Governor's Suite. Two of General Mier's army trucks arrived from Houston with enough food to get us through the next few days.

Early in the morning, Merski discovered me standing at the top of the capitol's front steps. I was drinking my third cup of hot tea, self-medicating my acute caffeine deprivation. Merski was the last person I wanted to see.

"Will," he said in a cheerful, energetic voice, "we're going to shoot the prisoners this morning. I want you to interrogate a few of them before they're executed."

I started to refuse. The idea of questioning a man just before he is going to be shot was abhorrent to me. I didn't think I was psychologically capable of it.

Then I looked into the colonel's face and I saw the face of death. The man who had chatted with me on the capitol steps the evening before was gone. Although Merski's face wore a jovial countenance this morning, the man who stood before me was devoid of all compassion, as indifferent to suffering as the Nazi bureaucrats who operated Auschwitz and Dachau.

If I cross this guy, I thought to myself, *he'll kill me.*

So I went to the horse corral and pointed to a prisoner sitting alone in a sunny spot with his back against the north wall of the capitol. Gordon's militiamen were on guard duty, and one of them put plastic handcuffs on the man I had chosen and shoved him along to one of the rear entrances to the capitol building. Together, the militiaman and I found a makeshift interrogation room that no one had crapped in—some long-departed Louisiana bureaucrat's office.

My prisoner gave his name as Robert Middleton. Although he was grimy and disheveled, I could tell he had shaved recently. He seemed a little cleaner than most of his comrades, and he wore horn-rimmed glasses that made him look more like a middle-aged professional person dressed for the weekend than a terrorist.

Middleton answered all my questions calmly and candidly, and I found myself starting to like the guy. He didn't fit the profile of the stereotypical southern redneck, so I asked him some personal questions—purely to satisfy my curiosity.

"I can tell you're an educated man, Mr. Middleton," I said. "Did you go to college?"

"Oh yeah. I got a business degree from Emory and an MBA from the Wharton School. Those were pretty good credentials in the old times. But my fancy degrees put me deep in debt. By the time I graduated, I'd taken out more than $200,000 in student loans."

"Did you get a job?"

"I got a good job. I was a financial analyst for a private equity fund in Atlanta, and I was making serious money. I had a pretty wife, three kids, and an expensive high-rise condo. I drove a Mercedes.

"But when the economy headed south, no one needed financial analysts or private equity funds. I didn't have any skills people need to survive in the new times. I hadn't learned a trade. I didn't know how to grow my own food. I had never fired a gun.

"My two youngest children died in one of the plagues, and my wife abandoned me and my only surviving son. The whole South was in chaos, and I knew my son and I would starve to death unless I joined the Nubians or the Redneckers.

"I tried joining the Nubians, but I wasn't a POC—a person of color—and I got turned down. If I had told them I was gay or transgender or something, I think they would have made an exception for me, but I was just a straight, white man, and I think the Nubians had seen enough guys like me.

"So," he continued, "I signed up with the New Rednecks.

"I want you to know that I have no political convictions whatsoever. I don't even like these people—they're all racists. And what have the Rednecks done for me?"

In response to my question, Middleton assured me that the New Redneck Army had not molested the farmsteads. "Our plan was to loot the farms and steal your food before we attacked Baton Rouge," he admitted. "But when your people discovered us at the L'Auberge Casino, we lost the element of surprise, so we immediately headed into Baton Rouge to get ready to attack. We didn't have time to stop and steal your food."

"Did you burn our farmhouses?" I asked.

"No, Mr. Burns, we didn't burn a single house. As I'm sure you know, the Redneckers are premier arsonists, but I think their scheme was to put the farmers to work growing food for their army. They figured it was in their interest to leave the farmhouses and barns intact."

These tidings seemed too good to be true, almost unbelievable. I had reconciled myself to the loss of Lâche Pas, and the news that my home might have survived the battle filled me with hope—a feeling I hadn't had in a long time.

Of course, Middleton might be lying to me, giving me good news in the hope that it would help him save his own skin.

But somehow, I knew Middleton wasn't lying. After all, I'd spent twenty-five years as a university professor, where I had been surrounded by bullshit artists—true masters of pious doublespeak. I had developed a pretty good knack for knowing when someone was deceiving me. I didn't think Middleton was a scammer.

In fact, Middleton had been so disarmingly candid that I felt I owed it to him to tell him he would probably be shot later in the day. I'd never delivered such dire news to anyone before, and I had no idea how he would react. Still, his response surprised me.

"Are you going to kill my son too?" he asked.

His question staggered me. "What are you talking about?" I responded. "Did you bring your son to Baton Rouge?"

"Of course, I brought him to Baton Rouge," Middleton snapped back. "He's fifteen years old, for Christ's sake. What was I supposed to do? Drop him off at boarding school?"

I tried to reassure him. "No, Mr. Middleton. The army isn't going to shoot your son. The army is ruthless, but as far as I know, it hasn't resorted to killing children."

My words gave him no reassurance. "I'm worried about him," Middleton confessed. "I haven't seen him since yesterday. I'm afraid he might have been killed in Spanish Town. Shot, maybe? Or burned up in the fire?"

"What's your kid's name?" I asked

"His name is Tom," Middleton replied.

I realized then that I wasn't tough enough for the world I lived in. I think most people would have broken off the conversation with Middleton and left him to his fate. But I had lost a son named Tom to Hurricane Maxine. I knew what it meant to lose a child. As Cole Goodnight might have put it, my heart was in the coffin with Robert Middleton.

"Look, Mr. Middleton, I'll try to find your son. What was he wearing the last time you saw him?"

"He was wearing a Yale T-shirt," Middleton replied. "God knows where he got it. Blue jeans and boots—leather work boots."

"He should be pretty easy to find," I assured him. "Not many Yalies around here."

I left immediately to search for Tom Middleton. I had told his father that the army didn't shoot children, but I wasn't absolutely sure I'd told him the truth. A fifteen-year-old kid is almost an adult. If the army caught him carrying a weapon, he might very well be slated for a firing squad. In fact, he might already be dead.

But as I walked out of the capitol, my sense of urgency diminished for a few seconds. I was bone tired. I was dirty, and I stank. I just wanted to find a quiet spot somewhere that didn't smell like shit and woodsmoke, lie down, and drift off to sleep.

But I kept moving. If Tom was a prisoner, he would be in the Pentagon Barracks. Had he been put in the horse corral, his dad would've already found him.

A plan formed in my mind. I decided to first look for Gordon. If I could get Tom Middleton released from the Pentagon Barracks, I would need Gordon's help to hide the kid until I could find Colonel Merski and persuade him not to execute him.

I found Gordon McIlhenny, my ever-steady brother-in-law, guarding the prisoners in the horse corral. Most of the farmers were with him. Like me, Gordon was sleep-deprived, and he looked awful—sooty face, filthy clothes, matted hair.

"What's up, brother-in-law?" Gordon asked, sounding a lot more cheerful than he looked.

I quickly told him I was looking for a fifteen-year-old boy because I wanted to assure his father—who was about to be shot—that his son was still alive.

"There are a few kids over at the Pentagon Barracks," Gordon informed me. "That's where the firing squads are working.

"But don't go over there unless you're prepared to be shocked. Children are milling around begging the army to spare their fathers—crying, screaming, trying to get to their dads. Wives calling out to their husbands . . . " Gordon's voice trailed off.

"But the army's not shooting kids, is it?"

"The army isn't shooting any young girls," Gordon corrected me. "But there are some teenage boys who are getting shot."

I ran over to the Pentagon Barracks, and Gordon's description didn't begin to describe the sorrow and terror that I saw. Soldiers were leading prisoners out of the Pentagon Barracks' courtyard, across River Road, and onto the concrete river levee, which had been built like steps leading down to the river.

I think Merski chose the levee for his killing ground because his soldiers could push the bodies into the Mississippi rather than burn or bury them. Soldiers simply lined up the prisoners on the levee's bottom step, shot them, and pushed them into the river.

I saw one soldier wearing chest waders standing in the shallows. He was pushing bodies into the current with a long pole. Very efficient.

Above all this, an improvised red flag was flying above the levee—the flag of no quarter. Merski had raised it in open defiance of international law.

My god, I said to myself. This is medieval. This is the way armies behaved during the Hundred Years' War.

I scanned the scene—the prisoners, the soldiers, the children—and I spotted a dirty teenager wearing a Yale T-shirt. To my horror, I could see he was in the group of men who were in line for the firing squad. Merski's troops—not Mier's—were the executioners, and I figured Merski had probably ordered his men to make no exceptions.

I spotted Sergeant Benoit, the fiddler in Merski's Cajun military band. He seemed to be in charge of the actual killing, and his face told me that Benoit had shut off all his human emotions.

"Sergeant Benoit," I said. "See that boy wearing the Yale T-shirt? He's just a kid. He's just a child. Let me get him out of the execution line."

But Benoit didn't seem to hear me, and he didn't look me in the eye. In fact, he shifted slightly and turned his back on me.

"For Christ's sake, Sergeant, that kid's only fifteen years old. You can't shoot a kid."

Then Benoit turned to look at me, and his eyes were as cold and hard as stones. "Mr. Burns, we caught that kid with a shotgun. He was shootin' at us. It don't matter how old he is. Our orders are to execute all prisoners who were carrying weapons. Thank god it'll be over soon."

I knew Benoit pretty well from casual connections over the years at St. Joan of Arc, our parish church. I considered him to be a decent man—a good father and husband. I had heard him play the fiddle at countless Cajun music events.

Today, however, he looked transformed. Sweat stains had made little rivulets in his grimy face. He was hollow-eyed, unshaven, and incredibly dirty from the fighting. His normally animated and cheerful voice was gone, and he spoke to me in a flat, deadened voice. He was clearly exhausted.

I suppose I, too, had been transformed by the siege and the ferocious fighting. I, too, was dirty and begrimed. In contrast to Benoit, however (who appeared to be in a trance), I had become nearly hysterical by the sight of so many bodies and the steady drumbeat of rifle fire from the killing squad.

I knew Sergeant Benoit was a heavy-duty Catholic. A daily communicant, in fact. I saw him at mass occasionally. I, on the other hand, was not a very good Catholic. In fact, I was a terrible Catholic. Nevertheless, in an act of desperation, I decided to appeal to Benoit as a co-religionist.

Big mistake.

"Sergeant Benoit," I said in a wheedling tone, "remember what Jesus said in the Bible, that it would be better to be drowned in the ocean than to hurt a child."

Benoit turned and cursed me. "Go fuck yourself, Mr. Burns," he responded savagely. "How the hell do you get off playing the religion card on me? Do I ever see you at mass?

"Do you think God is here today, Mr. Burns? Because he ain't. He's not here today."

"But how can you live with yourself if you shoot this kid?" I pleaded. "This fifteen-year-old child. This kid has a parent, and he has a name. His name is Tom."

"I'll go to confession when it's all over," Benoit replied cynically. "Father Kerry will absolve me."

"But Sergeant, the kid's cuffed. Let me take him to Colonel Merski and see what he says. I promise I won't release him unless Merski approves. If Colonel Merski says execute him, then by god, I'll shoot him myself."

"Alright, Mr. Burns, take him," Benoit muttered wearily. "But I'm not going down for this. If Merski raises hell, I'm gonna tell him that you helped a prisoner escape. You might wind up gettin' shot yourself."

"I understand, Sergeant," I replied. And then I raced over to the file of condemned prisoners and pulled Tom Middleton out of the execution line. I grabbed him by his plastic handcuffs, and we started running. "Let's go, Tom. Your father wants to see you."

THE MILITIA MUTINIES

In a few minutes, I was back at the horse corral, with Tom Middleton by my side. I was out of breath. It must have been fifty years since I had run that hard.

I quickly spotted Gordon, and I saw him talking with a group of six or seven farmers. They looked angry or distressed, maybe both.

"Gordon, this is Tom Middleton," I huffed. "His father's name is Robert Middleton. That's the dad leaning against the wall over there.

"I found Tom in the execution line. I managed to get Sergeant Benoit to release the kid to me, but he wasn't happy about it. In fact, he told me to fuck myself."

"Yeah, Benoit can be kind of prick sometimes," Gordon responded mildly, as if he were commenting on the weather. "I'm surprised he let you take the kid."

"Well, he might change his mind and show up here with a rifle team. I've got to hide Tom somewhere until I find Colonel Merski and ask him to give the kid a pardon."

"Sure, Will. There's a janitor's closet just inside the capitol. You can stash him in there. It stinks like hell; we've been using it as a latrine. Not likely anyone will want to even get close to that closet." Then Gordon drew his belt knife and cut Tom's plastic handcuffs.

Before I could spirit Tom Middleton away, his father saw him. He ran across the makeshift prison yard, pushing his comrades aside, and gave his son a fierce hug.

"Tom, Tom! You're alive!"

"Thanks to this man," Tom said, pointing to me. "The army was going to shoot me."

"Oh my god," Robert Middleton said repeatedly. "Oh my god. Oh my god." And then both father and son began weeping hysterically.

"Listen," I said. "I hate to break up this reunion, but some really bad guys may be looking for your son. We're kinda playing this by ear. I'm going to hide him out until things settle down."

I pulled the boy away from his father and guided him into the capitol building, where I quickly found the janitor's closet that Gordon told me about. But when I opened the door, the smell of urine and feces made us both gag.

Would I hide inside a pit toilet to keep from being killed? I asked myself. And my answer was no, and I think that was Tom's answer too. So I dragged him up several flights of stairs until I found the floor where Clotilde Savoie and her kids were sheltering with the civilians.

Like her husband Sonny, Clotilde was a Cajun Catholic, and she shared Sonny's Cajun accent—an accent I had always found appealing.

"Clotilde," I said, "you've got to help me hide this kid. The army had him lined up for a firing squad, but I got him out. They want to kill him as a terrorist, but you can see he's just a youngster. He's only here in Baton Rouge because his father is one of the Redneckers."

To my relief, Clotilde asked no questions. "Sure, Will. I'll find a place for him. Follow me."

She led us down a hallway to an empty office, one of the hundreds of tiny offices that honeycombed the capitol tower. It had a window but no furniture other than a single, straight-back chair.

I opened the window, hoping to catch a breeze, but the wind brought the sound of gunfire. Tom flinched every time he heard a volley from the firing squads. I decided to close the window.

"Stay here," I instructed Tom. "Don't leave this room unless Clotilde or I come for you. You might be here a long time."

"You're probably thirsty, cher," Clotilde said to the kid. "I'll bring you some water. And you're in shock so I'll bring you a blanket.

"I'll bring you something to read too, to help the time pass," she added. "Can you read?"

"Yeah," Tom replied. "I used to read a lot before Dad joined the Redneckers."

"Then I'm gonna bring you a Bible."

Clotilde left us for a few minutes and returned with a Bible, a plastic bottle of water, and a blanket. "Here," she said, handing Tom the Bible. "Start with Psalm 23. Dat will calm you down."

"And after you've read dat psalm, read the Book of Matthew, chapter 25."

By now, Tom Middleton was plainly in shock. I don't think he was listening to Clotilde's prattle.

"Are you a Christian, darlin'?" she asked Tom. "Catholic, maybe?"

"No, ma'am," Tom replied dazedly. Dad and I don't go to church."

"Well, if you can live by Matthew 25, you'll be alright," Clotilde said gently. "Don't worry about nothin' else."

"Mathew 25?" Tom said blankly. I could tell he had no idea what Clotilde was saying. She might as well have been speaking Swahili.

I was confused too. *What in the hell is she talking about?*

"Dat's the chapter where Jesus tells us to feed the hungry, give drink to the thirsty, and care for the sick," she said gently. "Them's the corporal works of mercy.

"Mr. Burns here performed a corporal work of mercy when he pulled you out of that firing-squad line," she explained. "Visiting the prisoner—that's another corporal work of mercy."

Then Clotilde turned to me. "Will, was you with Sonny when he died?"

"Yeah, Clotilde. Gordon and I were with him. The Redneckers shot him down on River Road. He died instantly. I don't think he suffered." I was glad that I could say that honestly.

"Well, dat's good," she said resignedly. "Where's his body?"

"Clotilde, I am so sorry to tell you this, but Gordon and I couldn't retrieve Sonny's body. People were shooting at us. Sonny's horse got shot. Gordon and I ran away."

"I understand," Clotilde replied. "But we'll have to find it, won't we?"

"Yeah, we'll have to find it."

I knew I should leave Tom and Clotilde and go looking for Colonel Merski, but I wanted to spend a few more minutes with them in that quiet sunny room—just a few more minutes before returning to the chaos and violence below. I felt calmed by Clotilde's serenity, which even the firing squads had not shaken. So I lingered.

"Clotilde," I asked, "aren't you one of the catechists at Joan of Arc? One of the people that brings new members into the Catholic Church?"

"Used to be, 'til Father Kerry fired me."

"Fired you? Why would he fire you?"

"Well, Sonny and I wasn't married in the Catholic Church, so Father Kerry said it didn't count an' Sonny and me was livin' in sin."

"But you can fix that, can't you? Just have Father Kerry give you a Catholic marriage."

"Well, there's another problem, Willoughby. I was married before I met Sonny, and I got a divorce. Somehow, Father Kerry found out about dat."

I hadn't expected the conversation to take this turn, and I grabbed Clotilde by the arm. "Stop right there, Clotilde. You don't have to tell me any of this. It's none of my goddamn business."

"No, that's okay. I got pregnant when I was seventeen, and I married this kid I went to high school with. Yeah, my oldest child's not Sonny's.

"But the marriage didn't work out, and we divorced after a couple of years. And then I met Sonny, and we had a pretty good life."

"Okay, I know divorce is a problem for guys like Father Kerry, but why would that keep you from being a catechist?"

"Well, the Catholic Church has an official rule: a divorced person can't be a catechist. In fact, when Father Kerry found out I was divorced, he wouldn't let me take communion."

"He's a vicious son of a bitch," I said, even though I knew Clotilde wasn't asking me for sympathy.

"Yeah, it was a shame, because I was a good catechist. I brought more than twenty people into the Church. It was my vocation, or at least I thought it was."

Clotilde was using the word vocation in the Catholic understanding of the word. By vocation, she meant a calling.

"You know, I just don't understand," she continued. "Father Kerry's diddling little boys in the rectory and he won't let me be a catechist."

And then Clotilde began to cry.

Jesus Christ! I thought to myself. *Another shock on an already shocking day.*

"I've heard rumors about Father Kerry, Clotilde, but you're telling me the rumors are true?"

"Oh, yeah, Willoughby. Father Kerry molested one of my nephews. I know dat for a fact."

"Did Father Kerry ever mess with any of your children?" I asked.

"No. Sonny told him that if he touched one of our kids, he'd cut his balls off."

Something about Clotilde's surprising revelation touched me to my core, stirred some old memory from my distant childhood—a memory that flickered for an instant in my consciousness and then was gone, a flickering memory of pain and humiliation. I felt tears welling up—tears for Clotilde and her family, tears for Tom Middleton, and tears for me.

This is no goddamn day to get weepy, I told myself, *and no time to be reflecting on my childhood, which had never done me any good.* I stifled memories that were rising to my consciousness and brusquely made my departure.

"Gotta go, Clotilde. Gotta find Colonel Merski."

I walked down the stairwell of the capitol tower for what seemed like the hundredth time and went back to the horse corral. I shook off my conversation with Clotilde about Father Kerry, but I filed it away in my mind to ponder later in the day.

When I got to the corral, I saw Gordon talking with Colonel Merski. Gordon was flanked by fifteen or twenty tense-looking farmers, all of them with their weapons at the ready—mostly shotguns and deer rifles. Merski had a half dozen soldiers by his side, and they, too, looked tense. I recognized one of the soldiers as Sergeant Guadalupe Gomez.

Something was definitely wrong; I could see that. I decided not to announce myself but to sidle up as close as I could to Merski and Gordon and listen to their conversation.

"Gordon," I heard Colonel Merski say, "I'm telling you for the last time. I want you and your men to escort the prisoners to the execution ground, and I want you to do it now."

"Colonel," Gordon replied, "that's not going to happen. The farm militia answered your call to come to Fort Sharpton and help defend it. We've done that. One of us got killed.

"But we're all decent people here; we aren't concentration camp guards. We're not going to help you shoot these prisoners.

"In fact, we're going to collect our families and go home. Get someone else to help you kill these men."

At that moment, Colonel Merski spotted me standing in the background, and he drew me into the confrontation.

"Will," he said, almost pleadingly, "help me persuade Gordon to follow my orders. There's work to be done here, and it needs to be done now. Tell these clodhoppers to escort the prisoners to the firing squads."

"Can't do it, Colonel," I replied. "I stand by my brother-in-law."

My insubordination sent Merski into a frenzy. "You motherfuckers," Merski hissed contemptuously. "You've all been fraternizing with the enemy. You're just a bunch of dumb, fuckin' rednecks who're feeling sorry for another bunch of dumb, fuckin' rednecks.

"Don't you realize that these assholes came to Baton Rouge to burn your farms, rape your wives, and steal your kids?" he raged. "If we let them go, they'll be back."

At that moment, it was easy for me to guess what must have been going through Merski's mind: First, he probably realized that he didn't have enough soldiers with him to back down the militia.

Second, he surely sensed—as I think we all sensed—that the prisoners were watching the situation unfold and had figured out that the farmers were not going to participate in a mass execution. Some of the prisoners were probably pondering whether now would be a good time to make a run for it. Third, I could see that Colonel Merski did not want to be humiliated in front of his own soldiers, who were all listening intently to the conversation between Merski and Gordon.

Seeing the dialogue had come to an impasse, Merski turned to Sergeant Gomez. "Sergeant, take your men, find Lieutenant Barkley, and tell her to get back here on the double with a platoon-strength unit. Bring two light machine guns."

Sergeant Gomez turned to follow Merski's order, but she stopped to ask a question. "Colonel, shouldn't a couple of us stay here with you?"

"No, Lupita," Merski replied, in a surprisingly kind, almost fatherly voice. "I want everyone to leave and form up under Lieutenant Barkley."

So Colonel Merski stood alone, facing a band of armed farmers, one hundred prisoners, and me. I could see he was unafraid. I wouldn't have been surprised if he had pulled out his pistol and shot Gordon and me on the spot. But that's not what he did.

"Willoughby," he said, turning to me, "you've always been a problem solver. Can you help us solve this problem?"

As I said before, sometimes my mind works fast, and sometimes it doesn't. I started to say, "I haven't got a fucking clue," but I knew I would have to do better than that. So I started talking, just making things up as I went along.

"Colonel, about a thousand Redneckers and Nubians attacked Fort Sharpton, and there's only about a hundred of 'em left. And maybe fifty Rednecker kids. They got here in all kinds of vehicles, including some school buses.

"Why not load the whole crowd up into three school buses and escort them to the state of Mississippi, somewhere east of the Pearl River? Put enough gas in the buses to get them to Mississippi, but not enough to come back here."

"You mean just leave 'em on the highway to starve to death?" Merski asked. "Wouldn't it be kinder just to shoot them? And I'm not giving 'em back their weapons. If they can't protect themselves, the comancheros will find them and kill them."

"Colonel," I responded, "the Redneckers must have brought some food with them, and I'll bet they've got water filtration equipment of some kind. Give them some MREs and a little water and turn them loose."

And then, with perfect timing, Gordon pitched in and backed my play. "You're right, Colonel. If the Redneckers don't have weapons, the comancheros will massacre them. Maybe we could give them a few rifles and shotguns—say ten pump shotguns and ten bolt-action rifles and a little ammunition. Then they could defend themselves, but they wouldn't have enough guns or ammo to attack us again."

Merski was a realist. He was also—as I discovered that morning—a psychopathic killer. But he was a realist.

"Okay, Willoughby, we can do that."

Then he turned to Gordon and raised his voice so that the other farmers could hear him. "You realize, of course," he told us all, "that you're putting your families in danger if we let these bastards go free. You people on the isolated homesteads are going to see these guys again. On some dark night, they will come for you and for your wives and your kids. And your softhearted compassion today won't save you."

At that moment, Lieutenant Barkley showed up with about twenty soldiers. She was carrying a machine gun, and it seemed to me she was pointing it in my direction.

"Lieutenant," Colonel Merski said, "we are paroling these prisoners. The militiamen are going to find some school buses to transport them to Mississippi. But if anyone tries to escape before we load these white-trash bastards on the buses, shoot them."

ANOTHER LEVEL OF EVIL

Finally, the long day—a long, murderous day—had come to an end. I wandered around the capitol grounds looking for Ranger Morales. I needed to know when the rangers were going back to Texas because I intended to go with them.

I found Adina sitting under a live oak tree east of the capitol building surrounded by her rangers. The rangers had spread a large blue tarp on the ground, and they were all sitting on it, intently cleaning their individual weapons. No one looked up when I approached.

"How did the rangers make out yesterday?" I asked Adina.

"We have three wounded," she replied. "Ranger Nguyen took a bullet in the stomach. We don't think she'll live. We're going to stay in Baton Rouge until she dies, but I think we will be on the road early tomorrow morning.

"You coming with us?" she asked.

"Oh yeah," I replied. "I'm going to break the news to my family and Colonel Merski as soon as I can find them.

"What do you think about the executions this morning?" I asked her.

Adina looked up from cleaning her pistol and wiped a strand of hair from her face. "War is war, Will. It's always been that way. What happened today is exactly like what happened after Goliad and the Alamo. And remember, the Americans killed a lot of Mexicans who were trying to surrender at San Jacinto Bayou, and that battle only lasted nineteen minutes.

"I heard you and your brother-in-law saved about a hundred Redneckers this morning," she continued. "I admire you for doing that. You know you might have gotten yourself shot."

"Yeah, it was a little tense for a few minutes," I admitted. "I was most worried about what Lieutenant Barkley was going to do with her machine gun."

Morales laughed. "It'd be a hell of a note to be executed by your own bodyguard!"

"Adina, I can't thank you enough for coming to Texas and joining the fight. The state of Louisiana owes you an eternal debt of gratitude."

Morales laughed again. "Well, don't erect any goddamn statue to me, Burnsie. Some numb-nut college student would just tear it down."

It was evening now, and I left the rangers to their gun-cleaning chores and looked around for Gordon. He and the militiamen had made their way down to Capitol Lake, and some men were bathing in the not-so-clean water.

Their family members had come down out of the capitol tower to join them, and there was a picnic atmosphere in the gathering dusk.

"Thanks, Gordon, for what you did today," I told Gordon when I found him. "You and the militia stopped the killing and saved a hundred men's lives."

"No, Will. We saved a hundred assholes' lives. Not the same thing. I hope we don't see any of those guys again.

"And anyway, you were the one who persuaded Merski to bus the bastards back to Mississippi. You talked him off the ledge just before his soldiers showed up."

"Yeah," I responded. "Colonel Merski's a lot more complicated than I figured him for. There was a moment there when I thought he was going to shoot us both.

"By the way," I continued, "where's Robert Middleton? Did he get reconnected with his son?"

"Robert Middleton and Tommy are right over there," Gordon pointed. "I told Merski we were putting them to work at Lâche Pas. Neither of 'em knows a fuckin' thing about farming, but you don't need to know much to slop hogs or shovel manure. I think they'll both work out fine."

"So," I said, "happy ending all around."

"I suppose," Gordon answered without enthusiasm. "Not so good for the people who got shot today."

I figured the time had come to break the news that I was leaving Lâche Pas and going to Texas.

"Gordon," I said, "I'm going to Texas, and I won't be back. Texas is going to become a nation, and I want to be part of it."

Gordon didn't look surprised. "I figured this day would come. Texas is where you always wanted to be. You've always got a home at the farm if you ever change your mind, but I don't think you'll ever be back."

"I'll be needing my Glock. Do you have it handy?"

"Yeah," Gordon replied. "I squirreled it away behind a wall in the governor's parking garage. Do you need it now?"

"I need it right now," I replied, sounding more vehement than I had intended.

Gordon looked startled at my response. "Willoughby, you don't even like guns. Why are you in such an all-fired hurry to get your Glock? Do you need to kill somebody tonight?"

"Don't ask me any questions, Gordon," I responded savagely. "Just get my fuckin' gun."

Gordon gazed into my eyes for a few seconds, but he asked me no more questions. He just turned and walked toward the parking garage.

A few minutes later, Gordon returned empty-handed.

"Where's my Glock?" I asked in an irritated voice.

Gordon pulled a small black revolver out of his pants pocket and gave it to me. "I'll give you your Glock tomorrow," he explained. "For now, take this revolver."

"What the hell is this?" I asked.

"It's a Ruger .38 special," Gordon replied. "And it's loaded, so be careful with it."

"Okay," I responded. "But why are you giving it to me?"

"Will," Gordon explained, as if he were talking with a five-year-old, "this is what you call a throw-down gun. I picked it up off the battlefield this morning. No one owns it. It's disposable. Kinda like a 'no deposit, no return' beer bottle. Use it once and throw it away."

"Thanks, Gordon," I said, suddenly grasping the significance of what he was telling me. "By the way, General Mier confiscated the shotgun you loaned me. I have no idea where it is now."

"No problem. We picked up dozens of shotguns on the battlefield today. I'll find a replacement. Some of those shotguns would probably make good throw-down guns," Gordon added.

It was late evening now. I faded into the darkness and began walking steadily toward Saint Joan of Arc Church, located a couple of miles east of the capitol. Merski had some sentries out, but I slipped past them without being seen. I headed east on Main Street, walking by the veterans' cemetery.

I was jittery. I knew Redneck stragglers might be lurking about, but I had the revolver. And I had one last thing to do before leaving for Texas.

I found Joan of Arc Church locked up and closed, but I walked around to the rectory, where I could see a candle's gleam inside. I eased up to a kitchen window and saw Father Kerry eating a solitary dinner—it looked like roast chicken and sweet potatoes. He had poured himself a glass of red wine from a bottle that sat on his table.

Father Kerry's parishioners had taken good care of their parish priest, I could see. Metal bars had been installed on the windows of his quarters and his front door was solid steel. The rectory was

Father Kerry's little fort. I couldn't get in by crawling through a window or knocking down a door, so I resorted to a ruse.

I began banging on the rectory's steel door. "Father Kerry! Father Kerry! I have an emergency! Jason Benoit is dying, and he's asking for last rites!"

I felt sure Father Kerry heard me, but when I walked back to the kitchen window, I saw that he kept eating, pausing occasionally to take a sip of wine.

"Father Kerry!" I called out. "You know Jason. He's a daily communicant. He's a Fourth Degree Knight. He's a Eucharistic minister. He's dying. He's begging for last rites."

Father Kerry kept on eating. Hmm, I thought. The old bastard's too sly for me.

I contemplated breaking a window and shooting at him through the bars, but just as I was about to do that, Father Kerry finished his meal, wiped his mouth with a white cloth napkin, and rose from his chair. He walked slowly to the rectory's front door, which he warily opened only a few inches.

"What do you mean," he said angrily, "interrupting my dinner hour?" I could tell he didn't recognize me.

"Father Kerry, Jason Benoit is dying. There was a big battle over at Fort Sharpton yesterday. You didn't hear it? Jason got shot, he's dying, and he's begging for last rites."

"Can't it wait until morning?" Father Kerry asked, in an irritated voice.

"No, Father, he's going to die. We've got to hurry. The army is sending a truck for you. It will be here any minute."

"Give me a moment to get my kit," he said grumpily. "It's in my study." As he spoke, he turned his back, and I slipped inside the door.

In a couple of minutes, Father Kerry returned from his study. "Is Mr. Benoit a Catholic in good standing?" he asked.

Father Kerry's question enraged me, and I dropped all pretense of being a deferential Catholic layperson. I began cursing.

"Father Kerry, you dumb motherfucker, what difference does that make? He's dying! He wants last rites! Don't you know who he is? He goes to mass every fuckin' day."

Curiously, Father Kerry ignored my profanity. "But if Mr. Benoit is not a Catholic in good standing," he lectured me, "he's not eligible for last rites."

That's when I pulled out the revolver. "Father Kerry," I snarled, "you rape little boys and you're a Catholic in good standing. What the fuck are you talking about?"

I don't think, even then, with my throw-down gun pointed at his face, that Father Kerry knew he was a dead man. He was outraged, and he was searching for something he could say that would put me in my place, which—in his opinion—was probably Hell.

"Have you gone to communion lately?" he asked me in a stern voice. "You know, of course, that if you take communion when you are not in a state of grace, you've committed a mortal sin. How many mortal sins have you committed?"

"I don't know, Father," I replied. "But I'm about to commit another one." Then I shot him in the chest.

Father Kerry staggered back but remained standing. Blood stained his black, clerical shirt and dripped from his mouth onto his Roman collar. I dragged him into the dining room and sat him down in his chair.

"You'll burn for this," he gurgled. "Murder is a mortal sin. You'll get the chair."

"I don't think so, Father," I replied. "The old times are over. Nobody cares if you live or die. And I won't get electrocuted because we ain't got no electricity."

"Besides," I added gratuitously, "aren't Catholics opposed to capital punishment? Didn't Pope Francis rule on that?"

Father Kerry said something in Latin—some special curse, I suspect. A secret curse the Vatican only gives out to insiders. But he slumped over in his chair before he could properly damn me, his head falling on his dinner plate.

I stood for a moment in the kitchen, waiting for my heart to stop pounding. Then I hurried to Father Kerry's bedroom and started rummaging through his dresser drawers and his clothes.

I didn't find what I was looking for, so I went to Father Kerry's study. Very impressive—bookshelves filled with scholarly books, including a huge biography of St. John Paul and the complete *Summa Theologica*, all five volumes. A large crucifix hung on the wall behind his desk, but I saw no images of the kind saints—St. Francis, for example, or St. Joseph, or St. Therese of Lisieux.

One drawer of his desk was locked, but I found Father Kerry's key ring hanging from a hook by the rectory's front door. I returned to the study and began inserting keys into the lock. After three tries, I found the one that unlocked the drawer.

Inside the drawer, I found file folders filled with child porn, each file dated by year. I hurriedly looked at the photos and I recognized Father Kerry in sexual poses with young boys, some of whom I knew. Several photos depicted Sergeant Benoit's son, age of about ten.

I spread the photos on the kitchen table by Father Kerry's body, and I placed the throw-down pistol in Father Kerry's dead hand. I wanted the scene to look like a suicide—a repentant priest who could not live with his sins.

But do people commit suicide by shooting themselves in the chest? I wondered. *Probably not.* Most people would shoot themselves in the head. So I had made a mistake that I could not fix.

Had I made any other mistakes? I asked myself. I quickly brought to mind all the film noir movies I had seen over the years. It seemed like the killer always got caught because he made a single mistake.

But I couldn't think of anything else I needed to do. I grabbed Father Kerry's wine bottle and left the house. As I walked back to Fort Sharpton, I sipped from the bottle until it was empty. It was a pretty good vintage. *One thing you've got to say about Father Kerry,* I reflected, *he knew his wine.*

I tossed the empty wine bottle over the cemetery fence and heard it break against a tombstone. Yet another mistake. Anyone investigating Father Kerry's death would see his half-empty wine glass and look for an open wine bottle.

When I got near the fort, I was challenged by a sentry. He was too far away to recognize me in the darkness, but he must have concluded I was not young when he heard the sound of my voice.

"What's the password?" he shouted.

"Beat Bama!" I shouted back.

"Nope," the sentry replied. "That's yesterday's password. But that's close enough. Pass by, old-timer."

GONE TO TEXAS

When I got back to the capitol grounds, I found Gordon with some farm families. They were sitting around an enormous bonfire, which they fed with broken-up furniture that they'd dragged out of the capitol building.

"Where ya been, Will?" Gordon asked.

"Well, if anybody wants to know, I've been sitting right here all evening. You can testify to that, can't you?"

"Yeah," Gordon replied. "I'll testify that you bored me for hours talking about your favorite movies."

"And what are my favorite movies, in case anyone asks?"

Gordon reeled them off: *The Big Lebowski, The Blues Brothers, Hud, Shane,* and the original *Stagecoach*—the one that John Ford directed.

"And what are my favorite movies?" he countered.

"*The Great Escape, Bullitt, Easy Rider,* and *The Godfather.*"

"*Godfather II,*" Gordon corrected me.

A few minutes later, I walked back into the capitol for the last time and climbed the stairs to my makeshift quarters in the capitol tower. I immediately fell asleep, giving no thought to the firing squads, the piles of bodies, Tom Middleton, or Father Kerry.

I woke early the next morning, found Gordon, and retrieved my Glock. I started to ask him why he had given me the throw-down gun, but I didn't.

Then I sought out Ranger Morales. She was saying her good-byes to Colonel Merski and Lieutenant Barkley. Merski could see immediately that I was going back to Texas, and he took one last opportunity to tease me.

"You'll come back to us, Will. You think the girls are prettier in Texas, but you'll soon discover that the prettiest girls on the planet live right here in Louisiana. It's that dirty Mississippi river water that gives them such beautiful complexions," he expounded in a lyrical voice. "And all that hazardous waste that's leaked out of the chemical plants over the years. It gives Louisiana girls that special glow."

I was glad Merski was kidding me; I took it as a sign that he didn't hold a grudge for my part in stopping the firing squads. Still, I declined to continue the joke.

"No, Colonel, my life is nearly over. I want to spend the years I've got left helping to build a decent society."

I tried to express my gratitude to Lieutenant Barkley. "Lieutenant," I said, "how can I thank you for being my bodyguard during these past few weeks? You kept me safe, and I know you would have taken a bullet for me."

Barkley said nothing. She simply gave me a brief hug and then snapped out a crisp military salute.

Just as I said my last farewell, Colonel Merski pulled me aside. "I sent Sergeant Benoit and a squad out before dawn this morning to patrol east of the city," he said in a low voice. "I asked Benoit to check on Father Kerry at Joan of Arc. No one's seen him since the Redneckers showed up."

Instantly, I was seized by stomach-churning fear. "Oh yeah?" I tried to sound casual, but my heart was pounding and my mouth was as dry as sandpaper. "How's Father Kerry doing?"

"Sergeant Benoit said he couldn't find the old bastard. The rectory door was unlocked, but Father Kerry wasn't there."

I didn't say anything. How could Sergeant Benoit have missed Father Kerry's body slumped over his dinner table?

"Sergeant Benoit suspects Father Kerry went over to the enemy," Merski continued. "But that doesn't seem plausible. The Rednecks aren't Catholic, are they, Will? Aren't they mostly Protestants?"

My mouth was so parched I didn't think I could speak, but I croaked out a response to Merski's question. "Yeah, I think so, Colonel. Baptists, Methodists, Presbyterians, maybe a few Episcopalians to give 'em a little class. I don't think many Rednecks are Catholic."

At that moment, I forced myself to look the Colonel in the eyes and I could see them twinkle. The son of a bitch *knew* I had killed Father Kerry. He was playing with me.

"Well, it doesn't really matter," Merski mused. "I never liked Father Kerry. He was a cranky motherfucker. I'm not going to spend any time looking for him."

I looked over Merski's shoulder and saw black smoke billowing up around a church steeple to the east. "Colonel Merski," I said. "I think Joan of Arc is on fire."

"No, Willoughby," Merski assured me. "Joan of Arc Church isn't on fire. It's the rectory. Sergeant Benoit torched it."

I couldn't think of anything I wanted to say in response to this revelation, so I kept my mouth shut.

"Benoit thinks the rectory could be a sniper's haven, so he burned it down," Merski explained.

"Did you order Sergeant Benoit to do that?" I asked.

"No, Will, Sergeant Benoit did that on his own initiative. You see, like you, Sergeant Benoit is a problem solver."

I made my way to Ranger Morales's caravan of black suburbans, which looked the worse for wear. In spite of the fact that all three vehicles were armored, I could see that they'd been shot up. The hood and front bumper of Morales's suburban looked the worst because Ranger Almaráz had used it as a battering ram on the I-10 bridge.

"Saddle up, Burnsie," Morales told me. "It's time to boogie back to Texas."

A body bag was strapped on the roof of Morales's suburban, secured with multiple bungee cords. Ranger Nguyen must have died in the night.

Soon, our ranger caravan left the carnage in Baton Rouge and headed west toward Texas. As we crossed the I-10 bridge, I looked down and saw corpses bobbing in the Mississippi—evidence of yesterday's mass executions.

"Catfish food," Chief Morales observed in a flat tone. I could see that she'd washed the smoke and grit off her face, but she was still dirty, and she looked exhausted. Listlessly, she watched the Louisiana landscape pass by for a while, but she fell into a lifeless torpor before we reached the town of Lafayette. PTSD, I decided.

I studied Adina's face as she gazed blankly out the SUV window. She was an attractive woman, and I could see a trace of the UT sorority girl on her drawn face. But there were a few streaks of grey in her hair and lines in her neck. The new times have been hard on everyone, I reflected, even Adina Morales, the fabled Texas Ranger who still held fast to the values and ideals of the old Texas.

When we reached the army's Sabine River checkpoint, Morales shook off her reverie and produced the pass that General Mier had given her. I walked with her as we stretched our legs in the Texas welcome center's empty parking lot.

When we were out of hearing of the other rangers, Morales unburdened herself to me. "Will," she said, "I am so sorry I took my rangers to Louisiana. What was I thinking?

"Ranger Nguyen was killed in Spanish Town. That's her in the body bag on top of our vehicle. She left a husband and two children in Houston.

"Ranger Rodríguez will probably lose an eye, and two more rangers were wounded. I'll regret the battle of Spanish Town for the rest of my life."

I tried clumsily to reassure her. "But Adina," I protested, "you and your rangers saved the day. If you hadn't cleared the I-10 bridge and charged into Spanish Town when you did, who knows how the battle might have turned out?"

But Ranger Morales just shook her head. "Ranger Nguyen didn't die for Texas, Burnsie. She died in a foreign war. How can I explain that to her husband and her kids?"

MILES AND MILES OF TEXAS

Within a week after leaving Louisiana with the Texas Rangers, I joined Adina Morales and Cole Goodnight in their crusade to round up support for the Texas Constitutional Convention. Together, we drove thousands of miles on Texas roads to meet our goal of holding an independence rally in all 254 counties.

I traveled through the state's former big cities—Dallas, Fort Worth, Houston, San Antonio, and El Paso—all just shadows of their former selves. I also visited a lot of small Texas towns with eccentric names: Happy and Smiley, Dime Box and Old Dime Box, Comfort, Friendship, Electra, and Rising Star. And I visited a few little towns that had taken the names of some of the world's great cities. There was Paris, Texas, and Athens, Texas; and there was a Dublin, a Bogota, and a Berlin.

As I cruised around the state in my LNG-powered pickup truck, I was struck anew by the diversity of Texas topography. I drove through the piney-woods country of East Texas, the rugged Texas Hill Country of the Edwards Plateau, and the Guadalupe Mountains of Big Bend. I passed over the Llano Estacado, where the land was as flat as a kitchen table. I drove through the Cross Timbers country, the Blackland prairie soil of northeast Texas, the high plains, and the Chihuahuan Desert.

And I loved it all. Texas had been staggered by the new times, and its people had suffered great hardships. But the Texans are a scrappy people, and everywhere I went, I saw Texans struggling to rebuild their way of life.

A sure sign of revival was the reemergence of the small-town Texas café. Wherever a few hundred people lived in close proximity, I usually found a humble restaurant where someone was smoking a brisket, scrambling huevos rancheros, or frying a chicken-fried steak.

And the Lone Star state's famous "hon" waitresses were not extinct. Every little Texas eatery seemed to have at least a couple of middle-aged matrons who addressed customers of all ages and genders as hon, honey, sweetie, sweetheart, or darlin'.

In Texas, everyone understands that these greetings are not flirtatious solicitations. Rather, calling a customer darlin' is merely a friendly welcome, which, like the rain, falls alike on the just and the unjust, the young and the old, the big tippers and the skinflints who don't tip at all. If you are a Texas waitress, you are licensed to call everyone darlin'.

And I was delighted to discover that the Texas dance halls were popping up, where people could hear "There Stands the Glass" and "Fraulein," and dance the two-step to country songs that only had one theme: the unhappy consequences of honky-tonking with the wrong woman.

I held some independence rallies on my own, but I often traveled with Adina or Cole. We found that double-teaming the crowd was usually more effective than having only one speaker. Whether we traveled alone or together, a Texas Ranger always accompanied us; an armed Texas lawman gave our rallies extra drama.

I had never been a great public speaker, but I learned long ago that I was a better speaker if I was talking on a subject that I care about, and I cared about the Texas Independence Movement.

Also, it helped that I almost always found a friendly audience.

After all, every Texan knew that the United States was a goner, and that Texas was on its own. In fact, I occasionally ran into an old codger who believed Texas had already become an independent nation.

"What?" an old-timer would ask incredulously. "You mean we're still part of the USA? Then why ain't I paying my federal income taxes? Why ain't I getting my mail? Where the hell is the president?"

Many people find a long automobile drive over the high plains to be mind-numbing, but I liked motoring across West Texas. For me, it was always a refreshingly serene experience—a Texas flatlander's version of yoga. I found the mesas, the flat vistas, and the blood-red sunsets far more beautiful than a rocky New England beach.

I even learned to love the wind farms that scarred the landscape.

In the old times, I despised the wind farms as ugly intrusions on the majestic Texas plains. But now I knew that the wind farms generated enough electricity to keep Texas from slipping back into the nineteenth century. They were as necessary for post-apocalyptic Texas as the windmills that pumped water for thirsty cattle herds back in the days of the cattle barons.

From time to time, I saw signs that nature was reclaiming the Texas plains. I often saw bobwhite quail crossing the highway in big coveys, a hundred birds or more. The antelope herds seemed bigger than they were a few years ago, and I occasionally saw wild long-horn cattle and even a few buffalo. Evidently, the longhorns and the buffalo had wandered away from the Wichita Mountains Wildlife Preserve in southwestern Oklahoma and were gradually increasing their numbers in the Texas Panhandle.

I knew, however, that paradise lost can never be recovered. Texans were living a hardscrabble existence in the new times. We all lived precarious lives. We needed a strong and honest democratic government if we were to survive.

THUGGERY IS AFOOT

About ten days before the constitutional convention was scheduled to begin, I drove back to Austin to help Cole and Adina prepare for the big event. Cole had appointed me to be the credentialing officer for the upcoming convention, and it was my job to resolve any disputes that arose out of the county-level delegate elections. I assigned myself a cubicle tucked away in the basement of the Texas capitol, where I heard various protests from people who were unhappy about the election outcomes.

One morning, I heard a challenge to Dallam County's delegate election. Dallam County was located on the high plains in the northwestern corner of the Texas Panhandle. In fact, Dalhart—Dallam County's county seat—is two hundred miles closer to Denver, Colorado than it is to Austin, Texas.

This particular dispute had a theological component. A Southern Baptist and an American Baptist won the first election, which was not surprising given the fact that the sole polling station was located in Dalhart's largest Baptist church.

Declaring the first election illegitimate, dissidents held a second election with the polling station moved to a different church. A Free Will Baptist and a Missionary Baptist won the second round of voting. To complicate things further, a Primitive Baptist had been on the ballot for both elections, and he argued that he had enough combined votes to be seated as one of Dallam County's official constitutional delegates.

I listened to impassioned harangues from five Texas Baptists for about an hour. Not only were the disputants arguing about the legitimacy of the two elections, but all five were trying to convert me to their particular brand of Baptist religion. Talking over one another, the Baptists quoted from scripture, warned me about the fires of hell, and implored me to be baptized by emersion. Soon, I developed a throbbing headache, which completely sapped my store of Christian charity.

Finally, I had heard enough. "I am a Catholic," I told the group, which left them all speechless. "And here is my final ruling: one delegate will be the Southern Baptist, and the other will be the Free Will Baptist. The Missionary Baptist and the American Baptist will be alternates."

"What about me?" the Primitive Baptist asked.

"Our rules only permit two delegates and two alternate delegates for each county. But here is what I'll do. I declare you to be an official convention observer, which entitles you to a reserved seat in the gallery.

"Now, go in peace, or I'll call the rangers and have you all escorted from the building."

To my surprise, my Solomonic ruling satisfied everybody. "Thank you, Mr. Burns," the Free Will Baptist said on behalf of the warring parties. "Now, can you recommend a place where we can get a good hamburger?"

"Sure," I said. "I recommend Dirty Martin's on Guadalupe Street. Dirty's has been in business for more than a hundred years, and that joint makes a good hamburger. You should try the Kumbak Burger or the Sissy Burger. But I gotta warn you, Dirty's serves beer."

"Beer is not a problem" the Southern Baptist assured me. "We're four hundred miles from home, and our preachers will never find out. But what's a Sissy Burger?"

"Basically," I explained, "it's a Kumback Burger with mayonnaise instead of mustard. And they put lettuce on the Sissy Burger. Maybe that's why they call it a Sissy Burger."

"Dirty Martin's it is," the Missionary Baptist declared, and all five Baptists left my office in good fellowship.

As soon as the Baptists were gone, I began searching through my desk for an over-the-counter pain reliever to knock out my headache. But I didn't find anything. *What fools we were to let the Chinese make all our Advil.*

Just then, Lieutenant Barkley walked in. She was wearing camo battle dress and carried a sidearm, but she had substituted a fatigue cap for her helmet, and she carried no rifle.

I greeted her warmly. "Lieutenant Barkley, it is very good to see you! What brings you here today?"

Barkley allowed herself the barest flicker of a smile, which made me forget for an instant that I had seen her kill almost a dozen people. But her first words were somber.

"General Mier and Colonel Merski sent me here to deliver a message," she said, a sense of urgency in her voice. "I'm under strict instructions to deliver the message to you personally and to watch you read it. Then I've been ordered to show the message to Mr. Goodnight and Ranger Morales. After the three of you have read it, my orders are to destroy the message."

"Mission impossible!" I said lightheartedly.

Barkley rebuked me with a severe frown. "This is no laughing matter, Mr. Burns. Read the message."

She handed me a hand-written note signed by General Mier and addressed to Cole Goodnight, Adina Morales, and me. I read it quickly.

Goodnight, Morales, and Burns—

Be advised that the Provisional Government considers the Texas Independence Movement to be an existential threat to the United States that must be stopped at any cost. All three of you are targeted for assassination. The Provisional Government has spies in Austin and at Forts Joplin and

Sharpton. You must take strong measures to protect your personal security and avoid exposing yourself to sniper fire or an assassin's explosive device.

—General Mier

"Okay," I said. "I get the picture. I'll find Cole and Adina. I think they're both in the capitol today."

Lieutenant Barkley and I walked upstairs to the Texas Secretary of State's office, where we found Goodnight and Morales poring over a large Texas map studded with colored pins showing which counties had held delegate elections. I was pleased to see that only a handful of counties had yet to choose their constitutional delegates.

Lieutenant Barkley did not explain why she was in Austin. She simply gave Cole and Adina the message from General Mier, which they read together while the lieutenant and I stood by.

"That's it?" Goodnight asked. "Do you have any additional information you can share with us?"

Lieutenant Barkley didn't answer. Instead, she retrieved General Mier's message, struck a match to it, and then watched it burn in a trashcan that was sitting beside Goodnight's desk.

"I have a second document for you to review," Barkley said as she handed over a one-page typed memorandum. "Operation Happy Trails," was written in capital letters at the top of the page. "Top Secret: For Your Eyes Only."

Cole, Adina, and I read the second document. We could see that it was a military order directed to General Mier and Colonel Merski. This is what the order said:

The Provisional Government has determined at the highest level that the Texas Independence Movement poses a severe threat to national security and must be stopped militarily. This order launches Operation Happy Trails and directs you to take all necessary measures to neutralize Roy Rogers, Dale Evans, and Pat Brady.

You are directed to lure these three individuals onto the USS Nancy anchored at the Port of Houston. Senior military

*officers will offer them the opportunity to publicly renounce
the Texas Independence Movement, cancel the upcoming
constitutional convention, and identify all persons who advo-
cate the secession of Texas from the United States. If they
refuse to comply, they are to be terminated with extreme prejudice without delay.*

"Whoa!" Morales exclaimed. "That's a hell of a document! I
presume 'terminate with extreme prejudice' is govspeak for 'assassinate,' am I right?"

"Yes, ma'am," Barkley replied as she took the document from
Morales. She tossed the order in the trashcan and set it ablaze.

"Roy Rodgers, I take it, is my code name," Goodnight said.
"Adina, you must be Dale Evans. And Willoughby, I think Pat Brady
must be your nom de guerre."

"Pat Brady!" I exclaimed indignantly. "Wasn't he the guy who
played Roy Roger's comical sidekick on that children's television
show? Drove a jeep named Nellybelle? That Pat Brady?"

"I think so," Goodnight replied, "but I'm not old enough to have
seen that particular television series." I saw him try to conceal a
smile.

"I get it that the government wants to kill us," Adina ventured,
"but I don't understand the silly code names. It seems so juvenile.
What are we to make of that, Lieutenant Barkley?"

"General Mier said that the policy wonks and strategic experts
in the Provisional Government were all trained at elite schools:
Harvard, Georgetown, Princeton, yada yada. He said they're all
idiots and think the code names are signs of sophisticated spycraft.
But the death threats are real."

"Okay, Lieutenant," Goodnight said. "What do you propose we
do about this?"

"General Mier and Colonel Merski told me to assure you that
they oppose this plot and will do everything they can to keep you
from being assassinated. They also said that you should not meet
with the feds on their turf because they plan to kill you."

"Of course," Morales replied, "but what do we *do*?"

"Mier and Merski have a plan, but they say it's highly risky."

Lieutenant Barkley then turned to me. "Mr. Burns, they want you to come to Fort Joplin. They said they need to use you as bait."

"Bait? What the hell does that mean?"

"I don't know, Mr. Burns. They didn't say. But I need to deliver you to Fort Joplin today for the plan to work."

Lieutenant Barkley then turned to address Cole and Adina.

"Mr. Goodnight and Ranger Morales, you need to separate and hide out for a few days. Don't tell anyone where you are going, and don't take anyone with you unless you trust them with your lives."

I quickly resigned myself to this new threat and decided to place my life in the hands of General Mier, Colonel Merski, and Lieutenant Barkley.

"Alright, Lieutenant," I said. "You've protected me so far. Let's get 'er done."

Cole grabbed me gently by my arm. "Wait a minute, Will. Don't go to Houston. The feds will shoot you on sight. You need to stay alive, at least until the constitutional convention. The future of Texas is at stake."

"No, Cole," I replied. "Mier and Merski's plan—whatever it is— is the only smart play. By helping us thwart this assassination plot, they're putting their own lives on the line. Merski and Mier wouldn't do that unless it was the only option. I've got to go to Houston with Lieutenant Barkley."

Adina agreed with me. "Burnsie is right, Cole. If our calculations are correct, Texas will be an independent nation in a few days. We've got to buy some time and stay above ground at least until the constitutional convention does its work."

"But why did Mier and Merski choose Willoughby to be the bait?" Goodnight asked. "Why not me?"

Lieutenant Barkley explained. "Frankly, Mr. Goodnight, General Mier and Colonel Merski consider Mr. Burns to be expendable. The Texas Independence Movement can carry on even if he's killed, but if you and Ranger Morales are assassinated, they think the movement will collapse."

Goodnight said nothing more, and neither did Morales. I was impressed by how quickly they analyzed the assassination plot and how decisively they responded. I think we all realized that there was nothing more to talk about.

I shook hands with my two stalwart comrades and followed Lieutenant Barkley out of the capitol to the armored Humvee I had seen before. Corporal Frizzell was driving, and I climbed aboard. Soon, we were headed toward Houston.

Lieutenant Barkley and I spoke very little on the long drive. We were each deep into our own thoughts, and I think we were both contemplating our mortality.

We drove by Weimar's Store on Highway 71 without stopping, although I would have liked to have picked up a few kolaches. After all, in Texas, men on death row are entitled to choose their last meal before they're executed. I vaguely remembered reading somewhere that a cheeseburger was the top choice for a condemned man's last meal, but I would choose a sausage-and-cheese kolache.

We pulled into Fort Joplin after nightfall, and Lieutenant Barkley immediately took me to General Mier's conference room. I found Mier and Merski drinking beer and eating brisket tacos. Based on the number of empties on the conference table, it appeared they were working their way through their second six-pack.

"Thanks for coming, Will," Mier said as he wiped his mouth on the sleeve of his camo uniform. "I take it you've read the two documents Lieutenant Barkley showed you."

I nodded.

"Lieutenant Barkley, you destroyed those documents, right?"

"Yes, sir," Barkley replied.

"Okay, then," Mier said, turning to me, "this is the situation. The navy has two ships anchored at the Port of Houston: the USNS *Harvey Milk*, which is a supply ship, and the USS *Nancy*, a Vietnam-War era destroyer. An elite army unit is on board the *Nancy*, and these troops are loyal to the Provisional Government.

"The navy wants me to lure you, Mr. Goodnight, and Ranger Morales onto the *Nancy*, where you will be assassinated.

"Colonel Merski and I can't stand by and let that happen, so we took the liberty of bullshitting the navy on your behalf. We told them that all three of you smelled a rat and refused to meet the government reps on a navy ship."

I was relieved by Mier's words because it meant that both he and Colonel Merski had committed themselves unconditionally on behalf of Cole, Adina, and me. By lying to the navy, they had put their own necks in the noose.

"But we also told them the three of you offered to meet with the feds at Fort Joplin if I would personally guarantee your safety, which of course I said I would do.

"So," Mier continued, "the feds expect to find Cole, Adina, and you here tomorrow morning to meet with a senior army officer, Colonel Bernard Lawless."

My ears perked up in surprise. "Colonel Lawless? Is he the guy you told me about back at Fort Sharpton—the guy who pays you for the oil the military gets from the Louisiana and Texas refineries?"

"That's the man," General Mier replied. "And you can trust him about as far as you can throw a hand grenade—and I don't think *you* can throw one very far."

At this point, Colonel Merski spoke up. "So tomorrow morning, Colonel Lawless will arrive here at Fort Joplin. We don't know if he will come alone or with a small escort, or whether his entourage will show up in force.

"When Lawless gets here, you tell him that Cole and Adina got cold feet, but that they gave you full authority to act on their behalf. Got that?"

I nodded again.

"We'll just play it by ear," Merski instructed. "You tell Colonel Lawless you will consider his proposal—whatever it is—and try to buy some time. That may work.

"On the other hand, the feds may have decided to assassinate you tomorrow here at the fort, regardless of what you say or do. I think the feds are assuming that General Mier and I will stand by and let that happen . . . which pisses me off."

"So what are you guys going to do if this Colonel Lawless tries to kill me?" I asked, trying to keep the fear out of my voice.

"Colonel Merski and I have a plan," General Mier assured me. "That's all we can tell you. Now get some rest. Tomorrow will be a busy day."

I checked myself in at the BOQ where I had spent several nights over the past few months, but I was too anxious to sleep. Finally, at about one in the morning, I got dressed and walked over to the infirmary.

I found a medic on duty and pleaded for a sleeping aid. "Do you have any Xanax?" I asked.

The medic just laughed at me. "Buddy, if I had Xanax, I'd be the richest guy in America. All I can offer you is a BC powder."

So I dissolved the BC powder in a glass of water and went back to my quarters. I decided to follow the ancient advice to count my blessings instead of sheep, and I finally fell into a deep slumber.

A soldier woke me at seven in the morning and gave me a hot beverage. "Colonel Merski said you are a *serious* caffeine addict, so I found you some instant coffee."

"Not bad," I said to myself and drank the coffee in three gulps. "You got any more of this stuff?"

"Let's get you some breakfast," the soldier replied.

We walked over to the mess hall, and I discovered I was ravenous. I ate three pancakes and drank another cup of instant coffee.

I still had a couple of hours before I was scheduled to meet Colonel Lawless, and I spent the time walking aimlessly around the grounds of Fort Joplin. On my previous visits, the fort had looked a lot like a college campus—which is what it had been back when the University of St. Thomas was a going concern.

But today, Fort Joplin was preparing for combat. Soldiers had built machine-gun emplacements at strategic points around the campus, each one bordered by piles of sandbags. I saw infantrymen with sniper rifles on the roofs of campus buildings, and every soldier was wearing a Kevlar vest and helmet.

I walked into General Mier's conference room at about 9:30 a.m. Mier and Merski were both checking their pistols, but they didn't seem nervous. Lieutenant Barkley was standing by, and I noticed she was carrying a stubby 9 mm submachine gun instead of her service rifle.

That struck me as odd.

THE FEDS TRY TO KILL ME

About a quarter before ten, I slipped out of General Mier's conference room and found a spot where I could see Fort Joplin's front gate. I was apprehensive, but I knew Lieutenant Barkley would be with me when I confronted Colonel Lawless. And I saw that General Mier's soldiers were preparing for a fight.

At exactly 10:00 a.m., two armored personnel carriers drove up to Fort Joplin's front gate, which was blocked by an enormous garbage truck. A lean army officer wearing a green beret and full battle dress got out of the lead vehicle and ordered the sentry on duty to move the garbage truck so the APCs could enter.

The sentry—a thin corporal who looked to be about eighteen years old—refused to comply. "I'm sorry, sir," the corporal explained deferentially, "but I cannot move the garbage truck without an order from my senior officer."

"Listen to me, you piece of shit. I'm Captain James Cabot Slocum, and *I'm* your senior officer. Now open the goddamned gate, or I'll put you under arrest."

Even from a distance, I could see that Captain Slocum had flustered the corporal, but the young soldier stood his ground. "I'll check with Captain Lubbock, sir. It'll only take a minute."

About ten minutes passed with Captain Slocum getting more and more agitated. Finally, Captain Lubbock appeared, strolling toward the front gate with an air of nonchalance. He was eating a donut, and he saluted the angry captain with the donut still in his hand.

"What can I do you for, Captain?" Lubbock asked genially, chewing while he talked.

"I tell you what you can do for me, asshole. You can move that garbage truck so my APCs can get through."

"No can do, Captain," Lubbock replied. "You see, the army leased these premises from the Catholic Church. Under the terms of our lease, we promised not to tear up the lawn. Those APCs, they must weigh twenty tons apiece. We can't let you park them inside the fort. They'll kill the grass. That's why we've got the gate blocked.

"You can park your vehicles over there in that old Walgreen's parking lot," Lubbock said casually, pointing toward the Walgreen's with the donut still in his hand.

"Don't worry," Lubbock added. "Nobody will steal them."

A few long minutes passed while Captain Slocum raged and swore at Captain Lubbock, who appeared to be utterly indifferent to Slocum's abusive language. In fact, Lubbock looked bored.

Finally, Captain Slocum walked back to consult with a tall, scrawny officer who had crawled out of the nearest of the two APCs. *That must be Colonel Lawless.*

Lawless was a very unimpressive-looking man. He had a narrow, almost concave chest and a prominent Adam's apple, and I could see the outlines of a potbelly under his ill-fitting camo battle dress. Like Captain Slocum, Lawless wore a green beret, but the cap made him look almost clownish. He was sweating profusely, and he wasn't carrying a weapon.

"If that guy's a Green Beret," I thought silently, "then the US Army is in real trouble."

Colonel Lawless walked up to Captain Lubbock, who was brushing donut crumbs off his uniform.

"Captain Lubbock," Lawless said in a nervous voice, "my authority comes directly from the highest level of the Provisional

Government. I'm ordering you to move that garbage truck and allow my vehicles to pass through."

"Like I told Captain Slocum, Colonel, no can do. Just park your rigs down the street somewhere."

To my surprise, Colonel Lawless didn't press the matter further.

"Then direct me to General Mier's office," Lawless said in exasperation.

"Sure, Colonel. General Mier is expecting you."

At that moment, heavily armed soldiers piled out of the APCs. They were all grim-faced and steely-eyed, but they looked a little disoriented. I think they had expected to remain concealed until their vehicles were inside the fort's perimeter. Instead, they were standing on Montrose Boulevard, completely exposed. I counted about twenty soldiers—not nearly enough to overpower the troops at Fort Joplin.

I noticed that Lawless was accompanied by two Green Berets who appeared to be his bodyguards. Both soldiers carried sidearms but not rifles. They looked like mean sonsabitches—like rottweilers straining to break free from their leashes so they could slash someone's throat.

I was beginning to see how things were going down, and I hurried over to General Mier's conference room. Mier and Merski were sitting at the conference table.

I joined them at the table, and I tried to look relaxed when Lawless and his escort soldiers arrived a couple of minutes later. Mier and Merski both rose and saluted when Lawless walked in, and they both shook hands with him.

"Have a seat, Colonel," Mier said in a friendly voice. "Let me introduce you to Willoughby Burns. He's the man you came to meet, correct?"

"Where are Cole Goodnight and Adina Morales?" Lawless asked. He looked confused.

"Colonel, Mr. Goodnight and Ranger Morales had a previous engagement," I explained, "and they asked me to convey their regrets. But they both authorized me to act on their behalf. I'll brief them on our meeting just as soon as I get back to Austin."

"Previous engagement?" Lawless asked in a peevish voice. "What previous engagement is more important than a meeting with a senior military officer on a matter of national security?"

What the hell? I thought to myself. I could see there was no point in trying to placate Colonel Lawless, so I tried to shake him up a little.

"The Cuero Turkey Trot," I replied. "Cole and Adina were named honorary parade marshals, so of course they had to show up."

General Mier joined in to back my play. "The Cuero Turkey Trot is a big-time festival in Texas, Colonel Lawless. Turkey races, turkey sausages, fried turkey legs, a carnival. I don't know, Willoughby. Do they crown a Turkey Queen?"

"I believe her proper title is Miss Turkey," I replied.

Colonel Lawless realized, of course, that General Mier and I were bantering with him, so he sat down at the conference table without saying anything further about the Cuero Turkey Trot. I noticed he chose a chair that kept him from getting between me and his two escorts, who remained standing.

Meanwhile, Lieutenant Barkley stood by the door and said nothing. She held her submachine gun at the ready with the barrel pointing toward the floor. She didn't look nervous, and that reassured me a little.

"Well, then," Lawless began, talking directly to me. "As I told Captain Lubbock, my orders come from the highest level of the Provisional Government. You are hereby directed to cease any effort to encourage Texas to secede from the United States. You are further directed to cancel your upcoming constitutional convention and to provide the army with the names of all secessionists."

I knew then that Colonel Lawless had not come to negotiate and that someone in authority had marked me for a fast-tracked assassination. Nevertheless, I played for time.

"Colonel, I think you are misinformed about the Texas Independence Movement. We are not secessionists because there is no government from which we could secede. Surely you know that.

"But I will convey your message to Mr. Goodnight and Ranger Morales just as soon as they return from Cuero. I'll be back in touch with you within a couple of days."

My delaying tactic didn't work. "That is unacceptable to the Provisional Government," Lawless said, his voice cracking a bit from anxiety. "If you do not immediately comply, my orders are to terminate this discussion with *extreme* prejudice."

I looked at the two Green Berets who were reaching for their handguns. *Oh my god*, I thought. *They're going to whack me!*

But the assassins hesitated for half a second. They certainly were prepared to kill me. In fact, I think they were looking forward to it. But they had trouble believing that Lawless had actually ordered them to kill an unarmed civilian in front of witnesses. They wanted one more confirmation before they pulled the trigger.

And Colonel Lawless gave it to them. "Yes," he said loudly. "I must end this discussion with extreme prejudice *right now.*"

The assassins went for their guns, but just a little too late. Lieutenant Barkley cut them down with her submachine gun before they could clear leather. She was apparently mindful of their body armor because she shot them both in the face.

Colonel Lawless's Green Beret rottweilers collapsed on the floor without a murmur. I looked at General Mier and Colonel Merski. They looked sad. They had crossed the Rubicon. They knew that Lieutenant Barkley's machine gun had turned them into mutineers, and there was no going back.

"Oh my," Colonel Lawless said, and then lost control of his bladder.

I looked over to Lieutenant Barkley, who appeared serene. In fact, she looked like she was about to ask if she could get us some sodas.

About a minute later, we heard gunfire coming from the direction of Fort Joplin's front gate. First, we heard a smattering of shots, then machine-gun fire, and then silence.

"Colonel Merski," General Mier said, "what say we go outside and see what the ruckus is about?"

Both men left the conference room with drawn pistols. "Lieutenant Barkley," Merski called back, "keep your eyes on Colonel Lawless. If he gives you any trouble—any trouble at all—you have my permission to kick him in the nuts with *extreme* prejudice."

Lieutenant Barkley told me to search Lawless for weapons,

which I did. His camo clothing smelled new to me, like it was being worn for the first time. And he also smelled of urine.

In about ten minutes, Merski and Mier returned. I could tell that they had made up their minds about something.

Without speaking, Merski bent down and shot both assassins in the head to make sure they were dead. This act, which surprised even General Mier, scared Colonel Lawless out of his wits. He began to weep.

"Colonel Lawless," Merski said as he sat down at the conference table, "didn't anyone ever tell you not to bring a knife to a gunfight? Did anyone think to do a little recon before you drove up in those APCs? Don't they teach the Green Berets basic infantry tactics anymore? Do you know that your troops are outnumbered ten to one?"

"I'm not a Green Beret," Lawless confessed. "I'm a JAG officer. I'm just an army lawyer delivering a message from my client. They told me to dress like a Green Beret for dramatic effect."

"I knew the moment I first laid eyes on you that you were nothing but a bagman," Merski replied contemptuously. "You look about as much like a Green Beret as my aunt Fanny."

General Mier spoke up. "Colonel Lawless, let me tell you what happened a few minutes ago at the front gate. Your Captain Slocum heard Lieutenant Barkley's machine gun and concluded that your assassination plot had failed. He ordered his men to fire on my soldiers. Slocum himself shot and killed Captain Lubbock, who was my senior staff officer, a good soldier, and a family man.

"Fortunately, only two soldiers obeyed Slocum's order and fired their weapons. Slocum soon realized he was hopelessly outnumbered and surrendered. We executed him on the spot for killing a fellow officer.

"In fact, I shot him myself. We're organizing a firing squad now, and we'll execute the other two soldiers in a few minutes."

Lawless's face turned pale when he heard this news, and he emitted a low, childlike moan. I could tell he was terrified.

Mier paused for a few seconds, allowing Colonel Lawless to contemplate what his own fate might be.

"Colonel Lawless, I've been in the army for thirty years," Mier continued. "I've served six combat tours, but this is the first time

I've seen American soldiers shooting at their comrades. Did you authorize Captain Slocum to attack my people?"

Before Lawless could answer, Mier answered his own question. "No, I don't think you did. You and Captain Slocum were just following orders from some high-ranking, anonymous turd in the Provisional Government. I'll probably never know who cooked up this assassination plot."

Colonel Lawless didn't answer. I don't think he even heard what General Mier had said. He just hung his head and remained silent.

"We also took seventeen prisoners," Mier continued. "Colonel Merski asked the prisoners whether they want to go back to the navy ships with you or throw in their lot with us. All seventeen decided to join us."

"Are you going to kill me too?" Lawless asked.

"No, we're not going to kill you," Merski replied. "Although I hate to pass up an opportunity to shoot a lawyer.

"But we're confiscating your APCs and all your weapons. As soon as we execute the soldiers who shot at us, we'll load all the bodies into a light truck. You can drive the truck back to the USS *Nancy*. You can keep your Green Beret costume, but General Mier wants his truck back. Just top off the tank and leave the key under the driver's seat."

Lawless bucked up a bit after Merski told him he wouldn't be shot. "The Provisional Government will retaliate, you know," Lawless said. "You are all mutineers—you and every soldier who followed your orders."

"Is that so?" Merski retorted. "Where did you get that idea? Did you learn about mutiny at Harvard Law School?"

"Princeton, actually," Lawless replied, a little pompously.

"Same difference," Merski said dismissively. "Did you happen to read the Declaration of Independence when you were at Princeton, or do the professors not teach that anymore?"

Colonel Lawless didn't answer. Instead, he turned to me. "And you," he snarled, "are a marked man. You won't live long enough to hold your pathetic constitutional convention."

Now General Mier rejoined the conversation. "I wouldn't be so sure about that, Colonel Lawless. Cause here's the thing: if the feds try to stop the Texas Independence Movement or take retaliatory action against Fort Joplin or Fort Sharpton, Colonel Merski and I are going to start blowing up the refineries."

"You wouldn't dare," Lawless smirked. I was impressed by how quickly he switched from stark terror to arrogance.

"Well, Colonel, I've dealt with liars and cowards all my life, and I find they have one thing in common. Because they themselves have no courage and no honor, they think everybody is a liar and a coward. You probably think I'm bluffing.

"So here is what Colonel Merski and I decided to do. We are going to blow up the Pasadena refinery this morning." Mier glanced at his watch. "In fact, my demolition people will start work in about an hour.

"So get your sorry ass in the truck I loaned you and take your dead back to the USS *Nancy*. You should have a good view of the fireworks in Pasadena from where she's anchored.

"And when you report back to your handlers in the Provisional Government, tell them what will happen if they try to assassinate Mr. Burns here, or Mr. Goodnight, or Ranger Morales. Tell them what will happen if they commit acts of sabotage in Texas or Louisiana, or attack Fort Joplin or Fort Sharpton.

"You need to tell the feds to maintain the status quo if they want to continue getting fuel and petroleum products from the refineries we're guarding."

At this point, Merski chimed in, making it clear—I suppose—that he and his Louisiana military base were solidly behind General Mier.

"So here's the deal," Merski said in a harsh and angry tone. "The Provisional Government will continue buying fuel from the Louisiana and Texas refineries, and it will continue paying in gold or silver. Don't even think about paying us with worthless US dollars. I wouldn't wipe my ass with that stuff.

"And the Provisional Government will leave us the hell alone. And by us, I mean Fort Sharpton, Fort Joplin, and the fuckin' Republic of Texas.

"Because if you mess with us again, I will personally hunt you down and kill you."

TEXAS COOKIN'

One of General Mier's soldiers gave Colonel Lawless a brief lesson on how to drive a truck with a standard transmission, and then Lawless drove through Fort Joplin's front gate with five body bags neatly stacked in the truck bed.

The truck jerked and bucked as he drove onto Montrose Boulevard, a sure sign that he had not figured out how to use the clutch to change gears.

"I need to get back to Austin," I told Mier and Merski. "Cole and Adina need to know what went down this morning."

"We'll send you back in the Humvee," Mier replied. "I hope the feds have abandoned their assassination plot, but you all three need to stay on your guard—at least until your constitutional convention is concluded. There may be more attempts on your lives."

I walked out to Fort Joplin's front gate and hopped into the waiting Humvee. This time, Sergeant McLaglen was my driver, with Corporal Frizzell manning the machine gun in the Humvee's turret.

Two armed soldiers were also in the vehicle—extra security, I assumed, in case the Provisional Government had sent assassins to waylay us on the highway.

"I'm driving you on Highway 290 today," Sergeant McLaglen explained. "I don't think your enemies will be expecting us to take that route."

After a half-hour or so, we put the city of Houston behind us. A few minutes later, we passed by the town of Brenham, the head-quarters of Blue Bell Creameries back in the old times.

"God, I miss Blue Bell ice cream," Sergeant McLaglen sighed. "Butter pecan."

"I miss Blue Bell's homemade vanilla," Corporal Frizzell volunteered.

"How about Blue Bell's vanilla bean?" I asked. "That was my favorite flavor."

Later, we drove into Elgin, famous for its barbecue. I smelled mesquite smoke as we passed by Southside Barbeque—still open for business! I knew everyone in the vehicle wanted McLaglen to pull over so we could chomp down on some ribs. But I was on an urgent errand, and I didn't suggest that we stop for lunch.

When I got back to the Texas capital, I saw that many of the delegates had already arrived. Some of the delegates had traveled great distances to cast their vote for Texas independence. The El Paso delegation had trekked almost six hundred miles to get to Austin, and the delegates from Dumas—on the northern edge of the Texas Panhandle—had journeyed nearly as far.

On the evening before the constitutional convention convened, I wandered over the capitol lawn, where the delegates and their families were eating their evening meals around cooking fires. Several vendors had set up an informal food court and were selling all kinds of traditional dishes: Vietnamese spring rolls, chapati from India, Greek shish kabobs, and German sausage on a stick—just to name a few.

I stopped at a booth where a grizzled Texan in a sweat-stained black Stetson was tending a barbecue pit shaped like a giant six-shooter. The pit grill comprised the pistol's mock cylinder. And of course, the pit's smokestack served as the pistol's smoking barrel.

"Whatcha want, mister?" the pit tender asked me. "Brisket, ribs, sausage, or a little of all three?"

"I'll have all three, and give me a fatty cut from that brisket."

"You got it. And do you want some sauce on your brisket?"

His question was casual, but I knew there was only one right answer. "No sauce for me," I replied. "Putting barbeque sauce on good brisket is like putting ketchup on a filet mignon."

My server seemed to like my answer, and he slapped an extra slice of brisket on my plate.

"Now we've got the Holy Trinity of sides, and you can have two. Which one do you not want?"

I knew the guy was telling me that the sides were pinto beans, potato salad, and coleslaw—the Holy Trinity of barbeque side dishes; but I would only get two. Apparently, it is illegal in Texas for barbeque joints to serve more than two side dishes to their customers.

But I was ready for this question too. "I'll skip the coleslaw," I said, and held out my plate to get a ladle of pinto beans and an ice cream scoop of potato salad.

After I finished my barbecue, I looked around for dessert. A Tejano family frying sopapillas in a blackened iron cooking pot stood off to the side, the children greedily watching the rising smoke in anticipation. Sopapillas—the perfect end to a barbeque meal. One of the children gave me two and shook a generous portion of powdered sugar on top. "No miel, señor. Lo siento."

"Está bien," I replied in my kindergarten-level Spanish.

I was too stuffed with barbecue and sopapillas to eat anything else, but I passed by several more food vendors selling other traditional foods: baklava, pita sandwiches, and cabrito. I bought a half dozen sweet tamales, which would be my breakfast in the morning.

Texas music of all varieties wafted over the capitol grounds. To my right, a Texas fiddle band played "Big Taters in Sandy Land," an old tune that may have crossed the Appalachians two hundred years ago. In the distance, a Tejano group pounded out corridos—narrative ballads about romance, adventure, and death in the borderlands.

I saw a large mariachi band—a dozen young musicians, both boys and girls—playing violins, guitars, cornets, and a guitarrón. The group strolled around the capitol grounds playing traditional mariachi favorites like "El Mariachi Loco," and "La Bamba," and other songs that were obscure to me. My Spanish-language skills were minimal, but I didn't have to understand the lyrics to be uplifted by music so joyful that I was reminded how glad I was to be alive.

All the mariachi performers were dressed in traditional charro attire. The men wore tight-fitting pantalóns and short, bolero jackets. The women wore ankle-length skirts and colorful peasant blouses. The whole group wore enormous sombreros that even Emiliano Zapata, the famous Mexican revolutionary, would have been proud to wear.

Last, I listened to a five-piece polka band from the German Hill Country: accordion, trombone, fiddle, clarinet, and—of course—a tuba. The male musicians were all wearing lederhosen, and the women were wearing traditional dirndl dresses. They played the old favorites: "Beer Barrel Polka," "Happy Valley Polka," and "In Heaven They Have No Beer."

Then, to my surprise, the band tooted out a polka version of the "Tennessee Waltz"—a schmaltzy, almost maudlin song, usually played to a slow waltz tempo. But the polka band kicked it up a notch, and Texans began polka dancing while the band's vocalist completely reinterpreted the melancholy lyrics. "Cheer up, buddy," he seemed to be singing. "Sure, your girl ran off with your best friend, but aren't you glad she's gone? Maybe you'll meet a nice German girl and learn to polka!"

At that moment, Adina Morales walked up to my side, and we listened for a few minutes to a cacophony of competing Texas bands—discordant, and yet strangely harmonious. She was wearing a traditional *huipil*—a white cotton dress with embroidered flowers decorating the neckline. She didn't say anything at first, and I noticed she wasn't wearing her sidearm.

A little later, Goodnight joined us, and the three of us stood silently in the gathering darkness, enjoying the music and the strong smell of mesquite smoke from the cooking fires. Goodnight was dressed this evening like a working cattleman: faded Levi jeans, an old checkered shirt, and scuffed-up western work boots.

After a moment, Adina reached out and grasped Cole and me each by the hand, an affectionate affirmation of our growing friendship over the past months. We were aware that the Texas Constitutional Convention would be convened on the morrow and that we were about to begin an epic and perhaps dangerous journey.

"The eyes of Texas are upon us," Goodnight said quietly.

"'Til Gabriel blows his goddamn horn," Morales replied.

THE EYES OF TEXAS ARE UPON YOU

Then the great day came. The day we had worked for. The day that Texas constitutional delegates would gather at the state capitol in Austin to cast their votes for independence from the United States.

Of course, the convention was not televised. Television died when the old times passed away, and most people claimed not to miss it. However, I saw a press section where a few scruffy-looking newspaper reporters were sitting. I suspected some of those reporters were spies for the Provisional Government, but it was impossible for me to determine which reporters were bona fide journalists and which ones might be enemy agents.

I considered the possibility that an assassin was in the audience. I was reassured to see so many Texas Rangers walking about; they were easy to pick out because none of them had removed their regulation Stetsons. I hoped there were some plainclothes officers sprinkled in the crowd.

After the convention was called to order, Cole Goodnight rose to the podium in the old Texas Senate chamber. The room was crowded with more than five hundred delegates—some sitting at the desks of the long-ago state senators, some sitting in the balcony, and some sitting on the window ledges. Goodnight stood for a moment and scanned the room intently as if he were looking for a particular individual. He did not have to call for silence; the room became absolutely still the moment he got to his feet.

"Ladies and gentlemen," he said in a calm but commanding voice, "*damas y cabelleros.* The eyes of Texas are upon each of you today.

"Having accepted the responsibility to be constitutional delegates, you cannot escape your duty to declare Texas an independent and sovereign nation, to ratify a constitution, and to form a national government.

"And before we take up the weighty matters before us and cast our votes, let us tell the world why we are taking this bold action.

"Texas is not seceding from the United States of America. We are not in rebellion. We have not done what the Californians did, which was to attack the civil authorities and the police and commit mass murder.

"Rather, Texans are rising from the ashes of the old American republic and recommitting ourselves to democratic government within the letter and the spirit of the United States Constitution.

"We are taking this grave step," Goodnight continued, "in order to defend our homes and families from our enemies both foreign and domestic. We are acting so that Texans can go back to work, grow our own food, and restart our businesses and industries without fear of being robbed, raped, or killed.

"We are forming a government so that we can get the mail service up and running and reopen our schools. We are declaring ourselves a new nation in order to reestablish our courts and justice system. We have come together to regulate our affairs and husband our natural resources for the benefit of the Texas people.

"We want the world to know that we are gathered today in the historic Texas capitol building as a diverse but united people. And let us reflect a moment on just how diverse we are.

"How many Hispanic delegates are here today?" Goodnight called out. A roar rose up from the senate floor and the gallery, with cries of "*¡Viva! ¡Viva! ¡Viva Tejas!*"

"How many African American delegates are here?" Another roar.

"How many Asians? How many are of Vietnamese heritage? How many can trace their roots to India, to Pakistan, to Korea, to China?"

Again, a roar swept up to Goodnight from the assembly.

"How many of you hail from Eastern Europe? From the Balkan states, from Ukraine, from Poland?

"And surely there are some Anglos and Celts. Who can trace their families back to Ireland, Germany, or Scandinavia?"

This was my cue to start yelling because my ancestors came from Germany and fought with George Washington even before they learned to speak English.

By now pandemonium had broken out among the delegates and the observers. Soon, the delegates and onlookers were chanting "Texas! Texas! Texas!" I also heard the high "yip yip!" of the *grito*, trilling ululations of women who had immigrated from the Middle East, and a few Anglos who were howling like stoned hippies at an old Willie Nelson concert.

And then the roll call of delegates began, and the delegates cast their votes.

The vote in favor of Texas independence was unanimous. Every delegate agreed that Texas needed to break away from the USA and form a new nation. But the vote to ratify the Texas Constitution was not unanimous; I hadn't expected it to be.

Twenty-one delegates voted no to the proposed new constitution and most of the dissenters stated their reasons. Pro-lifers voted no because the constitution did not outlaw abortions. Some pro-choice advocates went thumbs down because the constitution did not guarantee a woman's right to an abortion.

A few evangelical Christians cast negative votes because the constitution did not enshrine the traditional family. LGBTQ+ delegates said they could not approve a constitution that did not explicitly protect gay rights. And one unhappy delegate in the balcony muttered something about transgender bathrooms, but I couldn't tell if he was for or against them.

Nevertheless, the vote for independence was overwhelming. Most of the naysayers to the constitution walked out of the convention, so only jubilant and united delegates remained.

Next, the delegates voted to elect a provisional president. A Tejano wearing a straw cowboy hat rose to address the assembly in a booming, stentorian voice. "The delegates from El Paso County nominate Cole Goodnight, a native son of San Angelo, as provisional president of the nation of Texas."

A Vietnamese delegate from Houston seconded the nomination.

An awkward silence then fell over the convention chamber. It was clear that no one backed another candidate for the provisional president's job. Virtually everyone in the room wanted Goodnight to be the new nation's first leader.

After a couple of minutes, Adina whispered in my ear. "Will," she said, "ask if there are any other candidates."

I stood up and, in a loud voice, called out, "Are there any other nominations?" Then I sat down.

More silence and Adina whispered to me again. "Cole," she instructed, "make another call for other candidates to be nominated. We want to make sure everyone understands that Cole is the delegates' unanimous choice."

I rose to speak a second time. "I repeat," I said, "are there any other nominations?"

At that point, people started chanting, "Goodnight, Goodnight, Goodnight."

A delegate from Llano County yelled out over the din, "I call for a vote."

And I heard a Bosque County delegate shout from the balcony, "I second!"

I then called for a vote. "All in favor of electing Cole Goodnight as the Provisional President of Texas, say 'Aye.'" The entire assembly shouted, "Aye."

"Are there any nays?" I asked, hoping I had proceeded under *Robert's Rules of Order*.

I heard no dissenters. Cole Goodnight was unanimously elected president of the second Texas Republic.

After the applause and cheering died down, Goodnight rose to address the delegates. "You have placed a heavy responsibility on my shoulders," he said, "and I pledge my life and sacred honor to building Texas into a strong, secure, and prosperous nation.

"Within the next two years, the people of Texas will elect a new congress and a new president, and the nation's first elected president will nominate cabinet members. During the two years that I serve as your provisional president, I have selected Adina Morales to be Secretary of Defense, and Willoughby Burns as Secretary of State."

Adina and I rose when Goodnight called our names. Adina was wearing her 9 mm pistol, which was holstered at her waist, and a Texas Ranger badge pinned on her shirt. I wore a western yoke shirt, bootcut pants, my father's silverbelly Stetson, and his Nocona boots.

The delegates greeted Goodnight's cabinet choices with thunderous applause—not for me so much as for Chief Ranger Adina Morales. She stood modestly, holding her Stetson in both hands, and I basked in the reflection of the crowd's adulation for the nation's chief ranger and first Secretary of Defense.

As the convention drew to a close, I spotted three old friends sitting in the balcony: General Mier, Colonel Merski, and Lieutenant Barkley. I searched them out among the crowd of departing delegates and onlookers, and I found them in the capitol rotunda. All three were in their dress uniforms, medals arrayed on their coats, and shoes polished to an unnatural high shine.

I gave them all a fierce hug, keenly aware that they had saved my life a few days ago and probably the life of the Texas Republic.

"I see you are all in uniform," I commented. "So Colonel Lawless must not have gotten you kicked out of the army."

"As a matter of fact," General Mier explained, "we came out of the Front Gate Affair, as the fracas has become known, smelling like a rose—the yellow rose of Texas, you might say. All three of us were awarded the Bronze Star for heroism, and Lieutenant Barkley was promoted to captain."

"Congratulations! But what happened to Colonel Lawless?"

"He got promoted too. He's a two-star general now."

I was flabbergasted. "A two-star general? What's he in charge of?"

"Domestic terrorism, of course," Colonel Merski responded with a straight face.

"But how did Lawless explain those five bodies in the back of the truck you loaned him?"

"Well, we don't know all the details," Merski replied, "but apparently the good Colonel Lawless is quite a spin doctor. He told his superiors that some soldiers mutinied at Fort Joplin, but that he personally put down the insurrection with the loss of only five soldiers. And he gave the three of us some modest credit for helping him. That's why we got the medals."

I was incredulous. "But what about those two APCs you appropriated, and the seventeen soldiers who refused to go back to the USS *Nancy* with him? How did he spin that?"

"Not a problem," General Mier responded. "Colonel Lawless said Fort Sharpton obviously needed more resources to deal with any future insurrections that might erupt, so he gave us the APCs and permanently assigned the seventeen rebels to Fort Joplin."

"I'm confused," I confessed. "Lawless's job was to assassinate Cole, Adina, and me. And yet here we are today, doing exactly what the Provisional Government didn't want us to do—forming the Texas Republic."

"We're confused as well," Mier responded. "We think maybe Lawless persuaded the grand pooh-bahs in the Provisional Government to just wait you guys out.

"He probably said that the Texas Republic is bound to fail, so there's no point in provoking a public confrontation. Or maybe Lawless advised the Provisional Government spymasters to send in a team of assassins in a couple of months when you would probably think the threat is over and let your guard down."

"And nobody complained about you blowing up the Pasadena refinery?"

"But we didn't blow up the Pasadena refinery, Will. According to Colonel Lawless's report, the army wrote that off as an industrial accident."

"Only in America," was my sole comment.

"Yeah," General Mier replied. "Aren't you glad you don't live there anymore?

"If I can change the subject," Mier continued, "I would like to conduct some diplomatic business with you. Now that Texas is an independent nation, it has a foreign army on its soil. Namely my forces at Fort Joplin.

"Do you think we could get a treaty allowing the US Army to remain in Houston—a NATO kind of deal like the army used to have in Europe?"

"Absolutely, General Mier," I said. "I would do anything for Janis. Consider it a done deal."

And then I turned to Captain Barkley, who had said nothing while Mier and Merski updated me on the Front Gate Affair.

"Captain Barkley, you saved my life more than once. Would it be okay if I call you Wilhelmina?"

"Sure, Mr. Secretary. But my friends call me Willa."

ACKNOWLEDGMENTS

Anyone who publishes the first novel at the age of seventy-four has many people to thank. I would first like to thank Christie Leigh Babirad, Amy Goppert, Brittany Griffiths, Kelly Lydick Thomas Reale, Madelyn Schmidt, Sterling Zuelch, and all the people at Brown Books for their expert editing advice and suggestions.

I would also like to thank my family and friends who read early drafts of my novel and gave me encouragement and advice. I would never have finished the novel without their encouragement and support.

I would be remiss if I did not acknowledge my debt to James Howard Kunstler. I read his *World Made by Hand* novels, which are set in post-apocalyptic, upstate New York. These books prompted me to ponder what life might be like in the South when the petroleum age comes to an end. Mr. Kunstler's books inspired me to write *The Dixie Apocalypse*.

Finally, I wish to thank my wife, Kim, to whom I have dedicated this book, for her love and patience over the years. She brightens every day of my life.

ABOUT THE AUTHOR

Richard Fossey grew up in southwestern Oklahoma, and graduated with honors from the University of Texas School of Law. He practiced civil law in Anchorage, Alaska before attending Harvard University, where he obtained a doctorate in education administration and social policy. He taught education law and policy for many years at universities in Louisiana and Texas, where he held endowed professorships. He edited *Catholic Southwest*, a journal of Catholic history in the American Southwest, and was named Fellow of the Texas Catholic Historical Society in 2019. He lives in retirement with his wife Kim in Baton Rouge, Louisiana.

*Photo credited to Kevin Duffy.